After this harrowing day, Lang could... till his ton...

She'd never know wheth... kindness, his heart-stopping gaze and the hard, broad muscles beneath his shirt made her want to trust his sincerity. If he'd just take her in his arms, she might see her way to making a more certain judgment....

She took a deep breath, drawing in oxygen like courage. She'd made a fool of herself this day—surely one more bit of lunacy couldn't hurt. Maybe that way she could confine a lifetime's foibles to one neat twenty-four-hour period.

"May I ask you a favor?"

Lang's dark brows rose in curiosity. "Of course."

"Would you kiss me like there was no tomorrow?"

And who knows, she thought. There might not be. Because if Lang said no, she might die of embarrassment right there on her old spinster bed.

Dear Reader,

Welcome to Harlequin Historicals, Harlequin/Silhouette's *only* historical romance line! We offer four unforgettable love stories each month, in a range of time periods, settings and sensuality. And they're written by some of the best writers in the field!

We're very excited to bring you *The Outlaw's Bride,* a terrific Western by rising talent Liz Ireland. Some of you may know Liz from her contemporary romances for Harlequin. This is a heartwarming tale of two people who fall in love, despite the odds against them. Emma Colby scandalizes her small Texas town when she takes in an injured farmer, who is really a reputed outlaw. The two deny their feelings for each other—until the local sheriff brings things to a boil!

Deborah Simmons returns with a frothy new Regency romance, *The Gentleman Thief,* about a beautiful bluestocking who stirs up trouble when she investigates a jewel theft and finds herself scrutinizing—and falling for—an irresistible marquis. Carolyn Davidson's Western *The Bachelor Tax* features a least-likely-to-marry rancher who tries to avoid a local tax by proposing to the one woman he's *sure* will turn him down—the prim preacher's daughter....

My Lady Reluctant is a thrilling new medieval novel by Laurie Grant about a Norman lady who must travel to court to find a husband. En route, she is attacked by outlaws but rescued by a mysterious and handsome knight.... Don't miss it!

Enjoy! And come back again next month for four more choices of the best in historical romance.

Sincerely,

Tracy Farrell
Senior Editor

THE OUTLAW'S BRIDE

LIZ IRELAND

HARLEQUIN®

TORONTO • NEW YORK • LONDON
AMSTERDAM • PARIS • SYDNEY • HAMBURG
STOCKHOLM • ATHENS • TOKYO • MILAN • MADRID
PRAGUE • WARSAW • BUDAPEST • AUCKLAND

ISBN 0-373-29098-5

THE OUTLAW'S BRIDE

Copyright © 2000 by Elizabeth Bass

Please address questions and book requests to:
Harlequin Reader Service
U.S.: 3010 Walden Ave., P.O. Box 1325, Buffalo, NY 14269
Canadian: P.O. Box 609, Fort Erie, Ont. L2A 5X3

Chapter One

1882

"Oh, no! It's old Joe Spears!"

With stunning agility for one who was eight months pregnant, Lorna McCrae heaved herself out of the porch's rocking chair and, with her curly blond hair flying, scurried just inside the front door. She peered out fearfully, as if there were an army coming down the hill, not just one cranky old storekeeper.

Emma Colby, who was sitting on the top step of the porch enjoying the afternoon shade of the veranda that draped the length of the house like a comfortable old shawl, squinted at the approaching man on the mule. Usually a visitation from Joe Spears would strike dread in her heart, too, but Lorna's exaggerated reaction made her chuckle instead.

"Don't laugh, Emma. He's the biggest gossip in town!"

Emma stood. "Good. Maybe we'll be able to find out a little about what they're saying about us." Really, there was no maybe about it. Joe Spears, the proprietor of the Midday Mercantile, hadn't earned his knows-all-tells-all reputation by accident.

She squared her shoulders as the rider drew closer and

willed her lips to draw up in a welcoming smile. "Hello, Mr. Spears!" She tried to sound as if he were just the man she was hoping would lope down her path.

Joe's wiry frame descended from the mule as spryly as his seventy years and his lumbago would allow. He greeted her with a curt nod of his head. "Emma." His wide hat practically swallowed his scalp, but he pushed back the brim, giving her a better view of his wrinkly, grizzled old face. His watery blue eyes were still sharp. "You're lookin' poorly today. Kinda pale, and skinnier than usual, I'd say."

She kept smiling through his physical assessment. Joe wasn't known for flattery. "I'm doing well, thank you," she replied as if he'd just paid her a flowery compliment. "As well as I've been since…well, since Doc died."

For a moment the old man's wrinkles went slack, and he glanced nervously around at the large wood frame house and the massive live oak trees shading it, as if Dr. Colby's ghost might be haunting the place. "Hard to believe…"

"Yes, it is," she said, knowing what he meant without his even having to say it. It *was* hard to believe her father was gone, even though she herself had nursed him through two years of terrible illness. After three months, the absence of the wry, wise man who had been as much friend as father to her was still just sinking in.

Joe abruptly pulled an envelope from his jacket pocket. "I just happened to be in the post office and noticed this letter arrived for you from Galveston. Thought I'd bring it over."

Emma doubted that was his sole reason for the visit, but took the letter and tucked it into the pocket of her apron. "Thank you."

"Ain't you gonna read it?" Joe asked.

"Oh, I imagine so."

But she made no move to do so now, which seemed to vex Joe. "I never met a woman yet who could abide a sealed envelope."

Emma grinned. Apparently some men couldn't abide one, either.

His sharp eyes focused in on her pocket, as if trying to detect what the contents of the envelope might be. "I guess that letter would be from Rose Ellen."

She nodded. "Yes, I expect so."

Rose Ellen was her younger sister, who had married a businessman from Galveston seven years ago, breaking the heart of practically every man in Midday and three surrounding counties. Evidently her nuptials had left even Joe's craggy old heart tattered and torn.

"She's been writin' you every week since Doc died," he observed.

Emma nodded. The last one she'd barely skimmed. But then, she'd known what it would say. "Every week."

Joe practically quivered in frustration. "Folks in town are wondering what's going to happen with it all, Emma. I mean with the house and such. Oh, and you, of course."

She continued to smile. No one in town knew that her father had left the house, land and everything on it to Emma and nothing but good wishes to his younger daughter. Emma had been as astounded as Rose Ellen by the bequest. It made her feel uneasy. Why would her father have left her everything?

"I expect things will go on as they are," she told Joe. At least until she could settle on a course for her future.

Joe stamped his foot. "But that don't make sense! Aren't you all gonna have to sell the house? And what about all this land? Your father might have been too busy doctoring to farm it, but your grandfather made a good living off this acreage.''

"Then why would we think of selling it?" Emma asked him, blinking innocently.

"'Cause you can't split a house, not with you livin' here and Rose Ellen in Galveston!" Joe replied, as if her question had been plumb crazy. "And what good's land to a woman? Everybody in town's thinkin' you'll move to Galveston and help take care of Rose Ellen's little girl."

That's what Rose Ellen thought, too—that Emma should start behaving like a proper maiden aunt. "But I enjoy living right here," Emma said, tormenting the man.

"But you *cain't* live here," Joe argued, his spleen rising like a thermostat in July.

She stifled a laugh. "Why not?"

"'Cause you can't just live here all by your lonesome, Emma! That ain't right."

"But I'm not alone."

"And that's another thing!" Joe bellowed, getting, Emma suspected, to the real reason he'd ridden the mile from town. "Folks in town are wondering what Doc might have thought about the goings-on around here, Emma."

Her spine stiffened defensively. "My father taught me to be a nurse and a decent human being. He of all people would have approved."

"Doggonit, it ain't responsible!" He took off his hat and slapped it against his leg for emphasis. "A woman like you, livin' out here with some no-account pregnant girl! Everybody knows about Lorna McCrae! That girl's scandalous—and to think of a woman from an upstanding family like the Colbys taking in *her*…it's outrageous, that's what it is. Reverend Cathcart told me just the other day that Lorna's gonna be Topic A on his sermon this week."

Emma planted her fists on her hips and tapped her foot impatiently, perhaps to keep it from doing what would come naturally—booting Joe Spears's skinny hide back over the hill where he came from! He had to know that Lorna would be within earshot of this conversation.

"Good," she replied tartly. "A lot of lessons could be learned from Lorna's story. Especially if Reverend Cathcart brings up the subject of *who* got Lorna in her present condition and refuses to take responsibility for her. And while he's at it, the good reverend might mention something about her family, who never showed her an ounce of love, and tossed her out of the house when they discovered she tried to find understanding elsewhere."

"Never thought I'd hear you talk this way, Emma," Joe said curtly.

No, he never would have, because her father had done most of the talking for both of them while he'd been alive. Doc would have felt the same way she did, but she had to do her own talking now. "And I never thought I'd see the day when people in Midday turned their backs on people in need. What was Lorna supposed to do when her father kicked her out? Run away to a city, alone? What would happen to her there?"

"She shouldn't have got into trouble to begin with."

Emma tossed up her hands. She'd have more luck making the man's mule see reason! "I enjoy having Lorna here, and she's welcome to stay as long as she's got a mind to."

They stood in silence for a moment, Emma trying to rein in her anger and Joe no doubt contemplating how living alone soured a woman's temper. The man was as irritating as a poison oak rash. She took a breath, trying to remember that, while he was wrong and she was right, it would serve no useful purpose to antagonize Midday's most talkative resident. "Would you like some tea, Mr. Spears?" she forced herself to ask.

"No, thank you." Still, he didn't move. Apparently he wasn't finished. "I'm thinkin' you're takin' in this McCrae girl 'cause you're lonely and miss your pa. That's understandable, Emma. We're all heartbroken over Doc. But folks in town think you'd be better off in Galveston with Rose Ellen than takin' in strays."

"Lorna's not a puppy, Mr. Spears, she's a person. And I think I'm better equipped to know my business than folks in town." She felt her face heating with anger and took a deep breath. *Smile,* she told herself firmly. "Won't you at least have a sip of water from the pump?"

"No, thanks." Maybe he was still hoping that she would break down and read Rose Ellen's letter.

"Then I'm sure you'd like to sit for a moment and rest." She gestured to the rocker on the porch.

Joe watched her for a long moment, then suddenly laughed. "By golly, Miss Emma, for a spinster lady, you sure do have the mother hen in you!"

At first his words didn't quite register. She stared at him, feeling the heat seep out of her cheeks. *Spinster lady?* The words had slipped so easily from his lips!

"Well, I'm sorry I won't be able to report back that I made you see reason about that pregnant girl," Joe went on. "It's a durn shame, Emma."

As he turned and mounted back up on his mule, she barely heard his words. She was still too stunned.

"Bart's reminding everybody to keep their doors locked" was one sentence she did catch. Barton Sealy was the sheriff in Midday, and the secret love of Emma's life. Of course, he barely knew she existed, except that she was

Rose Ellen's older sister. Barton had been one of Rose Ellen's most ardent admirers, and Emma had been quietly jubilant when her sister chose wealth over the stunning good looks of their sheriff.

"Locked?" she repeated. "What for?"

Joe's jaw dropped. "Why, on account of the outlaw, of course! Haven't you heard?"

She hadn't, but Joe wasted no time telling her of the danger. An outlaw had been sighted fifteen miles away. No telling but that the man might show up right in Midday! Couldn't be too careful!

But as he regaled her with details, Emma was still only half listening. *Spinster lady.* True, she was almost twenty-nine—older than most women when they got married. Twenty-nine! But she didn't feel old...at least, not as old as Constance O'Hurlihy, Midday's most noted old maid, who tried to make up for the emptiness in her life with flair in her wardrobe. Good Lord, did everyone consider her to be a *spinster lady,* like Constance? Did Barton?

"Mind you take care," Joe insisted in parting.

She glanced up absently, her thoughts still far away. "Certainly. I will."

Joe and his mule ambled off toward the sunset, leaving Emma rooted to the porch. After a few moments Lorna came fluttering back outside.

"Oh, Emma! How terrible!"

Emma, still white with mortification to discover she was considered no better than a dusty old jar on the shelf, nodded. Terrible indeed! Where had the years gone? Then, seeing the telltale tear tracks down Lorna's cheeks, she realized that Lorna wasn't thinking about Emma's being called a spinster, but her own dilemma.

"Mr. Spears is right!" Lorna moaned. "I shouldn't have come here, bringing all my shame upon your house."

Emma's back stiffened in irritation once again. "Nonsense!"

"But didn't you hear what he said about Reverend Cathcart?" Her eyes brimmed with moisture and she flopped back down into the rocking chair. "I'm a fallen woman—a, a *Jezebel!*"

Emma rolled her eyes. Lorna was nothing if not theatrical. Then again, she was in a terrible position for a mere girl of seventeen. Emma patted her young friend on the shoulder. "Nonsense. You don't have a bad bone in your body."

Lorna hiccuped. "But you mustn't blame William, Emma."

William Sealy was the sheriff's younger brother. The Sealys were an old county family, and well off, while Lorna's family barely scratched out a living on a few sandy acres of land. But even given the difference in their economic positions and social ties, Emma was stunned by William's lack of chivalry. "I know you don't want to think ill of anyone, Lorna, but I can't help it. He's behaved abominably!" And to think he was Barton's own brother!

Poor Lorna shuddered with the effort to hold back tears for Emma's sake, but it was a fruitless battle. The effort only caused her to wail all the louder in her despair. "How could I have been such a fool!"

Emma attempted to calm her. "Don't blame yourself—it serves no purpose. You've just got to look forward to the future now, and having your baby."

Lorna nodded dutifully. "I know."

"Everything will work out, you'll see. You can stay here

for as long as you please. I don't care what people like Joe Spears say.''

Which was only partially a lie, Emma thought, the words *spinster lady* still ringing in her ears.

That night after Lorna was in bed, Emma poured herself a bracing cup of hot tea, laced it liberally with her father's medicinal brandy and swigged down a large gulp at once.

Once, her father had told her about a man he'd seen during the war who'd been so traumatized during battle that he hadn't been able to get the sound of cannon fire out of his head. Ever. Emma had never fully empathized with the poor soul until today. Even now, Joe Spears's reedy voice rang out in her own head as loudly as a cannon. *Spinster lady! Spinster lady! Spinster lady!* The words kept echoing in her mind, as if trying to find a comfortable place to settle in.

She *was* a spinster. All day she'd taken a fresh look at her life, from the bun on the top of her head to the tips of her practical flannel drawers, and the signs were there, all right. There wasn't a hair on her head or a square inch of fabric on her that sang of youthful abandon. She no longer had a spring in her step...if she ever had. Her cheeks couldn't be counted on to be rosy. And joie de vivre had long ago made way for practicality. Funny, while her father had been alive, she hadn't given the matter of her marital status more than an occasional thought, but now it was as if the old-maid label were branded on her. She felt exposed.

Thunder from a brewing storm clapped outside, and, fumbling, Emma took up Rose Ellen's letter. Her sister's missives were usually tedious, exasperating and mildly insulting, but perhaps this one would help get her mind off her newfound spinsterdom. She poured some more brandy, opened the envelope and was greeted by Rose Ellen's loopy, flowery hand.

Dear, dear Emma,

Emma harrumphed into her teacup. Two dears, no less!

I hope that all is well with you in your solitary existence. Naturally I will not regale you with all my problems. You know how my poor head has troubled me so since Daddy died. The doctor came yesterday afternoon and prescribed a powder, which exhausted me entirely. You, who have all the leisure in the world now, probably don't realize that with a growing daughter I no time to sleep all day. Though I am certain you are kept somewhat busy taking care of that large house Daddy left to you. You must be, since you haven't taken the time to answer my last two letters.

Emma looked at the nearly empty brandy bottle again. No, really, she'd had quite enough already.

Oh, Emma, why won't you come for a visit? I'm terribly worried at how lonely you must be, and I am sure you would be a better nurse to me than my darling Edward (he is useless with sick people). I know I told you about my swollen foot in my last letter. You will be shocked to hear I can no longer clasp the top three buttons on my shoes. And our new cook, Martha, is a wretched creature. Yesterday she let little Annalise help bake a cake—imagine a six-year-old covered head to toe in flour and you can envision the result! You are desperately needed here, Emma.

Since the day after their father had died, Emma had been pestered by her sister's requests that she move to Galveston. As far as she could tell, her sister hoped to secure a combination nanny-cook-slave for herself, something Emma had no intention of turning herself into. She had informed Rose Ellen of this twice already—but her sister had an uncanny knack for ignoring what was inconvenient.

Won't you please consider coming down for a while? Or better yet, why not sell that old place and live here indefinitely? Cooking and the care of Annalise, along with the proceeds from the sale of the house, would more than compensate Edward and me for having you live here. You wouldn't be a burden at all, and I'm sure you wouldn't be so lonely. I am becoming more enthusiastic about this plan as I write!

As if this weren't the very plan Emma had rejected several times already! One had to marvel at her sister's persistence. Rose Ellen would spare no effort to spare herself effort.

Why, with you here I am certain my headaches would go away completely, and perhaps I would no longer be run ragged on this poor foot of mine. Really, I can think of no reason on earth why you shouldn't come. There's nothing to keep you in Midday, and there are many more entertainments here for an older single woman. And who knows, Emma—in Galveston you might meet some older gentleman who would take a fancy to a woman like you. You shouldn't give up that hope, however slight it may be. But we all know in Midday there are no men who want to marry you, or it would have happened years ago.

Write to me as soon as possible with your answer, and I will have Edward make all the arrangements. Oh, I am so thrilled at the prospect of your coming! You cannot possibly understand how trying it has been taking care of this house and Annalise all by myself, especially with these headaches. I have simply been miserable.

Your loving sister,
Rose Ellen.

Emma folded the letter, shifted in her chair and reached for that brandy bottle. Of course she wouldn't consider going to Galveston to become Rose Ellen's indentured servant. That wasn't what disturbed her. No, it was her sister's choice of words—*older single woman*. Older than what? Methuselah?

In Midday there are no men who want to marry you, or it would have happened years ago....

Emma immediately thought of the handsome sheriff, Barton Sealy, and blushed. Whenever she dreamed of the future, his was the face that most often appeared in these fantasies. Of course, if word got out that she, plain Emma Colby, was sweet on Barton Sealy—a man far too handsome for his own good—she would never live down the humiliation of it. That's why her feelings for Barton, which had germinated even while he'd been courting Rose Ellen, had been her most tightly guarded secret.

She stood and paced across the kitchen. Before her father's death, no one had ever paid much attention to her—

not Rose Ellen and certainly not the people of Midday. But now that she was alone, and doing as she pleased, it seemed everyone in the world considered it their sacred duty to tell her what her future should be.

Of course, Joe Spears and Rose Ellen were right about one thing. She *had* been lonely after her father died. She'd rattled around the empty old house, haunted by its emptiness and her restless heart. After years of following her father on his rounds, and then caring for him in his sickness, she felt useless. She'd even begun to wonder if she wouldn't be better off in Galveston after all, sacrificing her freedom on the altar of Rose Ellen's headaches. Then one day Lorna had knocked on her door, needing her help and a place to stay, and Emma had immediately felt useful again.

And though the people of Midday might look with disdain upon her taking in Lorna, Emma began to understand how she might fill a need. Lorna needed somewhere to go to have her baby—why not here? Big cities had hospitals, so why shouldn't their rural community have somewhere to care for the needy, too? The only doctor now was Dr. Granby, but he lived in the next county. Wouldn't he be glad not to have to travel miles and miles to visit the sick in their far-flung houses when he could have them in one place?

The only problem was money. She had some that her father had left her, but that sum wouldn't last forever. She couldn't ask people who had even less to pay her; it would be like sucking blood from a turnip, anyway. What she needed was some means of making money...but how? She couldn't do any of the things that other women did to earn a living, like bake or sew or do laundry. At least, she couldn't do them particularly well. She was particularly bad at cooking. Poor Doc had uncomplainingly downed more half-baked, overcooked, or just plain burned meals than a body should be forced to eat in one lifetime.

Yet if she was going to go forward with this idea of a hospital, she had better learn to do something well enough that people would pay her for it. But what? What could possibly earn enough money for her to keep up a large house filled with sick people?

A loud *thunk* sounded, sending Emma shooting about three feet out of her chair.

"Heavens to Betsy!" She winced, and added a muttered, "Now I'm talking to myself." In a few weeks the good folks down in Midday could probably add *crazy* in front of the words *spinster lady* when they spoke of her. "Crazy spinster lady Emma Colby," they would whisper in hushed tones in the Midday Mercantile.

Emma laughed in spite of herself, stood and strode to the front door. Most likely a limb from the old oak out front had fallen on the porch, accounting for the clumping sound she'd heard. If it was a big branch she would wait until the morning to move it, but curiosity demanded that she check to see what kind of damage had been done.

She cracked the door, holding it firm against the pressure of the wind, and felt a cool rush of air burst past her. The storm was wilder than she had imagined, but so far it wasn't raining. She opened the door farther and poked her head out, savoring the feel of the bracing breeze on her cheeks. This blast was a welcome harbinger of spring, and the freshness of it brought a smile to her face as she surveyed her porch.

In a moment, the smile vanished in a gasp of surprise.

On the top step leading to the covered veranda lay a man, unconscious, on his side. His sprawled position, with his arm twisted awkwardly against a rail and his nose squashed into the pine floorboard, wasn't a comfortable way to have landed. Something must be very wrong with him.

She rushed forward and knelt by him, her hand darting out instinctively to capture his left wrist and check for a pulse. It was faint. She frowned, her years of working with her father rushing through her mind. What was the matter with him? She leaned closer to him, trying to get a closer look at his unshaven face, when the man she had assumed was unconscious suddenly grabbed her shoulder and pulled her toward him.

Emma let out another gasp as he drew her close and she found herself staring unblinkingly into two dark, piercing eyes. She couldn't speak—couldn't breathe.

"Angel," the man whispered, his voice a bare, throaty rasp. His hand reached up to her neck, and with firm pressure he pressed his lips against hers.

For one who appeared so close to death, his lips were surprisingly warm, and Emma was too stunned to pull away. All her life she'd dreamed of her first kiss. She'd always expected it would take place outdoors, on a moonlit night, maybe after a dance, with a man she'd admired for a long time. Perhaps the man would even be Barton Sealy. But now her first kiss was actually happening—and everything was all wrong!

A small frisson of heat shivered through her, making her thoughts spin in confusion, but before she could react, the moment was over. The man let out a groan and his head turned away. Emma recoiled slightly, and realized that the expected words of protest—and, in this instance, considering the man was a complete stranger, outrage—wouldn't be necessary. Her surprise swain was out cold.

She unwound his hand from her neck, and, taking hold of his far shoulder and hip, pushed with all her might to turn the man onto his back. He was so heavy, it took three tries to budge him. When she finally did have him laid out in front of her, she shrank back in shock.

She'd seen gunshot wounds before. Gruesome ones. Mortal wounds, even. But somehow nothing had ever looked so terrible as the sight of the dark stain radiating out across the entire front of this man's shirt. What little skin was visible on his bearded face was chalky white in the dim night—he had a dull waxen pallor. Emma's stomach turned, but she took a deep breath to fight against the nausea. This man needed help, and there was no one but herself to offer it to him.

First, she had to get him inside. Emma jumped to her feet and ran upstairs to her bedroom. She grabbed a woolen blanket from her chest and dashed straight down again, leaving the front door wide open. Working quickly, squinting against the wind, she spread the blanket and rolled the wounded man until he was fully on top of it. She was surprised again at how heavy he was. She stood at the top of the steps, gathered the two nearest corners of the blanket and put every bit of effort she had in her into pulling him up. After thirty seconds of huffing and puffing, she had budged him perhaps a foot. Wiping perspiration off her brow, she studied him, searching for anything that might lighten her load. Her gaze caught the gleam of a revolver on his hip. Bending, she unfastened his gun belt and tossed it aside, sending cold steel and slick leather clattering across the wooden floor into the shadows.

A silhouette darkened the front door and she heard a muffled yelp. Lorna stood there, equally transfixed by the wounded man and the gun Emma had just tossed aside.

"Maybe you can help me," Emma said, knowing activity might take Lorna's mind off more disturbing thoughts. "If you could lift his feet a little…"

As best she could in her condition, and with shaking hands, Lorna did as she was instructed. Together, inch by arduous inch, they tugged the man inside and lifted him onto the settee in the living room, which would have to serve as an operating table this night.

Lorna's blue eyes left the unconscious swarthy man for an instant and blinked up at Emma. "What do you think…?"

In spite of the long night ahead, Emma felt a grim lopsided smile tug at her lips. "I think I should have asked a few more questions about that outlaw Joe mentioned."

Chapter Two

Lang Tupper wasn't certain whether he was awake or dreaming. He knew he was lost, but he'd ridden for so long he didn't know where he'd ended up. He'd passed out someplace—that was all he could be sure of. And now he seemed to be hovering on the brink between life and death, between burning, restless, feverish pain and nothing. If he'd had a choice in the matter, he would have chosen the nothing. He could even hear a soft voice, an angel's voice beckoning him toward the sweet hereafter.

The pain in his chest seemed to be getting worse. Was that his wound, or his brother's betrayal festering in his heart? Amos's face appeared before him. Laughing, as he had so often as a boy. Then the laugh turned to a sneer. Amos as an adult. Lang's breath hitched. Sweat poured off him. He had to be alive to be sweating, right? Sweating was part of being on the run, a wanted man. He'd been sweating bricks for a solid day.

He gritted his teeth against the pain, and the angel's voice called to him again. What was she saying? That he'd had enough, that it was time to let go?

Letting go was hard. Which was peculiar, since to help

Amos he hadn't blinked an eye at letting go of the life he'd spent five painstaking years building for himself. The moment he'd stepped foot off the Wilkerson property to join the Gonzales gang, he'd known that no decent businessman would ever hire him, a farmhand turned outlaw, as foreman again. Without that kind of a job, most likely he would never again be able to earn enough to set himself up and start his own spread. But for his little brother's sake, the sacrifice had seemed worth it. Family looks after family, and since Amos was twelve, Lang had been all the family his brother had. He'd rescued him from schoolyard scrapes and barroom brawls, and he'd been prepared to rescue him again when he'd heard he'd gotten mixed up with a gang of outlaws.

Too late he realized that Amos might have gone beyond the rescuing stage. He just hadn't been able to accept it until, after the failed bank robbery, his own brother rode away, leaving Lang to die. But he hadn't died. He'd walked, and when he couldn't walk, he'd crawled.

It had taken two shots, two men, to bring him down. That's what he remembered most clearly. And one of them just might have come from his brother's gun.

The angel was hovering, and for a second the vision of Lucy came to him. Pretty, spoiled Lucy, in her robin's-egg-blue dress, laughing at him. That laughter had been as deadly in its own way as Amos's gun had been. Maybe his inability to judge people was his fatal flaw.

Another flash of white-hot pain shot through him. Lang felt his limbs thrash, heard his own voice cry out, and then the world went black again, except for the voice of that angel beckoning him to heaven...or was she telling him, in spite of everything, to live?

* * *

"Emma?"

Emma awakened with a jolt, half expecting a gun to be pointed in her face. Instead, Lorna knelt beside her, holding out a cup of steaming coffee.

"It's morning," Lorna whispered. She nodded anxiously toward the man covered by a pink woolen blanket, in case Emma had forgotten him. Small chance of that! The pale countenance of the desperado had haunted her fitful sleep. In her dream, she'd relived that brief, shocking pressure of his lips against hers again and again. Even now, her cheeks heated at the memory.

Their mysterious patient was exactly as Emma had left him just before dawn—asleep, helpless, his big body sprawled awkwardly on the parlor's dainty settee. She noted with some relief that there seemed to be a little more color in his skin than when last she'd checked. She expected a fever; that would at least mean he was strong enough that his body was beginning to fight back. She had been half prepared to discover he'd died during the night. She'd rarely seen a man lose so much blood and live, but this man apparently had strength to spare. And from the iron set of his jaw and the size of his wounds, she imagined he had plenty of fight in him, too.

Her gaze was riveted on him. He was so wild looking—more unkempt than any man she'd laid eyes on. His dark hair fell in long hanks, and his beard was scraggly and rough, as if he hadn't felt comfortable going into town to visit a barber for a while. His clothes, naturally, had been filthy with mud and blood; heaven only knew how long he had been crawling in the dirt before he'd come upon her house. With wounds in his side and one leg, it must have taken mammoth determination.

When she had stripped off his shirt, she'd been amazed that anyone so sick and helpless could appear so formidable. His muscles were lean but strong, like a cat's, and his skin had a dusting of the same dark hair that covered his head. Over the years she had seen many men naked, but until last night the male form itself had never given her much pause. The outlaw was as magnificent as the anatomy drawings in her father's medical books.

She blushed with shame to be thinking such things. Nurses shouldn't ogle—not even nurses who had been kissed by their patients! If she was going to let herself feel anything for the man, it should be fear. He was most likely an outlaw, and he'd already shown that, even sick, he could take her unawares.

Yet how could she fear someone after sharing such an ordeal with him? During what seemed like an endless night, she had opened up the stranger, pulled a bullet out of his side, cauterized his wounds and packed them—just as she had seen her father do. Only it had taken her own fingers, unaccustomed to being the ones performing the delicate tasks, much longer. And her father had never trembled as she had, or prayed aloud that his patient wouldn't die. She had, and still was. And she called on the stranger for help, too.

Live, she urged him silently as she had so often during the night. *Don't let yourself die. Don't disappoint me.*

"Do you *really* think he's the outlaw?" Lorna asked, as transfixed by the man's countenance as Emma was.

That was a question she hadn't allowed herself the luxury of pondering up to this moment, but now, as she stared at him openly in the bright light of morning, Emma wondered what she had done. Saved a criminal? "I'm afraid so."

She almost cracked a smile at the rightness of it. It just figured that the first man who would find her irresistibly kissable would be a broken-down outlaw!

"But he might not be," Lorna pointed out. "I mean...we don't know for sure that he is."

Emma frowned skeptically. "You mean despite the fact that there's an escaped outlaw in the area, this man might just happen to be a gunshot victim who has the appearance of a desperado?"

Lorna's cheeks reddened, and she sank her bulk down carefully on a nearby chair. "I guess it does sound far-fetched."

Emma shook her head. "As soon as I get him a little better, I'll have to turn him over to the sheriff."

To Barton Sealy. That prospect had its own appeal.

She allowed herself to imagine that shining moment when she would saddle up her father's horse and ride into town in a blaze of glory with the outlaw's body strapped over the back of her horse like a sack of potatoes.

"Here's your man," she would announce proudly to the stunned populace, all of them no doubt thinking, *Who would have thought the old spinster lady capable of such derring-do?*

The mob, of course, would be headed up by the handsome sheriff. In her mind Barton Sealy's twinkling blue eyes looked her over from head to toe with boundless admiration, as they never had in real life. "You're quite a woman, Miss Emma," he would say with a grin, flirting with her despite the rapt attention of the townspeople, not to mention the bound and gagged desperado just behind her. "I guess I never really appreciated how much of a woman until just this moment...."

"Emma?"

Lorna's voice intruded on her daydream, and Emma, flustered, snapped back to the present before the sheriff could fully express his newfound appreciation. ''Yes?''

''I said maybe this man was just a *victim* of the escaped outlaw.... Maybe that's why he was shot.'' Lorna glanced up at her hopefully.

Emma collapsed against the back of her chair and considered that unlikely explanation. Their man didn't have the appearance of a victim. ''He's not from around here,'' she pointed out. ''If he were a local, I would have seen him before.'' Practically every single man of marriageable age within fifty miles had been drawn to the Colby house like helpless moths to a blazing campfire to call on her little sister.

Nor was the man like any black sheep, long-lost cousin, or prodigal son she'd ever heard described. Having made the rounds with her father since she was a little girl, she had listened to all the stories of those who had gone west, or run off to sea, or even those who had escaped to big cities like New Orleans or St. Louis. She would have remembered tales of a gun-wielding panther of a man who had a face that appeared chiseled out of granite.

''I just thought...''

Emma smiled. Poor Lorna. She never wanted to think badly of anyone—not of the man who had abandoned her to the town's scorn, and not even of a stranger who was possibly a violent criminal. ''I know, you thought he might need somebody to stand by him. Who knows? Maybe he does.''

''Hello!''

At the sound of someone shouting outside, Lorna jumped, and her eyes widened fearfully. After having been kicked out of her own house and shunned by the entire

community, she was skittish about visitors. "Who do you
think could be coming by this time of morning?"

"Miss Emma?"

As suddenly as she recognized the visitor's voice, Emma
froze. "Barton Sealy!"

Lorna looked even more startled. "William's brother!"

As if fired to life by a cannon, Emma catapulted to the
window. At first she couldn't believe that she had heard
correctly. But when she peeked through the thick brocade
parlor curtains, she knew without a doubt that Barton
Sealy, at long last, had decided to pay her a visit.

Quaking with surprise, she jumped back from the window. "Nebuchadnezzar! I look terrible!" she exclaimed to
a flustered Lorna. After all, she'd had only a few hours'
sleep in a chair, and after she'd finished sewing up the
wounded man, she'd barely taken time to do the most per-
functory cleanup. Thank heavens she'd changed dresses!
Oh, but her hair...

"What if he's come on account of William?" Lorna's
fretful gaze was owl wide. "Barton's so intimidating! I
don't want to talk to him."

"You won't have to," Emma promised, also feeling
trepidation—but not because of William and Lorna's predicament. Her dream man had arrived on her doorstep—
and she probably looked like an unmade bed! "Just stay
here. I'll handle everything."

Emma skidded past the settee and again caught sight of
the outlaw, who—Lorna's anxiety and her own fluttery
heart to the contrary—was no doubt the real reason for the
sheriff's unexpected visit. Thank goodness Barton had
come! Her legs shook as she sprinted to the front door.
Until just this moment, she hadn't realized how fearful she
had been with the dangerous stranger under her roof.

She sprinted outside before the sheriff had made it to the top step of the porch, the one where she'd found the outlaw. Where he'd kissed her. The thought caused heat to rise in her cheeks. She definitely needed to drive that little incident out of her head.

"Miss Emma!"

Emma caught her breath, sure from Barton's surprised gaze that she looked as wild and flustered as she felt inside. The sheriff himself did nothing to steady the flutter of her heartbeat. To call Barton Sealy handsome was an indecent understatement. His blond hair and blue eyes, his broad shoulders and lean, muscular physique caused feminine pulses all over the county to leap out of control. He had the added dash, acknowledged in his confident grin, of being perfectly aware that he was irresistible, which made him insufferable at times, as well.

But to Emma, everything about him, right down to his masculine conceit, was absolutely wonderful. If only he could get that brother of his to straighten up! Maybe this was her chance to convince him to. She was bound to have some sort of influence with the sheriff once she showed him what she had hidden in her parlor.

"What brings you here, Sheriff?" As if she had to ask! She wasn't under the delusion that after all these years he had come to *see* her. Only one thing—only one *man*—had drawn him here. The outlaw.

He took off his hat and looked at her almost shyly. "I came to check up on you."

His reply stunned her into silence.

Her? She could hardly believe her ears! She could count on the fingers of one hand the number of men who had made the trip out to the Colby house just on her account.

The sheriff, still grinning, explained, "That was a mighty fierce storm last night."

Emma had a hard time breathing. He'd been worried about her? *Her?*

"Oh, y-yes…I know," she stammered, seeing her opening. "You wouldn't believe what I've been through!" Her tone lacked the bravado she'd imagined. Now she knew why Rose Ellen had always acted like a goose when anything in pants trudged up on the porch. It was that giddy, fluttery feeling that just the right pair of blue eyes could set off inside.

"Long night?" One of his eyes blinked at her so fast she wasn't sure it actually was a wink.

"You have no idea.…"

"Oh?" His smile broadened, causing her stomach to do a gravity-defying somersault. How could she know whether or not he was flirting with her? She'd had so little of that activity aimed at her. But he certainly seemed to be. Incredible!

"Yes.…" Emma said numbly.

"Rose Ellen always said you were skittish during a storm."

Hearing her sister's name out of the blue was like having ice water thrown in her face. And those lithe tummy somersaults suddenly tumbled into awkward heavy flops. "Rose Ellen?" Inside Emma's heart, slim hope evaporated like a dewdrop in July.

"Joe Spears told me you'd received a letter from your sister yesterday," Barton said, nudging a floor plank shyly with his boot tip. "Well, he said letters had been comin' from her real regular. And I was just wondering…"

Emma crossed her arms, holding in her crushing disappointment as best she could. "Yes?"

Barton took an eager step forward. "Well, Miss Emma, how *is* Rose Ellen?"

"Fine." Emma bit out the word.

His eyes lit up. "Is she coming for a visit any time soon?"

Emma almost wailed aloud at the very idea. The last thing she felt like contemplating right this moment was Rose Ellen and her aches and pains and domestic troubles. "Not that I know of."

"I got to thinking about it last night," Barton continued, scratching his wealth of blond hair, oblivious to Emma's letdown. "I thought maybe, since she's been writin' you all the time, Rose Ellen was having a bad spell at home. You know, I never did trust that fella she got herself hitched to...."

Emma pursed her lips. Actually, she herself had been stunned that Rose Ellen had had the sense to marry a man like Edward Douglas, when she'd had the choice of practically every type of male flesh in boot leather. "Edward Douglas is a fine man."

Barton blinked. "Well, naturally.... I didn't mean to say anything against him."

Just that he was untrustworthy, Emma thought with growing frustration. When it came to Rose Ellen, men just couldn't keep their good sense nailed down. And leave it to Rose Ellen to steal her thunder! Just when she was about to have her moment of glory in handing an infamous outlaw over to the man she had secretly been sweet on for years and years, the mere memory of Rose Ellen was shadowing her triumph. In fact, all the excitement she'd anticipated when thinking of relinquishing the outlaw was disappearing, even though it *was* her big chance to finally make an impression.

Finally sensing Emma's shift in mood, the sheriff shuffled his feet. "Of course, it wasn't on account of Rose Ellen that I rode all the way out here."

No, of course not. There was Rose Ellen, and there was the outlaw. Wouldn't he be surprised to discover who'd caught him!

He cleared his throat. "At the store yesterday Joe said you'd mentioned my brother's name in connection with that McCrae woman."

Emma blinked, flabbergasted. Not only was he not interested in her, he apparently wasn't too interested in that desperado on her settee, either!

Her reply was stiff. "I don't recall ever mentioning William's name."

"Hang it, Emma—Joe told several people that you said plain as day that William was shirking his responsibilities by not marrying that woman."

If he called Lorna "that woman" one more time, Emma was certain she was going to have a conniption. "And isn't he?"

"He is not. There's no telling what lies that McCrae woman would tell to get herself out of trouble, but she has no call mixing my brother up in her problems."

For a moment Emma saw red. Then she took a deep breath. She wasn't certain what upset her more—hearing Lorna slandered, or having the insults come from Barton Sealy, whom she'd always admired. For the past few weeks, she'd hoped Barton might help William do right by Lorna. "I think you'd better go, Sheriff."

"Darn it, Emma, this shouldn't be your concern! If you weren't so mule headed, you'd see she's taking advantage of you."

"Mule headed!" Did everyone in Midday think they

could give her marching orders? "It's the good folks at the Midday Mercantile who are being mules—petty, back-biting mules! If they had one-tenth the Christian spirit they all claim to have, they would see that Lorna is the victim here and do something to help her, not just talk about her."

As her words sank in, the sheriff's eyes narrowed, and he looked away, staring off at her pastureland. Good. Maybe he would go.

Except...

The outlaw! Emma shuffled her feet and forced herself not to send a nervous glance toward the parlor. Here she was expelling the sheriff from her home, when reason told her she needed him there. But despite her trepidation about being left alone again with the outlaw, stubbornness welled in her. She couldn't turn the outlaw over to the sheriff. Absolutely not...yet. A man who couldn't see the truth in his own domestic matters couldn't be allowed to handle a fragile life-and-death situation. Her patient was weak, and there was no doctor in town. Why should she have gone to all the trouble to save a man's life, only to have him hauled off to the filthy jail where he would most likely die within a day?

And after all, as Lorna had said, they weren't absolutely certain that the man *was* the outlaw. But the minute Barton got a look at the scruffy, wild-looking person, the lawman was certain to act on the assumption that the criminal had been caught. She'd be signing her patient's death warrant—in which case she might as well have let him bleed to death on her porch steps last night.

She wished the sheriff would leave. Of course, once he was gone, she would have sealed her fate. Aiding and abetting a criminal. She might claim that she didn't know for absolute certain he was a criminal, but would anyone believe her? After all, they hanged Mary Surratt just for renting a room to John Wilkes Booth!

She realized suddenly she had another problem. Even if her patient awoke and told her his name, she couldn't be certain he was the man the sheriff was looking for unless she knew the outlaw's name, too. And how was she going to get that information without tipping her hand?

She cleared her throat and changed the subject as casually as she could. "Has there been any sign of the desperado?"

The sheriff's head swung around, but those dazzling blue eyes looked vacant. "Huh?"

"You know…the desperado on the loose?"

"Oh! Well, now, Miss Emma, I doubt we'll see that rascal around here." Barton rocked cockily on his heels.

Emma might have laughed at the man's hubris if the situation hadn't been so fraught with peril. She needed to find out just how dangerous her desperado was. "What exactly is this man wanted for?" After all, his crime could have been something relatively harmless, in which case she shouldn't be so worried about housing him in her parlor. "Did he steal something? A horse, maybe?"

"He stole a horse, sure," Barton said. "A dappled gray mare."

A smile of relief tugged at her lips. If that was all—

"Not to mention, he murdered a bank clerk during a robbery."

She swallowed. *Murder.* "What…what is his name?"

"Lang Tupper."

She nodded solemnly, committing the name to memory. She had a feeling it would come in handy.

The sheriff laughed. "But if you run into him, Miss

Emma, you go ahead and shoot first and worry about his name later.''

"Heaven forbid any such a thing would ever happen!'' Emma cried, a quaking hand rising to her breast. She tilted her head and asked, "But if it *were* to happen...how would I know this outlaw if I saw him?''

"Oh, you'd know him. They say he's a big man, and dark. You can always tell a killer.''

She managed a wan smile, but had to look away to steady her nerves. Big and dark summed up her patient pretty well. Heavens! What should she do?

Unfortunately, at that moment her gaze landed on the gun belt she had tossed aside last night while trying to move the man, and this set off a new flurry of hysteria inside her. The sheriff was standing five feet from the outlaw's gun, which was barely hidden from view by her rocking chair. If he saw the gun, the whole matter would be out of her hands.

"Oh, my!'' she exclaimed.

Barton looked at her sharply. "Something wrong?''

"No...only I have some things I need to do,'' she said, edging back toward the door. "I don't mean to be unneighborly....''

The sheriff's face remained a blank. "Anything I can help you with?''

"No, goodness. I'm just...just spring cleaning.''

He winked. "Well, be careful. You might be doing spring cleaning, but you're no spring chicken anymore.''

Emma stood stunned for a moment. *No spring chicken?* Was the entire world conspiring to make her feel like an old maid? She recoiled, banging her head on the door frame behind her. Pain pierced her scalp. "Ouch!''

Barton's hand clamped down on her arm. "Land's sake, are you all right?"

"Yes!" She jumped away from him. Suddenly she didn't want to spend another second in his company. And the gun...she had to get rid of that gun!

Instead of freeing her, however, Barton tightened his grip as he dragged her over to the dreaded rocking chair. If he saw the gun and put two and two together, the sheriff would know that she'd been hiding the criminal from him. Would she, too, go to jail?

"I've never seen a woman so jittery!" Barton exclaimed as he sat her down in the rocker.

Emma held her breath as she saw his booted foot land not more than four inches away from the gun belt. She threw the back of her hand against her forehead, sure her secret was about to be discovered. Sure her life behind bars was about to begin...

"Ever since Doc passed away...my nerves..."

Barton's face was a mask of remorse. "Of course. You've probably been under a strain."

"Yes, I have." She was so nervous, it was a wonder she could speak at all.

"Everyone in town's remarked on it. Maybe it's the strain that caused you to do something crazy like take in that McCrae woman."

Emma stiffened, but when in the next instant she heard a groan from inside, she positively froze. The sheriff turned toward the front door. Emma faked a yawn, loudly mimicking the noise from inside, hoping to divert his attention.

He did look at her—and why wouldn't he? She'd just emitted a noise that sounded like a moose mating call as much as a yawn.

"Well, I guess I'd better be getting back," the sheriff

said quickly. He took a few steps, then turned, raking her up and down with his gaze. Emma rocked forward and held her breath, praying the gun belt was well hidden beneath her skirts.

"Was there something else you wanted?" She was such a bundle of nerves she was ready to toss him bodily back on his horse if need be.

He sawed his jaw back and forth for a moment. "Well…just remember me to your sister, won't you?"

She crossed her arms, holding in her distaste for that request. Some men didn't know when they were licked! "I certainly will."

He nodded, clapped his hat back on his head and strolled over to his gelding. To Emma, it seemed that he was taking an inordinate amount of time mounting up, but then she began to wonder if her sheriff weren't just a tad slow-witted—not an admirable trait for a lawman. Why hadn't she noticed this before?

When the sheriff finally trotted away and disappeared from sight, she spun on her heel and dashed inside. As she approached her patient, the jittery nerves she'd had with the sheriff fell away from her, replaced by another, more cautious feeling, mixed with a firm sense of purpose, as she touched her hand to the man's warm forehead. Fever.

No wonder he'd groaned. He had also turned over, and now a long, thick leg dangled over the side of the settee like a fallen branch.

A big man… Dark… You can always tell a killer….

Pushing the troubling words aside, she turned and marched upstairs to her room to fetch some more blankets. As always, she felt most comfortable when she was busy making herself useful. Even if the man she was making herself useful to was an outlaw.

Lorna's boots clattered behind her on the stairs as she came back down. "Is the sheriff gone?"

Emma nodded.

"Did he say anything about William?"

She decided a gentle lie was in order. "We didn't discuss William."

Blue eyes widened as they looked at her. "And you didn't tell the sheriff about the outlaw?"

"No," Emma admitted. "Our visitor won't be able to cause any harm in the state he's in. Right now he's as helpless as a kitten." She gave Lang Tupper's muscled physique a quick inspection, remembering the forceful way he'd caught her by surprise last night and pulled her lips down to his. *Kitten?* More like a feral jungle cat...

She added quickly, "But just in case he awakes, I'm going to hide his gun...and Doc's old rifle...and anything else that seems even remotely related to weaponry."

Chapter Three

"Mr. Tupper?"

Through a dense fog of fatigue Lang could hear the sweet voice calling to him again. The sound had an almost musical quality to it, reminding him of the gentle coo of the mourning dove, or lullabies women sang to their children.

"Mr. Tupper, can you hear me?"

His eyelids flickered against a blinding light. Then a shadow appeared, and he was able to keep his eyes open. The shadow looming over him was the angel with the voice—a pretty woman, real respectable, too, if he wasn't mistaken. His whole body hurt, from the roots of his hair to the soles of his feet, which felt as though they had walked six hundred miles. And maybe they had. He didn't know where in tarnation he'd landed himself.

"I'm Emma Colby." And as if this Emma Colby had the uncanny ability to read his thoughts she added, "You're in my home."

Tilting his head, he glanced away from Emma Colby's wide, luminous green eyes to the room around him. A carved wood clock ticked on a mantel, and his head seemed to pound in time with it. Confusion blurred his thoughts. All around were the trappings of the good life—fancy curtains, finely carved furniture, a rug with deep pile. How the hell had he ended up here?

"I found you on my doorstep." He turned his head back to Emma Colby, amazed. *Could* she read his mind? "You were hurt."

That was pretty damned obvious! His consciousness honed in on the burning pain in his side and his right leg.

"You were shot just below your ribs, Mr. Tupper. I removed the bullet. I also tended to the wound on your leg."

"You patched me up?" Lang had never met a lady doctor before.

She nodded. "This morning you developed a severe fever, but you seem to have pulled through nicely."

Shot. In a blast almost as strong as a gunshot, he remembered the tumbling sequence of events that had led to Amos's betrayal. And now, after all his effort to get away, it appeared he'd reached the end of the line. He couldn't move, much less work up the spunk to run.

His gun. His hand moved defensively to his hip, where it grasped nothing but pink woolen blanket. He glanced around, looking for his weapon and trying to see who besides Emma Colby he had to contend with. Banged up as he was, he wouldn't be much good without a gun.

"I'm sorry if the settee is uncomfortable. I wasn't able to move you upstairs." The woman smiled. "We had enough trouble just getting you into the parlor."

Having such a radiant smile focused on him was unbelievable. Before he'd passed out, his best guess had been that he'd awaken in a jail cell, or, more preferably, at the pearly gates. Never would he have expected to be lying in front of a woman in what was probably the nicest house he'd ever stepped foot in.

Then that word sank in. She'd said *we*. "You've got somebody else here?"

Her smile remained frozen. "Yes—there's Lorna."

Drawn to an almost undetectable sound, Lang looked at the door leading out of the room in time to fasten upon a pair of round blue eyes, which rounded even more when they discovered he was staring into them. In a flash, the blond head disappeared. Apparently Lorna was shy. And no one to be afraid of.

He frowned. "You two women dragged me in here all by yourselves?"

"Yes, we did."

Emma Colby didn't appear big enough to haul a grown man's deadweight very far, and he doubted the blonde was much bigger. He looked her over from the crown of her head to her slim shoulders and frame to her little feet encased in small, sturdy black boots. "I've put you to too much trouble."

"You weren't so difficult to manage." She blushed under his visual assessment.

Lang shook his head in amazement. He was still free—and living to see a pretty woman blush! He looked toward the door, and listened for any more sounds coming from the house. There was nothing but the unholy loud ticking of a clock. He truly was alone in a house with two ladies, at least one of whom seemed to know quite a bit about doctoring. Things could definitely be worse. Much worse. He screwed his lips into a grin.

The woman named Emma averted her eyes. "Are you thirsty, Mr. Tupper?"

Deep inside, he froze. *Mr. Tupper*... She'd said his name before, he remembered now. She knew who he was. Did she also know he was wanted by the law?

How else *would* she know his name?

Lorna's frightened blue eyes peeking at him made more sense now. That wasn't just shyness making a complete stranger regard him as if he were a dangerous character. To think—he'd gone from law-abiding farmer to desperado in the space of a month! If it had been anybody else, the absurdity of the situation might have had him in stitches. As it was, the only stitches he could produce were the ones over his mangled body parts.

He studied Emma Colby's profile. "Mr. Tupper" she called him, and she'd said his name with relative calm. There was no accusation in her tone. And yet he wore nothing that would reveal his identity, carried no letters that might have familiarized her with the name Lang Tupper. So the only way Miss Emma Colby could know him was through reputation...as an outlaw.

He knit his brows together and scrutinized her intently. Now that he got a better look at her, he could tell she was a little on the mousy side. Not nearly so pretty as Lucy— not that being unlike that other woman was necessarily a bad thing, he thought a little bitterly. Emma's hair was a light brown color, like fallen leaves, and her cheeks had a fine dusting of freckles. Her mouth, when it wasn't smiling, was nothing extraordinary. But her eyes, wide set and green, shone like precious gemstones with a rare intelligence. And beneath that calm of hers, he detected tension.

She was testing him. But what did she expect him to say? More interestingly, what did she *want* him to say?

Lang knew one thing—he hadn't come this far only to be handed over to the law by an earnest female. "Maybe you're confused...or I am. What name did you call me?"

"Tupper," she said, cocking her head a little as she watched him. "You said that name in your sleep. Lang Tupper, I believe you said."

"But my name's…Johann," he said. "Johann Archibald."

Johann had been one of the hands on the Wilkerson farm where Lang was foreman—though just how he'd sprung to mind at this juncture Lang couldn't say. But perhaps the thought of being saddled with the crazy name made his next wince more than a little convincing.

Emma gasped and leapt forward, kneeling next to him, close enough that he could smell a trace of perfume in the air. The sweetness of it—of her—made him squirm guiltily.

"Try not to move," Emma commanded gently, and her touch was just as gentle as her voice. He looked her up and down, admiring her concentration as she checked the dressing on his wound. Surprisingly, he felt a quick pang of desire as her fingers brushed his skin. That had to be a sign of health!

"You *must* be an angel." Though it came from his own lips, the comment surprised him.

Emma practically shot six feet into the air. "An angel!" she exclaimed, her cheeks pink. "How silly! I'm merely looking after you."

"And I appreciate it," he said truthfully, covering her shaking hand with his own.

She lifted the blanket back over him and pulled away. "And what do you do, Mr. Archibald, that makes a man want to shoot at you?"

He laughed. "What makes you think it was a man?"

Her lips twisted wryly. "Just a guess. Am I wrong?"

"No.…" He thought for a moment. Having a man shoot him did sound more plausible than some altercation with a woman. Also a little more dignified. "I must confess, Miss Colby…it is Miss, isn't it?"

Her cheeks flamed crimson, and for a moment he wondered if he'd insulted her in some way. "Yes."

"I'm not the most sterling character. I'm a...gambler."

"Ah!"

"Yes—you see, I got in a little over my head in a black-jack game back in San Antone...." He shrugged, deciding that providing more detail was just liable to trip him up later on. "I suppose you can guess the rest."

"Mmm." He wished she were a little more readable— he couldn't tell whether or not she was actually buying the load of nonsense he was selling her. "You're still a little feverish." The observation brought her to her feet. "I'll get you some water."

"Much obliged," he said with relief as he watched her walk quickly away. "But Miss Colby?"

She turned at the doorway, raising an eyebrow. "Yes?"

"Since you saved my life, I'd take it kindly if you just called me Johann."

"All right...Johann." She smiled, turned, then disappeared.

Lang sank down against his pillow, so tired, but fighting the urge to fall back asleep. Maybe this thin disguise would buy him some more time, time he needed to get better...and to find his gun. And to his way of thinking, some time with Emma Colby wouldn't be half bad, either. He allowed himself to smile as he thought about her trim figure, her soft hands, her gentle voice. And those eyes. Green like the first shoots of spring grass. She had a serene look about her that made the troubled, frantic past month of his life fly out of his mind. Miss Emma Colby had obviously lived a sheltered kind of existence.

He looked around him, doubt creeping into his thoughts. She was holed up in nice digs for a single lady. But where had she learned to deal unflinchingly with near-dead men and how to clean up bullet wounds? He frowned. As long as he had more holes in him than a worm-eaten fence post, he couldn't be too cocksure about anything. Maybe Emma had bought the story about his being Johann Archibald, gambler, but she'd looked relieved when he'd said it…as if she'd been glad to know he wasn't Tupper. Which meant that she definitely knew who Lang Tupper was.

Which led to an interesting question. If Emma did know who Lang Tupper was, and if she'd assumed he was that man, why had she bothered to save the life of an outlaw?

"Oh, Emma, what are we going to do?"

Emma crossed the kitchen, steeling herself against the plaintive sound of Lorna's trembly voice. Maybe it was best, she decided, simply to play innocent. "Do? About what?"

"About…" Lorna lowered her voice, though their visitor was well out of hearing range, and probably sound asleep. *"The outlaw…"*

Emma let out a careless laugh, hoping it sounded somewhat close to genuine. "You can rest easy about that. The man's not a desperado, just a gambler." Lord forgive her for lying, but Lorna had enough to worry about without adding Mr. Tupper to her list of woes.

Lorna frowned. "How do you know?"

"Because he told me so. His name is Johann Archibald."

The young woman digested this information slowly, watching absently as Emma crossed the kitchen putting together a tea tray for her patient. Her possibly criminal patient. She, for one, wasn't buying that gambling story…but neither was she ready to turn the man in. She told herself that she simply wanted to wait for him to get a little better. But there was something else she was waiting for, too.

A hint, maybe. How could a man seem so kind and innocent, and not *be* innocent?

"Well..." Lorna let out a sigh. "I suppose if he says he's a gambler, he must be one."

Emma nearly dropped her teapot. Was it any wonder the girl was in her predicament? She'd never met anyone so gullible. Probably she believed everything William Sealy said to her, too!

Lorna looked up at her, tears brimming. "I suppose I should be glad he's not a completely reputable man. Otherwise he'd never want to be in the...same...house—" her shoulders began to shake and her words came out in tortured sobs "—as...*me!*"

Emma put her teapot down with a clatter and scurried to Lorna's side. "You shouldn't talk like that! I've told you before, *you're* not the one who should be ashamed!"

Weeping outright, Lorna nodded her head and flapped her hands furiously to regain control.

Emma fumed at how unfair the world was. "Oh, I wish I could get my hands on that William Sealy! What I wouldn't like to say to that cad!"

Lorna looked horrified. "Emma, you wouldn't!"

"Not if you don't want me to," Emma raced on heatedly, "but I swear to you, Lorna, even that outlaw in there has more honor than that boy who broke your heart!"

Lorna gaped at her in teary confusion. "But you said the visitor *wasn't* an outlaw."

"Oh, I meant..." Emma swallowed, reminding herself that she shouldn't get so carried away in righteous indignation as long as she suspected she was hiding a criminal under her roof. "Well, even if he *were* an outlaw, he would have more honor than William Sealy."

Lorna nodded. "You're right. You're always right."

Always? Emma shivered. Was she right now? Had it been right to turn away the sheriff without letting him know about the man draped across her settee? Would she live to regret the impulsive decision to become the stranger's silent accomplice?

Would you have done so if he hadn't kissed you?

That last tantalizing question worried her more than anything. She'd always been so wise about men, had never let herself be carried away or made a fool of. Was she allowing her reason to be swept away now because her patient had strong arms and a pair of the most gorgeous brown eyes she'd ever seen?

She shook her head, clearing it of these terrible questions, and focused her attention back on Lorna. "You need to stop moping and carry your head high, Lorna. The world won't respect you if you don't respect yourself."

Dutifully, Lorna lifted her tear-streaked face. Her chin was wrinkled from the effort it took her to keep a stiff upper lip. "All right, Emma. I'll try."

"And don't worry about Mr. Archibald. I'll take care of him."

Lorna nodded. "Well, of course I'm not worried." She blinked as if the idea were plumb crazy. "There's nothing to fear about having a gambler in the house, is there?"

"Just the sheriff showing up again," Emma muttered to herself as she carried the tea tray out of the kitchen.

"I think it's time to move you upstairs, Johann."

Now that his fever seemed to be under control, Emma definitely wanted to get Mr. Archibald out of sight.

Her suggestion brought a smile to her patient's face. "I sure wouldn't mind sleeping in a real bed. I'm afraid I'm about ten sizes too big for this parlor contraption."

She couldn't help laughing. Considering how weak he must feel, and *who* he probably was, Mr. Archibald was one of the most pleasant invalids she'd ever met. In fact, it was his affability that made her doubt sometimes who he really was. Outlaws, she imagined, were sinister creatures with bad manners and no humor; despite his rough looks, Mr. Archibald seemed almost refined in his manners.

She was a little dismayed at how much she enjoyed talking to him. She still felt anxious at the way he'd grabbed her the night she'd found him, and sometimes when he looked at her, the kiss would spring to mind, making her cheeks warm and bringing a flurry of unfamiliar sensations. Again and again she had to remind herself she was being a goose. It would be one thing if she were remembering a kiss from a real beau. But her man had been losing consciousness and probably hadn't even meant to kiss her. It had been an involuntary reaction, like a twitch.

"It's most neighborly of you to take me in like this, Emma."

"It's nothing." Nothing law-abiding, she feared.

His eyes warmed. "I owe you my life. That's something—to me, at least."

She heard a note of desolation in his tone, and a sharp stab of sadness spiked her heart for him. Whoever he was, gambler or outlaw, he'd obviously seen trouble. "I'm sure you must have people somewhere who will be glad to hear that you're well. When you're feeling better, I'll write a letter for you."

She also wanted to advise him not to give her any more hints that he was alone in the world, a wanted man. She felt better thinking of him simply as Johann Archibald. A ridiculous name—and yet it was pleasantly different than Lang Tupper, the name she was trying to tuck safely into the back of her mind. "No one would have done any less than I have."

He chuckled, then pushed himself up with a wince. "Pretty, modest and talented to boot."

Pretty. Her gaze flew to his, wondering if he was thinking of their kiss.... But his gaze wasn't lascivious, just flattering. He seemed to have forgotten all about the liberty he'd taken with her. If only *she* could! She didn't know what to say. No one had called her pretty in...well, she wasn't sure how long. Lately she'd become more accustomed to comments like those she'd received from Joe. That she was thin, pale and spinstery. But Johann wasn't looking at her as if she were a spinster.

"Not many people would have known how to treat a wound like mine, ma'am," he went on. "Fortune must have been smiling on me to lead me up to your porch. Just how did you learn to care for the sick?"

"My father was a doctor. He died a few months ago."

Eyes the color of rich chocolate stared at her with piercing understanding. "I'm sorry."

She wondered whether he, too, had lost someone close to him. That would account for the sadness around his dark eyes. She wondered...

Well, the question that leapt immediately to her mind was if he had lost a wife or sweetheart...or whether he had one still. As if that was any of her business! She was interested only in taking care of him, healing him. The trouble was those eyes of his. They had been bothering her ever since he'd awakened. No one she'd ever known had stared at her so closely; it was unnerving. What was he trying to learn? And how could she become so undone by a simple gaze?

"Lorna, could you come here for a moment?" she called

out. Maybe having a third party in the room would calm her nerves.

In a second, Lorna was there beside them.

"I'm afraid I'll be too heavy for you two ladies." Johann looked up at Emma, obviously upset at having to lean on two women, one of whom was eight months pregnant.

"Nonsense!" Emma exclaimed. "You certainly can't make it upstairs by yourself. You've been prone for a day, and you lost a great deal of blood."

When the two of them pulled Johann upright, his skin turned clammy and his face went green, and he stopped complaining about having to accept help. "Take a moment to gather your breath," Emma instructed him as she and Lorna positioned themselves on either side of him, like two human crutches.

He obediently did as he was told, but when they finally began to move, she became acutely aware of the strong arm propped over her shoulder. The man was all muscle, and the press of his body against hers made her feel jittery as a cat during a hailstorm.

Emma pitched forward and probably would have fallen flat on her nose if Johann hadn't grabbed her sleeve and pulled her back. Thank goodness Lorna was holding *him* up or they might have toppled as easily as a line of dominoes.

"Mind the rug," he instructed her. "Can't have one of my crutches crumbling on me."

They made faster progress than Emma had anticipated, yet it was still too slow for her taste. If only she had a magic carpet that would fly Johann Archibald up these stairs, which took so much effort and might prolong their journey…and their bodily contact. A hot flush had come over her skin when she'd felt his hand catch her arm, and she was intensely aware of it there still. She hoped no one detected how flustered she was.

In bumbling lockstep, they continued the arduous ascent. It took Emma only a few steps to realize how weak Johann must really be. It felt as if he were leaning his full weight against her and Lorna. Then, when they had nearly reached the top of the stairs, a heavy knock sounded at the door. Emma froze, and for a moment it felt as if her very heart had stopped beating. Her gaze flew to Lorna's.

"Do you think it's the sheriff again?" Lorna asked, terrified at the idea of having to see William's brother.

"The sheriff!" Johann's eyes were wide with shock, and he swallowed in astonishment. *"Again?"* For all the world, he looked ready to forget the pain in his leg and sprint as far and as fast as he could. "When was he here before?"

"Yesterday," Lorna replied. "Emma didn't invite him in the house."

"I suppose I should offer him tea today." Emma did not want their visitor to get the impression that they were hostile to law and order. "But first we need to get you settled." She tried not to think about the fact that Johann's alarmed reaction to offering a lawman tea would have been just what she might have expected from the outlaw Lang Tupper.

The rest of the journey proceeded considerably faster. Johann had composed himself, but the thought of a sheriff being at her door put a spring in his limp. When Emma had deposited Johann inside her father's bedroom door, she turned to Lorna. "Do you think you can manage from here?"

Lorna nodded. "Of course." Still believing Mr. Archibald was just a gambler, she had no reason to be afraid that there was about to be a gunfight.

Was there about to be a gunfight?

The knock sounded at the front door again, more forcefully this time, causing all three of them to jump. "You'd better go, Emma!"

"Yes, Emma," their patient said, having regained his composure a little. "Don't keep your guest waiting on my account." She caught his gaze and was surprised to find a teasing humor in it. Would an outlaw be able to laugh at a time like this?

Realizing she didn't have time to sit around contemplating the character of desperadoes, Emma shut the door firmly behind her and flew down the stairs. If her visitor was the sheriff, back to ask questions he should have been asking yesterday, what would she say to him? Would he be able to read the lie in her eyes if she told him she hadn't seen the outlaw?

Taking a deep breath, she pulled the door open—to find not the sheriff but a man in coveralls holding a small boy wrapped in a woolen blanket. Emma recognized the farmer immediately as Cal Winters, an old widower whose large family her father had treated many times over the years. And the child in his arms—that must be his youngest, Davy. She'd attended his birth with her father, who had brought the boy into the world but hadn't been able to save Mrs. Winters that night.

Emma welcomed him, relieved that he wasn't the sheriff.

"I brung Davy," the man said gruffly as he crossed the threshold. "I brung him 'cause I didn't know where else to turn, Miss Emma."

"Of course!" She led the two of them into the parlor, whipped the old blanket off the settee and gestured to Cal to lay Davy across it. One in, one out, she thought, astonished that her nursing services had so suddenly come into vogue.

"I heard what you done for the McCrae girl and I thought it was a good thing."

Emma looked at the man with surprise, and respect. "You're about the only one, it seems."

"Ain't everybody who understands other people's misfortunes, I guess," Cal said sadly. "Anyways, when my boy came down sick with the pox, you were the only one I could think of to turn to. We don't have any money, you see. And since your pa...well, there ain't no doctor."

"I understand," Emma said, bending to examine Davy. The boy seemed small for his age, though he had a healthy mop of white-blond hair on his head and intelligent blue eyes. A simple touch to his forehead told her he had a fever, and his face and thin arms were covered with bumps she recognized from much experience, including her own. "It's chicken pox, all right."

"I ain't gonna die, am I, Miss Emma?" The boy's voice was a singular mixture of dread and morbid curiosity.

She looked down into the young boy's eyes and bit back a laugh. "No, you're not. You're just going to stay in bed and try not to scratch." Davy appeared immensely relieved to hear his young life would be spared. Emma looked up at the boy's father. "No need to worry, Mr. Winters. Just keep him in bed, watch him and make sure he stays well covered until the fever breaks. Plenty of water to drink, too."

Cal shuffled his feet. "I, uh, guess there's no other way...."

Emma frowned. "No other way to what?"

His careworn eyes met hers beseechingly. "See, it's plowin' time, and all my children are out in the fields.

That's why I brung Davy here, Miss Emma. I was hoping…''

Emma understood immediately. ''You were hoping I would take him,'' she guessed. The Winterses were poor— getting their crops in meant life and death to them, and with no mother, there would be no one to look after Davy at home. The other children couldn't be spared from work, and even if they could, chances were with Davy near, his siblings would become infected with the chicken pox, too. Which would only multiply Cal's dilemma.

She didn't hesitate. ''I'd be glad to keep Davy here, if you'll allow me. I'm sure he'll be fine in a matter of weeks.''

Davy, his eyes flying open at this news, looked around the parlor in wonder. ''I get to stay here?''

Emma laughed. Never had she looked at the parlor as if it were a veritable fairyland.

Davy's father sent his son a stern gaze. ''Mind you behave, and do what Miss Emma tells you.''

''He can stay in…'' Emma suddenly remembered her house was filling up quickly. Lorna was in Rose Ellen's old room, and now there was probably an outlaw living where her father used to reside.

Mr. Archibald! What was she going to do about him? It was one thing putting herself and Lorna in danger. They could take care of themselves. Or in any case, they were adults. But what of Davy? He was just a boy. Could she really have Mr. Winters entrust his son to her care when she was harboring someone who was most likely a fugitive?

Then again, could she bear to turn Davy away? That would be a hardship on his family. Besides, she seriously doubted that Mr. Archibald would harm any of them…especially while he was seriously ill himself. He didn't have access to his weapon. The house was relatively safe.

"I'm sure I'll be bringing him back to you in about two weeks' time," she assured Cal. "He won't be sick for long."

Cal was pleased. "I'm much obliged, Emma. I don't know how we'll repay you."

"Don't worry about that." She waited for the father to give his son parting instructions to behave and mind her, then, after he refused what refreshments she offered, she ushered him to the front door. "I'll take good care of your son for you, Mr. Winters."

He tipped his hat and rode off, and Emma returned to Davy. "I need to get you up to your room."

"My own room?" He shook his full head of white hair in wonderment.

"Yes, indeed. And once you're settled, and sleep for a little bit, I'll bring you some soup."

In a moment, Lorna came down the stairs. "What is it? Can I help?"

Emma looked up, suddenly remembering one drawback to taking in Davy. "Have you had chicken pox?"

Lorna nodded. "When I was little."

That was good. "That leaves Mr. Archibald. I hope he's had them already. How is he settling in?"

Davy didn't give Lorna time to answer. "Mr. Archibald? Who's he?"

Emma combed back the boy's thick hair with her hand. "A nice man who's staying here, too. He's sick, like you are."

"Does he itch, too?"

Emma and Lorna chuckled. "No," Emma replied as she reached down and pulled Davy into her arms to carry him upstairs. "He's a different kind of sick."

"He's lucky," Davy grumbled. "Does he get soup, too?"

Emma nodded. "If he behaves."

"Royal flush!" Emma crowed triumphantly.

Lang inspected his paltry two pairs then stared back at Emma's winning hand. Then he compared the dwindling pile of matchsticks on his side of the coverlet to the virtual mountain of matches next to Emma. "I've fallen in with a cardsharp!"

She laughed at him. "I can see how you might have gotten into trouble gambling. You need to change professions."

Truer words were never spoken. The one he'd been practicing for the past month—bank robbing—hadn't worked out so well. "How on earth did you learn to play cards like that?"

"My father taught me." Her eyes shone with memory. "Doc and I used to play every evening about this time, just about sunset. I hadn't realized how I missed those times! He was never so easy to beat, though." Her impish glee at winning made Emma seem as girlish as Lorna. "Davy puts up a better fight than you do!"

Lang loved to see Emma laugh—something she'd been doing a lot more of this evening, now that he was stowed safely away in an upstairs bedroom. He felt a lot better himself with the new arrangement, even given that there was now another person in the house to worry about. "I need to hold a powwow with this youngster," he said, feigning aggrievement. "I'm half inclined to think you're cheating."

"And I'm half inclined to think that you're not really a gambler at all."

Lang's poker face was truly tested in the sharp scrutiny

of those green eyes. She wasn't teasing any longer. He itched to look away, but he didn't, forcing himself to remain smiling. How much did she know? Her words made him wary, which he supposed he should have remained all along. He couldn't afford to let his guard down—even before sweet, generous Emma Colby.

Sweet, sly Emma Colby.

He looked up at her and let out a dramatic sigh. "All right, all right. If you must know the truth, I've been letting you win."

"*Letting* me!" The words were practically a shriek of outrage. "That's the most preposterous thing I've ever heard!"

"It would hardly be right for me to play at full speed. I'm a guest, and after all, you've been so kind...."

"That's the most feeble excuse for poor playing I've ever heard," she scoffed.

"How was I to know that beneath that sweet, pretty, innocent exterior beat the heart of a unrepentant card fiend?"

"Now I know you're lying. That's the second time you've said I was pretty. I suspect you're trying to flatter me into losing to you!"

She wasn't so far from the truth, but he couldn't let one misperception pass. "But I *do* think you're pretty. There's nothing deceptive in my saying so."

She blushed.

"Aren't you accustomed to men speaking their minds to you?"

"Yes, but unfortunately that's not what they usually say!"

He laughed, then suddenly marveled at the luck he'd had. Was he really lying in a warm bed, laughing with a pretty woman? Miraculous! Two days ago he'd thought his life was over. "Then these Midday men ought to be horse-whipped. Why should a girl like yourself still be trotting around unmarried?"

His words appeared to shock her down to her toes. "You're very forward, aren't you?"

"It's best to be direct, if you want answers."

She sighed and fastened a level stare on him. "Part of what's wrong, I suspect, is that I'm not a girl anymore. I'm an…" She swallowed. "An old maid."

He barked out a sharp laugh.

She stiffened. "I've heard it from a very good authority."

"I've known girls younger than you who look twice as old." He'd also known a girl twice as beautiful yet at the same time less dazzling. Lucy. The thought of her threatened to bring his spirits low. Why should he keep thinking of that sad history now when he had myriad other problems to deal with? Maybe it was because no woman since Lucy had captured his eye…until Emma. But that probably had to do more with the fact that Emma was so singular. She'd saved his life.

He looked away, trying to put all thoughts of women out of his head. With one foot in the gallows, he had no time for that nonsense now. Thinking of Emma, entertaining ideas about how shocked she would be to learn that he daydreamed about feeling her lips beneath his, was pointless. He couldn't kiss her. He had nothing—just had a life of running ahead of him, which didn't seem much of a life at all.

And as if to underline this fact, at that moment Emma peered out the window to watch something in the pasture below. Lang, too, looked out…and felt his heart sink in his chest. Below them, a dappled gray mare grazed on fresh shoots of grass. His memory wasn't so far gone that he didn't remember the stolen horse that had saved his life, and probably had almost cost him it, as well.

"Nice animal." The description of the horse a bank robber had stolen was probably all over by now. In his mind he was packing his bags, wondering how he would escape. *If* he could escape.

"Thank you," Emma said.

His head whipped around to gape at her. Could he have heard her correctly? Had she just claimed ownership of his stolen nag?

Emma shrugged her thin shoulders. "The trouble is, she always wants to graze too close to the house." She looked at him, her eyes sharp, surely missing none of the confusion in his face. "I should put her up in the barn, don't you think?"

Lang nodded his head numbly. "That would be a good idea."

They played another hand, and the subject of the mare was never raised again. Lang began to think that maybe he remembered wrong and the little mare did belong to Emma. Maybe she didn't even suspect who he really was....

But suddenly, subtly, Emma let him know that he couldn't live under this delusion for long. "I'd better check on Lorna soon," she said as she dealt out a last hand. "She's so nervous these days...."

Something in the change in Emma's tone made him stiffen. "Why? Because her time's coming?"

Green eyes met his flatly. "Because of the outlaw."

The air between them crackled with tension.

"Outlaw?" he asked, scratching his uncomfortable beard. "I, uh, guess I haven't heard." He glanced at the cards she'd dealt him, still face down on the coverlet. His hands felt too heavy to pick them up.

"It's all anyone talks about," Emma said.

"What's this fella done?"

She picked up her cards and inspected them. "Murder, they say."

The room began to spin. Lang was certain he'd heard her wrong, but her eyes told him he hadn't. *Murder?* As if bank robbing and horse thieving weren't enough! "Who…" His mouth was so dry he could barely rasp out a question. "Who did he murder?"

"A bank clerk."

Lang ran through the day of the robbery over and over in his mind; but he would have remembered killing someone. He'd never done serious harm to another person in his life. And the only person who'd been shot that day was himself.

Then he remembered. Moments before his brother and his cohorts had run out of the bank, *two* shots had been fired in quick succession. The sound of the first gunshot had so surprised Lang, he'd turned to see who had fired. Then the second shot had struck him. Now he couldn't be sure from whose gun either bullet had come, but he was fairly certain Amos had been behind him. Amos, who didn't want a big brother's interference.

And Lang looked just enough like Amos to confuse a witness…. The light-headed queasiness he'd experienced when trying to walk up those stairs returned.

"Murder," he breathed, his voice reedy and thin.

"Terrible business." Emma clucked her tongue. "The sheriff was here just yesterday telling me about it."

Lang bit his lip. Maybe he should turn himself in, and tell the truth. He shouldn't be lying here taking advantage of Emma's kindness when he was a wanted man. For murder. Good God! Sweat poured out of him.

"I sure could use a drink," he said.

Emma looked over at the full water pitcher by his side. He frowned. "I mean something with teeth."

"Oh." Emma frowned. "I had some brandy—medicinal brandy, mind you—but..."

Just his luck. "You probably used it all the night I arrived."

Faint color touched her cheeks, which made him wonder if he hadn't been the recipient of the last drops of spirits. "Well...yes."

Never in his life had he had a real craving for liquor— but just this moment his thirst for it was fierce. Drowning himself in alcohol was all he could think of to do to forget—forget Amos, forget the past month, forget that his life, his future, was ruined. Maybe if he drank enough, he would gather up the nerve to march into town to see Emma's friend the sheriff and turn himself in, and make his future that much shorter. He felt sick. Never had he expected to finish his life at the end of a rope.

"Mr. Archibald, is there something wrong? You haven't looked at your cards!"

Emma's pretty face, those intelligent eyes, inspected him. She knew. He knew she knew. So why was she hiding him? Did she pity him for some reason he couldn't fathom?

He looked at her lips and thought of another way to forget his troubles. How easily he could imagine leaving all thought behind and losing himself in the pleasures of her lips, her flesh. He could almost sense the fresh scent of verbena he would smell when he buried his face in her hair. Or maybe she would prefer camellias. He'd never felt so weak, so much at someone else's mercy.

"Mr. Archibald." Emma said his name and reached out to him.

He pulled his hand back, pulled himself together and

gathered his cards in his shaky fist. When he could focus at all, he found himself looking at an inside straight.

Lucky. It was hard to believe that anything in his life could turn lucky at this point.

"Don't they sell whiskey in Midday?"

Emma glanced up at him, surprised. "Of course, but…"

"I'll wager this hand against a flask of rye."

"This hand?" she asked. "You mean gambling?"

He looked at the Mount Everest of matchsticks on her side of the coverlet and almost laughed. What did *she* have to be nervous about? "Surely you don't have anything against a friendly bet?"

"But you couldn't expect *me* to buy whiskey!" She eyed him as if he'd turned lunatic on her. "I have my reputation to consider! Why, the store's run by the biggest gossip in town, and all the ladies gather there."

He waved off her argument. "Are you going to let a bunch of old crows dictate what you can have in your own house?"

"Well, no—"

"And who cares if a storekeeper knows you like to take a little nip now and then?"

Her cheeks were red. "But I don't!"

"You can't let other people tell you how to live for the rest of your life."

"But I don't!" she repeated indignantly.

He slapped the covers. "Then just march into that store and announce for the world to hear that you need a bottle of spirits…large size."

She gazed at him seriously. "Alcohol would make you feel better?"

Pickling himself was as good a way as any to blot out his troubles. He nodded. "Or are you afraid I might leave when you go to town?"

"I don't think you'll be going anywhere for a while, Mr. Archibald. You could barely make it up a flight of stairs."

"I mend quickly."

"You sound as if you'd like to make a fast getaway," she said, eyeing him closely.

Lang laughed uncomfortably at her use of desperado lingo. "Personally, I'd like to stay forever...but of course I can't."

"Of course." She looked almost disappointed.

And, oddly, at the thought of leaving Emma, his gut felt a stab of regret that made him blurt impulsively, "If I lose this hand, Miss Emma, I promise I'll tell you all about myself, and how I got here, and where I'm headed."

Her eyes glittered in open curiosity, and she glanced with a certain smug assurance at the disparity of their matchsticks. "All right, Mr. Archibald, you have yourself a wager."

Lang looked into Emma's green eyes, shocked to find he wanted to confide in her...almost as much as he wanted that whiskey.

Chapter Four

"**Y**ou want a bottle of *what?*"

As if he hadn't heard her! Emma lifted her chin and leveled her gaze on Joe Spears, whose sharp eyes were squinting at her in disapproval. Johann was right. Did she really want this old man telling her how to live her life?

Definitely not!

"Rye whiskey," she repeated.

"Lord-a-mercy!" Joe blinked in amazement.

"Your largest bottle," Emma added defiantly, drawing open stares from Mrs. Dunston and her married daughter Sara. To her right Emma was flanked by Constance O'Hurlihy, who was wearing a perfectly ridiculous hat topped by a pert bird that stared out like a third set of eyes, and who closed in on Emma with gray arched brows. Emma didn't care if they all thought she was peculiar, or had gone to Hades in a handcart, nor was she going to offer any explanations. If they wanted to believe she was a tippling old spinster, so be it. This was her declaration of independence.

Of course, she couldn't help asking herself, was she really independent when she was taking orders from an outlaw? She had few illusions left where Johann Archibald was concerned. The horse now housed in her barn exactly matched the dappled gray mare described on the Wanted poster—which also sported Johann's image—outside the post office and on selected poles around town. If Johann Archibald wasn't Lang Tupper, she wasn't Emma Colby. And if there was anything she was sure of right at this moment, with grizzled Joe gaping at her as if she'd just asked for a bottle of opium, not whiskey, it was that she was Emma Colby.

Joe let out a bark and scratched his rough gray grizzled face. "Women these days! I guess I've lived to see everything!"

Emma smiled placidly. "Doc always said he'd never live in a house without a bottle of spirits. It has many medicinal properties, you know."

As always when she spoke of her father, Joe looked more reverent. "Doc said that, did he?"

"Yes, indeed. It does a lot more for headaches and insomnia than those pink pills you're selling. And as for female complaints—"

Joe, horrified at the thought of having to hear one word about "female complaints," raised his hands in a gesture of surrender. "All right, all right," he muttered, turning and reaching for what looked like a gallon jug. "I suppose old Doc knew what he was talking about. Not his fault he couldn't do nothin' for my lumbago."

"Maybe you should take a sip now and then," Emma suggested pertly.

He snorted. "I might try a slug, at that."

Mrs. Dunston sidled closer to Emma. "I'll just bet your buying spirits has to do with that McCrae girl!"

Joe, who had butted heads with Emma on the subject of Lorna once before, nearly dropped the large glass bottle as the ladies circled around her like a hostile tribe.

"*Lorna* doesn't imbibe," Emma assured them, attempting to hold on to her temper.

The three ladies exchanged skeptical glances, and the thin-lipped Constance smirked. "It's comforting to know there's something she'll say no to."

Emma's blood reached boiling point.

"Here's your bottle, Emma!" Joe interjected from behind the counter, obviously trying to avoid bloodshed in his store. Or maybe he was just trying to angle for a better view.

Emma wasn't ready to walk away from the self-righteous cluster. What did they know of Lorna and her problems? "Lorna has been so kind and helpful to me, I'm going to ask her to be my assistant."

Three unblinking sets of eyes—not to mention that bird on Constance's hat—gaped at her in astonishment. "Your assistant in *what?*" Mrs. Dunston asked.

"The hospital I intend to start here."

The store fell so silent one could have heard an ant cough.

"You, Emma?" Sara piped up. "A hospital? Here?"

Emma's lips turned up in a grin. "Yes, Sara. And when my facility is up and running, you might consider coming by to have your hearing checked."

Constance bustled forward, wagging a long bony finger in Emma's face. "That's the most outrageous idea I've ever heard! Why does Midday need a hospital? Folks around here get taken care of just fine at home, by their own people, just as it should be."

"Not all of them, Constance."

Sara put a hand on her arm condescendingly. "Naturally, Emma, since your dear father died you've been lonely, but there's no call for you to start taking up queer notions."

"That's what I told her," Joe said, "but she don't listen."

"Lord-a-mercy!" Mrs. Dunston cried, as if the horror of it was just beginning to sink in. "A hospital, right here in Midday. Why, I've got a cousin from Philadelphia and she said those places do nothing but attract riffraff and breed pestilence!"

They all needed a good bashing on the head with a Florence Nightingale primer.

Constance's thin lips twisted sourly. "It would set a bad example for a young gentlewoman like yourself to work alone among sick people all day, Emma. I'm not sure it's even proper!"

"No one mentioned propriety when I used to make the rounds with my father," Emma pointed out.

"Well, no…naturally," Mrs. Dunston stuttered in response. "Your father could be trusted to know what was best, of course."

But *she* couldn't, was the implication. Emma began to see red again. How were women alone supposed to make useful lives for themselves if the world wouldn't allow them to make their own decisions? She supposed that's why single women like Constance were encouraged to embrace the most restrictive, small-minded viewpoint, to discourage them from thinking for themselves. Like men. But the thought of turning into Constance O'Hurlihy terrified Emma more than becoming Midday's pariah.

"You always were the strangest girl, Emma," Sara said, holding her head loftily. "But I never thought you'd show such poor judgment."

She and Sara had been schoolmates, but right now Emma felt as if she had been reared on another planet from Sara. "Some of the less fortunate around Midday might not think it's poor judgment," she said sharply. "Those are the people who concern me."

"Well!" exclaimed Mrs. Dunston, drawing up in offense. All three women were huddled together, gaping at her like offended peahens.

"Thank you for the whiskey, Joe." Emma turned to him. She had to hold herself back from running out the door, but she wasn't going to give the ladies the satisfaction of seeing how much they ruffled her.

"I don't stock that much liquor, you know," Joe grumbled, looking almost disappointed that she was averting an all-out social war. "Didn't used to at all till Arvin died and his barroom shut down."

"Maybe you should consider stocking more," Emma advised. "In fact, you could turn this whole place into a very fine saloon. All it needs is velvet curtains, mirrors and pictures of unclad women."

She spun on her heel and bit back a smile, leaving the store clutching her bottle close to hide the fact that her hands were shaking. She could practically feel the shocked glares burning into her back as the door slapped closed behind her.

It was silly, but she felt a rush of pride after the confrontation. All her life she'd been meek and dutiful, devoting her life to studying, and taking care of others, taking care of her father. She'd never done a daring thing in her life, and certainly had never sassed anyone. Now look at her—helping the outcast! Consorting with outlaws! Buying liquor! She was out of control, sliding down an icy slope, free-falling off the mountain of dull Midday respectability.

Worse yet, she was glad. She'd been avoiding coming to town since her father died; now she wondered why. She was alone, but she wasn't powerless. She had money, for the time being, and she owned property—and she intended to use both for the town's good, even if Midday had to be drawn kicking and screaming into acceptance of her hospital.

She marched down the street with a grin until she passed a pole and came face-to-face with Johann's steely glare. Only it wasn't Johann's, really. The expression on the man's face was mean, direct, ruthless, as if the sketch had been drawn of Johann's evil twin. The prime difference between them was that the man in the picture was clean shaven, with a deep cleft in his chin, and Johann had a dark scraggly beard—she doubted she'd recognize him without it. The picture also contained none of the brooding sadness she'd seen in Johann's expression, or the teasing brilliance of his eyes when he played cards with her, or the shock and disbelief that had crossed his face when she'd told him that Lang Tupper was wanted for murder.

It was that last expression that stuck in her mind the most. Because if Johann were really the coldhearted murderer pictured here on this pole, he wouldn't have blinked an eye at being informed he was wanted for murder. In fact, if Johann were the vicious desperado the authorities were searching for, she had little doubt that she would have been a goner already.

How, then, to explain Johann's arrival at her house on the very night the law was searching for him, and his wounds, and his similarity to the Wanted portrait?

There was a one-hundred-dollar reward on his head, and she would have liked to believe that the lure of that money didn't tempt her. But it did. She would need money for her hospital. The only thing preventing her from marching right up to Barton Sealy and offering up her houseguest was that niggling doubt. Johann Archibald...or Lang Tupper? Why didn't the two fit together better? In spite of all the damning evidence, she couldn't envision her patient as a vicious murderer.

And maybe, she thought guiltily, maybe one other reason she didn't throw her guest to the sheriff was that kiss. The one Johann had forgotten but she couldn't. Something in him had reached out to her that night; he'd captured more than her lips. There was just the tiniest corner of her heart that couldn't help but respond to the kiss, and more important, to the way his eyes looked her up and down like no other man's ever had. Though she knew it was wrong to feel even a sliver of attraction to a man who was a desperado. It was ridiculous. Some might even say pathetic.

Emma frowned, wondering if he would still be there when she returned to the house. Probably, she decided. Where would he go, and how? He knew she'd put his horse in the barn, out of sight, but he was still so weak he'd nearly passed out that morning when she'd changed the dressing on his wound. She doubted he'd survive long on horseback.

No, he was definitely going to have to stay with her a while. Her pulse jumped with guilty pleasure at the thought. She'd enjoyed playing cards with him. She even liked the way he flirted with her—though she was sure it was just his way of manipulating her. No man had bothered to flirt with her before. How could they? Most of her life she had been flanked by Rose Ellen, and a man would have had to be blind not to prefer her younger sister to herself. If given the opportunity, Johann would probably be no different. Rose Ellen had that effect on the opposite sex, which just proved that the average man didn't care one whit whether a woman had sense or not. Expecting a man to resist a pretty face was like expecting a dog not to roll in a cow pie.

After a quick peek around the empty block, she reached out and snatched the picture off the pole. In the next block, outside the sheriff's office, she removed another one. It was lunacy, but she couldn't help herself. The more people who saw the picture, the more likelihood there seemed of Johann's being caught. She had to do what she could to prevent that from happening, at least till she knew how he'd come to be a desperado. A man deserved that much.

When she had taken down all the posters she could find on Main Street, she turned toward the livery stable, where she'd left her wagon. As she was walking past the town's small hotel, a stage was letting off its passengers. A child hopped down from the cab, making Emma smile. The girl appeared to be six years old—just the age her niece would be. In fact, this little girl even *looked* like Annalise, although Emma hadn't seen her for two years. She had dark brown hair cascading in neat ringlets around her pudgy face, and sparkling blue eyes fringed with long dark lashes. Her blue velvet dress and hair ribbons matched her eyes. Rosebud lips pursed at the world with a tentative, almost skeptical frown not often seen in a girl that age.

Emma tilted her head, then felt the blood drain out of her cheeks. The similarity was too uncanny! That *was* Rose Ellen's daughter, she was sure of it! But where was Rose Ellen?

She surged forward just in time to see her sister disembark from the stagecoach. At the sight, she froze in shock—and confusion. What was Rose Ellen doing in Midday?

Her sister, beautifully dressed as always, wore a deep blue traveling frock much the same color as her daughter's, with velvet cuffs and piping along the hem. Rose Ellen's dark, luxurious hair was done up in one of those elaborate styles with cascading curls that Emma could only marvel at, since twirling her hair into a simple bun was a feat for her. But Rose Ellen had always been able to copy styles out of magazines with just a few glances and a couple of hairpins.

Naturally, she sported a fashionable hat that matched her dress perfectly; this one had a veil of blue netting that covered her face, making her look older and more distinguished than Emma could remember. Not that it mattered. Rose Ellen, with her beautiful skin and pampered life, was one of those women who only seemed to become more lovely as the years went by. Her eager, plump, youthful look had given way to a more angular grace, which turned more heads than ever. Certainly there was no shortage of men taking note of her this morning. Emma counted no less than five pairs of hands helping her to step down from the carriage—even the driver, who looked as if he couldn't care less whether ladies tripped coming down from his coach or not, had leapt off his perch to come to Rose Ellen's aid.

And Rose Ellen accepted help in this simple task with open delight that made the men all the more glad they'd come to her rescue. No wonder males loved her!

Emma snapped out of her trance when Rose Ellen looked up and met her gaze. "Emma!" her sister cried, running forward. She grabbed her by the shoulders and kissed the air above one of Emma's cheeks. "Dear, dear Emma!"

Numb, Emma accepted the embrace, though she felt conflicted as always around Rose Ellen. She had genuine affection for her sister, who after all had been the companion of her youth; then again, why did she always feel like a barn wren next to Rose Ellen's swanlike glory?

"I'm so glad you came to greet me!" Rose Ellen said,

as if this meeting could have possibly been planned. Why hadn't Rose Ellen given her some warning?

"Rose Ellen, what on earth are you doing here?"

Rose Ellen laughed. "Why, I would think it would be obvious! I've come for a visit!"

Clammy panic stole over her. "V-visit?"

"Of course! You never wrote me back, not for weeks and weeks, and I was so-o-o worried that you were rattling around that old house just dying of loneliness that I entered into a little correspondence with my old friend Janine Littlefield."

And Janine, who was Joe Spears's niece by marriage, would know everything that happened in Midday.

Rose Ellen's expression turned mournful. "Emma, Janine said you'd taken in a…well, some wretched girl so insignificant I'd never even heard of her!"

To cover her anger, Emma turned to her niece and smiled. "Hello, Annalise. Do you remember me?"

The little girl lifted her chin and frowned gravely. Deep dimples appeared in her chubby cheeks. "Of course, you're Aunt Emma. Mama says I'm supposed to try hard to be nice to you."

Emma laughed. "The effort won't be too prodigious, I hope."

The little girl's lips turned into a pout. "What's prodigious?"

Rose Ellen tapped her foot impatiently at the distraction her daughter posed. "We'll explain later, honey." She turned back to her sister. "Emma, aren't you even going to tell me who this strange woman is living in the house Daddy left to you?"

Emma swung little Annalise up into her arms. The girl didn't look pleased. With Rose Ellen and her daughter both glaring at her unsmilingly, Emma felt as if she were seeing double. "Her name's Lorna McCrae. You've heard of the McCraes, Rose Ellen. The family's been here for years."

"Where?"

"Out toward Little Sandy."

Rose Ellen's big blue eyes nearly popped out of her head. "Little Sandy!" she exclaimed in horror. Little Sandy was where many poor farmers lived, trying to scrape a living off land that was not the best quality. "Oh, Emma! How could you?"

"She's a very nice person, Rose Ellen."

From Rose Ellen's expression, Emma could tell that being a nice person held as little weight as ever. "That's all fine and good, but what right does that give her to impose on your kindness?"

"I enjoy having her company."

"I knew your living in that big empty house was going to have a harmful effect on you! You're lonely, and now you're behaving foolishly!"

Emma managed a sickly half smile and clutched her whiskey bottle so tightly she feared it would shatter. *The big empty house?* Empty except for a sick boy, a pregnant girl and an outlaw...

"Maybe this isn't the best time and place to be having a private discussion." More than anything, Emma wished she could put Rose Ellen and Annalise on the next stage south out of town, but that wouldn't be till tomorrow. And she doubted she could force her sister to leave that quickly.

"We won't be able to have any privacy at home, now that woman is there," Rose Ellen grumbled as they started toward the wagon. She carried her own bags only reluctantly, when she noticed that Emma's arms were already full with Annalise and the large bag. She clucked her tongue at Emma's continued silence. "Although I suppose our house—excuse me, *your* house—is sufficiently large for four people to rattle around in without being too much of a bother.''

Emma smiled, in spite of the barb. ''I might as well tell you now, Rose Ellen, that there won't just be four of us.''

Rose Ellen blinked in dismay. ''Oh?''

''I'm taking care of a little boy. He's sick.''

Rose Ellen shot her a dubious look. ''Who are his family?''

Emma swallowed. ''Do you remember Cal Winters, the farmer?''

Her sister dropped her bags and planted her hands on her hips. ''Emma, have you lost your mind?''

''And you might as well know, there's someone else.''

''Someone else!'' By this time, Rose Ellen almost seemed to relish the enormity of her sister's folly. ''Who?''

Emma sucked in a deep breath and gathered her courage. ''You see, I've taken in a…'' The word *stranger* seemed insufficient; it raised more questions than it answered. Naturally, *outlaw* was unthinkable. It would send Rose Ellen running to the sheriff lickety-split. ''A boarder.''

''A boarder!'' Rose Ellen repeated, thunderstruck. ''Then it's worse than Janine had the courage to tell me!'' Clearly, she considered a single woman taking in strangers for pay to be the height of bad taste. Pity and disgust mixed in her expression. ''A boarder—oh, Emma! Whatever possessed you?''

Faced with the prospect of having an outlaw in the same house with her sister, Emma was beginning to wonder that herself.

The gun wasn't in the kitchen, or the parlor, or anywhere that he could see. Lang hobbled over to the little secretary in the corner of the dining room and shamelessly began searching through drawers that weren't his to open—something he never would have dreamed of doing a month ago. But now was different. He was a wanted man.

He was pretty sure he'd had the gun when he arrived at the Colby house. He'd had it when he'd stolen the horse to make his getaway, and he doubted he would have let it go in his flight. He especially wouldn't have let it get away from him if he'd known what he was wanted for.

Murder.

The word rang again and again in his mind. Wanted for murder. Not just robbery, or horse thieving, which could cost him his life anyway; but murder. Lawmen, bounty hunters and just ordinary folks would be looking for him. There was probably a price on his head. Nowhere would be safe—maybe not even here, if Emma Colby finally got some sense and decided to kick him out or to bring the sheriff back with her.

He prayed that wouldn't happen. But if it did, he wanted to be ready. And he wanted to be armed. His first instinct had been to surrender to the authorities. But on second thought he decided he should wait. He was innocent, but innocent men had been hanged before.

Collapsing into the dainty chair to partially relieve the sharp pains shooting through his leg and his side, he took a deep breath and realized the little nooks and drawers in front of him were far too small to conceal a weapon. He would have to drag himself into another room, maybe even outside, if he wanted to discover where Emma had hidden that blasted gun.

He buried his head in his hands, dreading the pain and effort that endeavor would cost him, when his gaze was caught by loopy, large script on paper. "But we all know in Midday there are no men who want to marry you, or it would have happened years ago." He skimmed the rest of the insulting missive and let out a disbelieving grunt when he read the closing. "Your loving sister, Rose Ellen."

Loving! It struck him then that as different as he and Emma Colby were in so many ways, they had one misfortune in common—sibling problems!

Absorbed, he read through the entire offensive letter this time, forgetting that Emma Colby's correspondence was absolutely none of his business. He didn't understand it. This sister of hers treated Emma like a lackey—Emma, who was coolheaded and competent and didn't look eager to take direction from anyone. And not only that, but the sore-footed Rose Ellen seemed to imply that Emma was a hopeless old dowd.

He looked up, but didn't see the room in front of him. Instead, he envisioned Emma's green eyes, her wide mouth, which usually was turned up in either a friendly smile...or a skeptical smirk. True, she wasn't outrageously beautiful; her looks were more understated, more subdued than striking. But she had certain features other women would envy. Her lithe frame, for one, which at times seemed too delicate, and yet was deceptively strong. And her pale skin was something other women would douse themselves in oils and buttermilk and who knows what all to replicate. Her hair was straight and light brown—there was no denying its plainness, yet it created a perfect frame for those green eyes.

Her eyes were what had first caught his attention. The intelligence in them, the caring. No other woman he'd known had eyes like Emma's; but then, no woman he'd ever known could sew up a man's wounds and nurse him back from the brink of oblivion. He owed his life to Emma. Maybe that's why she seemed beautiful to him, and why he couldn't stop thinking about her. Maybe that's why he would have gladly strangled Rose Ellen on Emma's behalf.

"Mr. Archibald!" Lorna's screech from the stairway startled him guiltily to his feet. "What are you doing out of bed?"

He opened his mouth, but no answer came. He'd almost forgotten about the other woman living in the house.

"You shouldn't be up and about for a week, at least!"

"A week!" How could he stay in a damned bed for a week when the area was probably crawling with people looking for him? "I can't stay in bed for a week."

"Not even for a day, apparently." Lorna bustled her bulk over to him with surprising ease and tugged him out of the chair as if he were a child. "You must give yourself time to recover."

"I was restless," he said in his own defense, as the pert, bulky blonde began dragging him back toward the staircase.

"Emma would have a fit if she knew you were out of your room."

Emma. "Does she boss you around, too?"

Lorna looked at him as if he'd just uttered a sacrilege. "I'm happy to be here, and I'm grateful to Emma. She took me in when even my own folks wouldn't have me."

He tried not to look at her swollen belly, though it was hard to avoid it. So that's the way it was. They were both of them Emma's outcasts.

"If Emma says jump, I'll jump," Lorna continued, "and you'd be wise to, also."

Lang wasn't accustomed to taking orders unless he was paid to—and sometimes even then it rankled. That's why he'd been scrimping and saving for so long to buy his own spread. Because he yearned to be his own boss, to take orders from no one, to answer only to himself. But now look at him. Hunted like a rabbit. Hiding out in the most unlikely of places. And taking orders from women.

He sighed and started the nearly impossible climb up the stairs. Descending had been a slow, painful process, but nothing like getting back up. Shards of white-hot pain shot through him, and his skin felt clammy and hot all at the same time. It was hard to breathe, even. If it weren't for leaning half his weight on the banister and the other half on Lorna, he wasn't positive he would have made it. Maybe he did need to recuperate a little longer, much as it annoyed him to wait it out. At any rate, it would take something pretty damn important to make him tackle these steps again any time soon.

When they got to the top, Lorna exclaimed brightly, "There! That wasn't so bad!"

As soon as the spots cleared from his eyes, he nodded numbly, still trying to catch his breath. "Not so…bad."

"Can you make it the rest of the way on your own?" she asked him. "I'm busy in the kitchen."

He swallowed and leaned against the newel post for support. "Of course."

Lang watched in awe as she bustled back down the stairs. Never again would he take simple mobility for granted—even Lorna was an object of envy, although she hobbled along with her weight thrown back to counterbalance the bundle her body was carrying.

He turned and shuffled along the landing. While he was up, he decided he might as well search a little longer for his gun. He opened the first door he came to, and was stunned to find a rifle pointed straight at him.

"Put 'em up, mister!"

Actually, it was a broom doubling as a rifle.

After the first wave of surprise left him, Lang bit back a smile and did as ordered, ignoring the stitch that sent fire shooting through his gut. He'd almost forgotten about the boy with chicken pox Emma had told him about. His fellow invalid.

Only when his arms were straight up did the little boy relax the broom and lean back against his pillows in the bed. "What's your business here, mister?"

Lang limped forward. "I'm on the run from a notorious female duo."

The little boy giggled, and Lang noted that he was missing one front tooth. "Did you get wounded?"

Lang nodded, then, grinning, he lifted his shirt to show the massive bandage that slashed across his chest.

The boy's round eyes bugged in awe. "Holy smokes! They must have got you good!"

He grinned. "You'd better do exactly what Emma says."

The kid sized him up, as if trying to see whether to believe him. "Does Miss Emma make you stay in bed, too?" he asked, rubbing his arm.

Lang nodded. "And I'm not allowed to scratch."

The boy dropped his hand. "I'm not supposed to, either, but I itch something awful!"

Lang came closer and dropped down on the side of the bed. "I guess we're in the same boat. Bossed by women."

The boy shrugged. "I don't mind. Yesterday I got three cookies, and I got a bed all to myself—do you?"

Lang nodded.

"This house is so big—it's like a castle. Have you ever seen a castle?"

He shook his head.

"I intend to see a castle and all sorts of things when I grow up," the boy announced. "I'm gonna be a Texas Ranger!"

A future lawman! Just what he needed. "Your name's Davy, isn't it?"

"Sure is! Like Davy Crockett. Did you know him?"

That question brought a laugh. He felt old, but luckily he didn't predate the battle at the Alamo. "We never met."

Davy frowned. "There's lots of people still alive who knew him, I bet. If I'm a Ranger, I'll bet I'll meet up with some. I'll bet I'll meet up with all sorts of people—Indians and outlaws, even!"

"I wouldn't be surprised." How pleased the kid would be to know how close he was to a genuine outlaw already.

"What's your name?"

"Johann Archibald," he said.

The boy wrinkled his nose. "What are you, a schoolteacher or something?"

"No, a gambler."

Davy's face brightened considerably. "I bet you've run into an outlaw!"

Lang nodded, frowning. His own brother, for one. His own brother, who was once as young and innocent and exuberant as Davy. The depression he'd been fighting since Emma had informed him he was wanted as a murderer returned.

"Maybe someday soon I'll tell you about outlaws, Davy, but right now, shouldn't you take a nap? You've got to rest to get better. You can't fight outlaws with chicken pox."

The boy sank against the pillows. "Shucks, I don't know if I wanna get better, really. I like it here! Don't you like Miss Emma, Johann?"

"Sure." He swallowed. Much more than he ought to.

"My daddy says Miss Emma's better'n a doctor."

Lang tilted his head. "Is your daddy coming back to see you any time soon?" He felt he should be more prepared for the next round of visitors.

Davy lifted his head proudly. "He's too busy with plowin' and plantin'. But he'll be here once that's done."

Lang nodded. A few weeks, probably. He should be mended by then.

Hoofbeats and the rumbling of wagon wheels heralded Emma's return, and Lang stepped over to the window. When he looked out, his heart sank. She wasn't alone.

All the way from Midday, Rose Ellen had been alternately scolding, whining, pouting and lecturing. "I told you that you'd be lonely all by yourself. You'd have been better off in Galveston with me. At least then you'd be respectable!"

Emma bristled. "I'm respectable now."

Rose Ellen turned on her with cold eyes. "Being nurse-maid to two poverty-stricken people whose families won't even take care of them? Cooking and doing laundry for some stranger from who knows where? What do you really know about this Mr. Archibald, Emma?"

"He's been a perfect gentleman so far...."

"Oh, Emma, you are so naive!" Rose Ellen exclaimed. "You know nothing about men. They often make a good impression at first, but it's breeding that tells in the end."

Like with William Sealy? Emma thought bitterly, though she said nothing. Rose Ellen would never side with a share-cropper's daughter like Lorna McCrae over a scion of the Sealy family.

Rose Ellen straightened determinedly. "Well! I can see it's just my God-given duty to get rid of all these hangers-on and convince you to go back to Galveston with me, where I can keep you company and take care of you. Yes, take care of you, Emma—don't look at me like that! Older isn't necessarily wiser, you know."

Emma sighed. Could she say nothing to convince her

sister that she wasn't going to Galveston? Would no ever
be enough?

Dreading their return to the house and having to expose
Lorna and Davy to her sister—not to mention dealing with
the Johann Archibald problem—Emma had allowed the
horses to lumber back to the house at their leisure. But
now the house was in sight, and there was no putting off
the inevitable. She tapped one of the horse's rumps lightly
with the crop and the animals trotted forward.

"I swear all the jostling from traveling has given me the
most terrible headache!" Rose Ellen said. "Maybe when
we get to the house you could give me one of those headache powders. Oh, and a toddy! You always know just
what to do for my headaches."

Emma smiled tightly. Usually she was proud of her nursing ability. But the prospect of waiting on her sister hand
and foot was not appealing. In fact, she dreaded it. But
there was no ignoring Rose Ellen's demands. Rose Ellen
had a knack for sapping all attention away from others and
toward herself. In fact, now that Emma recalled her life
before Rose Ellen's marriage, much of her time had been
spent catering to Rose Ellen's whims, and taking care of
Rose Ellen's needs. Certainly, a great deal of effort had
been expended in Rose Ellen's social life, which had been
lively, at least by Midday standards. Sometimes it seemed
as though Emma had spent the first half of her life watching Rose Ellen live hers.

She blushed lightly as the reed-thin voice of her conscience reminded her that she should be ashamed to hold
such petty resentments against her own flesh and blood.
And yet, she couldn't deny that she dreaded having Rose
Ellen's needs supersede her own, as they always did. And
most of all—something she could barely admit even to
herself—she dreaded the moment when Johann laid eyes

on her sister. Her beautiful sister, whom no man had ever been able to resist...

"I swear, Emma, I'd forgotten how quiet you are! I never know what you're thinking."

As the wagon pulled up to the front of the house, Emma sighed, pulled up on the reins, then turned to her sister. Maybe it was best just to be honest...sort of. "I'll tell you straight, Rose Ellen. You probably won't like the way I run my household, and you won't approve of the people I have staying with me, but nothing you say will make me change."

Her sister bridled in astonished anger. "Well! It's clear I got here just in time! Thank heavens Janine warned me about you, Emma. It's clear you've lost your mind, or at least your manners!"

Emma took a breath to gather her patience. "I'm just warning you not to say a mean word to Lorna, or Davy."

"And what about your boarder?"

"Mr. Archibald is an invalid, and doesn't like to be disturbed. You probably won't even see him."

Rose Ellen shook her head, but for the first time in her life had the good sense not to argue. Instead, she turned to her daughter. "Did you hear, Annalise? You're not to bother Mr. Archibald!"

Annalise nodded. "Yes, ma'am."

Emma took in the girl's somber expression and felt a piercing pain in her heart. So far she hadn't seen the girl crack a smile, and she never spoke unless spoken to. Annalise, too, had spent her life in the shadow of the force that was Rose Ellen, and obviously the experience had been just as spirit-withering for her as it had been for Emma.

Annalise dutifully got up and began gathering things from the wagon. Emma helped them both down, noting that Rose Ellen didn't make a move to carry her own things this time.

"At least I can look forward to sleeping in my old bed again," Rose Ellen said with false brightness.

Emma winced. "Oh…well…"

Rose Ellen shot her a look of utter disbelief. "You haven't put Mr. Archibald in my room!"

"No, he's in Daddy's."

"What? The best room in the house?"

"Well…he *is* paying," she lied.

Rose Ellen frowned. "If it's that girl, we'll just tell her to move."

Lorna was now sleeping in the attic room. "I'm afraid Davy is the one in your room."

Rose Ellen shrugged. "Even better. Little boys can sleep anywhere."

"But he's ill. With chicken pox."

"So? Annalise has had chicken pox. There's nothing to fear."

"*You* haven't had them, Rose Ellen," Emma reminded her.

Rose Ellen blinked. "Good heavens! You mean I might end up catching a disease from some little pauper boy?"

"We'll just have to be careful," Emma assured her.

But there was much more to be careful about than just Davy and his chicken pox. For starters, she had to make sure her sister never laid eyes on the outlaw, who would be staying just one room away.

Now, how was she going to manage that?

Chapter Five

Despite Emma's best intentions, and her vows to be conciliatory and patient, her nerves began to unravel from the moment Rose Ellen stepped foot in the house.

Everyone was on edge. Lorna sensed immediately that Emma's sister didn't approve of her and didn't want her in her family's home, which set her off crying. She cried whenever she saw Emma, or Rose Ellen, or even Annalise. Annalise was shocked at the idea of having to share a small spare room with her mother, and displeased with the loose state of affairs in Aunt Emma's household. She spent the balance of the day on the verge of tears herself, and everywhere Emma turned, it seemed that she was faced with her niece's disapproving scowl.

But at least Annalise was silent. Rose Ellen, on the other hand, was very vocal. Though she kept her promise not to say anything—*overtly*—to Lorna, she managed to make her feelings known by venting her rage at the house in general.

"Honestly, Emma!" she exclaimed the minute she entered the kitchen. "Those new curtains are so tacked together and cheap looking! Wherever did you get them?"

"I made them," Lorna confessed, bursting into a flood of tears.

It took twenty minutes of Emma's consoling to convince Lorna that the yellow-checked curtains were sweet and just right for the room—which they were. But Rose Ellen, she discovered, who usually couldn't stand old things, expected everything in her ancestral home to stay just as it had always been, with Emma serving as curator.

"What happened to Daddy's old chair?" she asked in outrage, seeing that the item was missing from the parlor. The worn-out old chair now resided in the spare bedroom.

"I moved it upstairs," Emma said.

"By yourself?"

"Lorna helped me."

Rose Ellen's piercing gaze of disapproval alighted on Lorna only for an instant, but an instant was all it took to dissolve Lorna onto the settee in a pool of tears. Emma spent ten more minutes explaining that it wasn't Lorna's fault—she would have moved the old chair nevertheless. The truth was, after their father's death, she hadn't been able to bear looking at it empty. It had made her feel so alone.

Now when she was bumping into hysterical people wherever she turned, it was hard to believe she'd ever been alone. And in the back of her mind was always the fear that her "boarder," the reclusive Mr. Archibald, would be discovered.

"I'd better check on Mr. Archibald." She grabbed the wrapped whiskey bottle, eager to get away from the tension permeating the downstairs.

Lorna ran after Emma as she headed for the stairs. "Emma, there's something I have to tell you."

Emma turned a little more sharply than she should have. Her sympathies were all with Lorna, but her patience with everyone was wearing thin. "Honestly, Lorna, I was tired of looking at that old battered chair every day. I swear it."

Lorna shook her head. "It's not about the chair, it's about..." She lowered her voice. "Mr. Archibald."

Emma's brows shot up in inquiry. "What about him?"

"With your sister showing up and all, I almost forgot to tell you. While you were away, I caught Mr. Archibald downstairs, snooping around your desk."

"Snooping!" Emma frowned.

"Don't you think he was just hunting for cards...or poker chips, or something like that?"

They should be so lucky! There was no telling what an outlaw would be searching for...but Emma could guess at several likely possibilities.

"I made him go upstairs immediately," Lorna explained. "And I don't think he'll be back down again any time soon. He almost didn't make it back up the stairs again at all. The poor man tried to hide it, but by the time he reached the landing he looked greener than a tree frog."

Emma pursed her lips. None of this was good news—except perhaps that Johann wouldn't be in any shape to leave. While that suited her feminine interest, it also worried her. How long could she shelter a wanted man in her house with so many people about, especially when he seemed to be getting restless?

She marched upstairs and rapped lightly at his door. When she heard "Come in," she pushed the door open and found him sitting up in bed. There was no evidence of the man's having looked like a frog mere hours before. His color was improved. And his smile—a row of even white teeth gleaming out at her from beneath his dark rugged growth of beard—made her heart skip erratically in her chest.

She slipped inside and leaned against the shut door, holding up the bag. "As you requested."

"Ah, the spoils of victory!"

Emma skirted the bed and sat down in the chair by the window. She took the preposterously large bottle out of the bag and held it up for his approval.

He laughed. "Why didn't you just bring a whole keg?"

She lifted her chin. "I hope you appreciate the scandal I created at the mercantile. Folks in town now believe I'm a tippling spinster."

Again that grin sent her heart into unnerving palpitations. "Why didn't you just explain that you had a new gentleman friend who enjoys his liquor?"

"They wouldn't have believed me."

"Why not?"

"Because I've never had a gentleman friend," she confessed. Immediately she regretted it. Why should she tell this man anything at all about her personal history?

"I can't believe that."

Discussing her nonexistent love life with a desperado wasn't something she wanted to do, and gazing into his coal-dark eyes made her so tongue-tied she doubted she could carry the conversation much further anyway. She looked down at her hands. "We have some visitors."

"I noticed." He nodded toward the bottle and glass on the table beside her. "Feel free to pour a glass for me at any time, by the way."

She opened the bottle and poured the whiskey into a large glass. "It's my sister, Rose Ellen."

A frown creased Johann's brow, and for a moment it almost seemed as if he had a prior acquaintance with her sister. "Is that what all that caterwauling downstairs is about?"

"You heard all the way up here?"

"I wouldn't be surprised if that woman's voice could be heard all the way up to Montana."

Emma took a generous slug of the whiskey herself. "I

didn't expect her, or of course I would have told you. And by the way, I explained to her that you were a boarder.''

His dark brows arched with interest. "A lie, Emma?"

She shifted uncomfortably on the stiff spindly chair. "I didn't feel like explaining your mysterious appearance on my doorstep. You see, Rose Ellen is the suspicious type. Rose Ellen might think you aren't who you say you are."

For a moment their gazes met and held; then Emma finished off the glass. She set the empty down on the table and leaned back, feeling somewhat more relaxed. "I'd appreciate it if you didn't contradict my story. I've also explained to my sister that you are an invalid, which you are. You shouldn't be getting out of bed."

"Lorna tattled?"

She nodded, noting that he didn't look the least bit remorseful for having flown his coop. "She said you looked as if you were searching for something."

His eyes sparked with curiosity. "Do you think I'm a thief?"

She didn't know what to say. Reason told her that he absolutely was a thief—he'd murdered someone during a bank robbery, the posters had said. And yet he didn't seem like a murderer, or a bank robber, or even so much as a lowly pickpocket. "What were you doing downstairs?"

He shrugged. "I'm not used to being penned up like this."

A jail cell would be much worse, she thought.

Maybe it was good that there were more people in the house. He would be more likely to keep to himself if he feared who might be standing just outside his door. "You're not to leave this room again until I tell you you're well enough."

He grinned. "Yes, ma'am."

"My sister used to be the sheriff's sweetheart, you know," she added for good measure.

He let out a rough chuckle. "I never met a lawman yet who had good taste in women."

She regarded him closely and felt a grin tug at her lips. Whiskey was potent stuff, and it was going straight to her head. It made her want to finish that conversation she'd been afraid to finish just minutes before. "Why don't you believe I've never had a gentleman friend?"

He didn't hurry his answer, which pleased her. He didn't strike her as a silver-tongued slicker who would say anything just to get what he wanted. "Maybe because I've been around you enough to know that you've got qualities any man in his right mind would look for in a woman. If you haven't had gentlemen come calling on you before now, my only answer is that the men around here must all be crazy."

"Or maybe they were sidetracked," she said, coming to a realization.

He frowned at her in question.

She poured another glass of spirits, but this time was careful to hand it to him instead of tossing it down herself. She had an inkling that she would regret having said as much as she had already. "If you met my sister, you'd understand. No man can resist her."

"I could," he answered, taking a slug.

She shook her head. "Rose Ellen has a magical effect on men. You've never seen her up close. She's very beautiful."

"She needs to be, with a personality that reduces grown women to tears."

"It's just that Rose Ellen has certain standards...." Emma didn't know why she was standing up for her sister. Maybe it was just reflex, like poking someone's elbow.

Hearing someone speak ill of a family member naturally made her leap to the defensive.

"And no one ever meets them," Johann finished for her.

She smiled. "No, no one ever does." Some part of her wanted to think that Johann, or Lang, or whoever he was, was different, that he would not fall for Rose Ellen's undeniable charms. But she wasn't a fool. The past was all the proof she needed that Johann would fall for her sister like a boulder dropping off a cliff.

But what did she care if a man who was undoubtedly an outlaw had a weakness for her sister? She stood resolutely, determined not to let her pride sting when the inevitable meeting took place.

She just hoped it didn't take place too soon.

"I'd better check on Davy," she said.

"He was hoping for licorice whips."

She grinned. "He'll get them."

"Then he'll be a happy boy."

Just then, a crash shattered the silence in the house below them, followed by muffled words in a harsh tone, then quick footsteps and a familiar anguished wail.

"It will be nice to have one happy person in the house," Emma muttered with a sigh as she left the room.

Lang sat in bed rubbing his itchy beard and brooding. About the only advantage of Emma's sister's arrival was that now, instead of agonizing about being wanted for murder, he discovered that his mind was focused on a whole new dilemma. Namely, the pros and cons of living just over the Colby dining room.

He hadn't met Rose Ellen yet and already he disliked her intensely. Part of his animosity stemmed from having read the insulting remarks she'd written to Emma. Of course, he wasn't supposed to have looked at those any more than he should have been eavesdropping on the conversation downstairs now. But that didn't change the fact that Rose Ellen was an arrogant snob who didn't appreciate her sister's worth.

He drummed his fingers and listened some more to the spirited discussion going on below. It was mostly a one-sided affair, with Rose Ellen alternately asking Emma to wait on her hand and foot and then berating her for her bad judgment. For instance, for taking in a boarder.

Him. He had to agree with Rose Ellen on that one.

Restless, he climbed out of bed. He couldn't pace very well with his leg being what it was, so he lowered himself into Emma's spindly little chair and drummed his fingers angrily against the table. He didn't like to think of Emma being browbeaten, or belittled. In her letter, Rose Ellen had repeatedly told Emma she should give up her house—giving the proceeds to Rose Ellen, naturally—and live in Galveston. Maybe she was here now to make her appeal in person. Would Emma back down? He sensed that Emma at her core was a stubborn, independent creature. Then again, that sister of hers seemed to have the personality of a tornado.

It shouldn't matter to him so much anyway, he thought to himself. He stood again, and went to the bureau. On top of it lay a shaving cup, brush and razor on a small silver plate. This beard of his was driving him crazy!

Rashly he filled the washbasin with water and began shaving off the dense facial hair, feeling more human as the skin beneath became exposed. And for a few minutes he was able to concentrate on the task of shaving, not on the sounds of argument below.

But when he was finished, his thoughts drifted back to Emma. He turned and eyed the bag the whiskey had arrived in. There was something still inside it. Curious, he reached in and brought out a stack of thick folded paper. He unfolded one of them and gaped in astonishment at what he saw.

Amos!

It spooked him at first to see his brother so clearly—the lanky hair, the severe jaw, the cold, steely eyes. It was like suddenly having a bad dream come to life. For the past few days, that's what his month with Amos had seemed like—a bad dream. Here was evidence that his time with Amos's gang of cohorts had had definite repercussions. The picture resembled himself, especially now that he was clean shaven, and bore his name underneath. To anyone who recognized him, there was an offer of a hundred-dollar reward.

Lang felt sick.

He hobbled to the mirror, examining his face. His hair was actually darker than Amos's, and curlier, but that was something a crude drawing couldn't really capture. Anyone looking at him, then this picture, might very well believe that he was the killer advertised in it.

He was holding the picture up, still examining it against his own image, when a cold realization occurred to him. Emma. She'd gone to town today and pulled down these posters herself, in broad daylight. And there was only one reason she would have done such a thing—she knew the picture was of him, and she wanted to protect him.

The hand that was holding the poster dropped to his side, and he stared at his reflection, thunderstruck. Why would Emma Colby want to save his worthless hide? She knew it wasn't lawful to aid a criminal. Why would she put her own reputation on the line to keep him from harm?

He had known mostly good luck all his life. True, the last month had been rough, and he was in a spot now, but he wasn't one to moan and complain and pretend his problems weren't of his own making. Overall, he'd been dealt a fair hand. But running into Emma Colby...nothing so fortuitous had ever happened to him before. What had he done to deserve her help, and how was he ever going to repay her? At the best of times he'd been poor, and now he didn't have two sticks to rub together.

Downstairs, another dining-room skirmish erupted. It would be a miracle if those people finished their meal in one piece, he thought wryly.

Then, slowly, as he stared at his newly tidied self in the mirror, an idea occurred to him. In the wardrobe was a suit of clothes, plus boots and a cane. A gentleman's outfit.

Maybe there *was* a way to repay Emma's kindness...

They should have skipped dessert. Lorna, whose appetite varied from birdlike to ravenous, was just picking at her plate. Annalise announced she didn't like apples, even in pie, and Rose Ellen ate half of her piece, declared the crust heavy, which as Emma's handiwork it naturally was, and pushed her plate away. Nervously Emma gulped down her piece and felt it settle in a lump in her stomach.

She was just about to suggest they give up on the meal altogether when she heard someone descending the staircase. All three women looked up; Lorna and Emma exchanged alarmed glances.

Rose Ellen shot Emma a suspicious look. "That must be Mr. Archibald. I thought you said he was an invalid."

"He is," Emma croaked, discovering her throat had gone bone-dry. It went even drier when Johann appeared.

At least, she *assumed* this was Johann.

The man she'd rescued had disappeared, and in his place was an even more devastatingly handsome impostor. He towered in the doorway, tall and distinguished, though he leaned slightly on his cane. The dark brown suit and snowy white shirt, which Emma recognized immediately as her father's, suited him to a T. His dark hair was combed back neatly, but had a rakish wave in it she suspected no barber could tame. His jaw, once host to an unruly crop of whiskers, was now clean shaven and smooth, making Emma wonder what it would feel like to touch. She could see now the straight, almost severe line of his jaw, the dimple on one side of his mouth...and the cleft in his chin.

She sucked in a breath, remembering the deep cleft chin in the Wanted posters. Strangely, though, his clean-cut look made him appear less like the wanted man than ever, though some of his features were strikingly similar. The one feature that made her absolutely certain in her heart that a terrible mistake had been made, however, was his gaze. His dark eyes were even more startlingly intense without his beard, yet they were also warm and kind...and they were boring right into her.

She blushed, and as she did, panic began to set in. What was he doing down here? To anyone who didn't know better, he was a dead ringer for the man wanted for murder. Didn't he realize what a risk he was taking? What if her sister had seen a poster somewhere along the road?

She glanced quickly at her sister, and saw that Rose Ellen, for all her distaste at Emma's taking in a boarder, was viewing *this particular boarder* with intense interest. She'd shifted in her chair—turned to gape, actually—and now had a gleam in her blue eyes that Emma remembered all too well.

Emma stiffened. The meeting she'd hoped to postpone was now at hand. She looked back at Johann, swallowed with effort and forced herself to sound somewhat pleasant. "Mr. Archibald! I had no idea you were coming down to join us this evening."

He grinned broadly—but it wasn't the smile she knew.

This was different. A politician's smile. "What man could resist the temptation of being entertained by four lovely ladies?"

Lorna smiled anxiously, Annalise's frown lessened in severity and Rose Ellen practically glowed in the presence of this new male arrival. Only Emma seemed unmoved by his ingratiating remark. She knew what was coming, and made the formal introductions to her sister and her niece with little enthusiasm.

"Oh, Mr. Archibald, I've heard so much about you!" Rose Ellen exclaimed in a voice that was a cross between a squeal and a simper. She patted the empty seat next to her. "You must come sit by me." Being a boarder of unknown origin, apparently, wasn't such a terrible offense now that she had determined that he was also good-looking.

Emma stewed.

And Johann, that traitor, did as he was told, grinning from ear to ear. Emma bridled in her chair, and had a difficult time keeping herself from glowering at the man as he sat down opposite her. The hypocrite! Just hours ago he'd said that he wouldn't be swayed by Rose Ellen's dubious charms—and now look at him! He even scooted his chair over a few inches to get closer to her.

Oblivious, he shot Emma a sunny smile and then turned back to her sister. "What, exactly, did Emma tell you about me?"

Rose Ellen's smile froze in place, and she shifted uncomfortably. All Emma had really told her was that Mr. Archibald was an invalid, and a boarder, both of which had made him repugnant to her before. Now that she saw that the man had Adonislike qualities to compensate, she was obviously desperate to give him the benefit of the doubt. "Oh, you know Emma..."

Johann flicked Emma an intimate grin. "Yes, I do."

Emma blushed, and Rose Ellen glanced anxiously between the two of them. "Emma's so tight-lipped, she never tells me anything."

Johann's gaze fell back on Rose Ellen. "Really? But just seconds ago you said she told you all about me."

Emma grinned as her sister froze, obviously flustered speechless. "I think Rose Ellen was trying to be cordial, Mr. Archibald."

Johann looked at Rose Ellen in amazement. "Really? From what I've heard from upstairs today, courtesy doesn't seem to be your finest quality."

Rose Ellen gawked at the man with such slack-jawed amazement that Emma almost felt sorry for her. Lorna ducked her head to hide a chuckle as a flush crept into Rose Ellen's cheeks.

Before Rose Ellen could lift a protest at such ill treatment, however, Johann spoke again in a voice that was practically a purr. "Now I know why they call you Rose Ellen. Your cheeks become rosy when you're..." He frowned and looked at her with almost scientific interest. "What would you say you're feeling? Embarrassment? Anger?"

Rose Ellen's blue eyes shot daggers at Johann. "It doesn't matter! I'm called Rose Ellen because that's my name."

He laughed at her. *Laughed at her!* Emma felt an almost triumphant glee at her sister's expense. "I see you're not the intellectual type. That's good. Smart women always have a harder time finding husbands, you know."

Rose Ellen sent him a withering, haughty look. "Well, I don't have to be intelligent—*I* was married almost seven years ago!"

Emma and Lorna looked at each other, hiding silent

laughter behind their napkins, which caused Rose Ellen to glance quickly around the table in confusion. "I meant…" Her voice trailed away.

"Of course," Johann interjected smoothly, "a woman as lovely as yourself was bound to be snatched up quickly."

This comment placated Rose Ellen somewhat, although for perhaps the first time in her life, she seemed a little more wary of speaking.

Though she reserved a little pity for her sister, Emma felt satisfaction to have her sister silenced after this long day. And by Johann—who she'd feared would fall salivating at Rose Ellen's feet, as so many others had before him! Is that why he had come down? To give Rose Ellen her comeuppance?

She was glad he had, but still felt nervous at his taking such a risk. The fewer people who saw him, the better. Of course, Rose Ellen didn't seem to suspect there was anything amiss with him yet, which wasn't surprising. Cleaned up and in his new clothes, Johann seemed as respectable as a judge. Even his cane gave him a look of distinction. By his appearance, no one would ever guess that he'd distinguished himself only during a bank robbery.

She cut a wedge of pie and shoved it across the table to him. Her signature leathery crust would at least keep his mouth occupied for a while. "Have some pie, Mr. Archibald."

He grinned at her, obviously enjoying himself way too much. "I thought we'd agreed that you'd call me Johann."

She caught a strange stare from her sister, then nodded. "Of course."

He bit into the pie, and after registering just the briefest moment of discomfort he let out a sound that was just between rapture and ecstasy. "Mmm-mmm!" He turned to Rose Ellen. "Isn't this the best pie you've had in your life?"

Rose Ellen of the heavy crust complaints blinked hesitantly. "It was yummy," she agreed, teeth gritted.

"It certainly is!" Johann exclaimed. He shot Emma a look that was half open admiration and half tongue-in-cheek humor. What an actor! "You must be the best cook in the county, or perhaps the entire state. Isn't that right, Rose Ellen?"

At first it didn't look as if Rose Ellen would be able to manage complimenting her sister in public, but she finally produced a stiff nod.

Satisfied, Johann turned back to Emma. "Talented, big-hearted, and good-looking to boot."

Emma blushed, knowing she should have been furious at Johann for the impression he was giving Rose Ellen. Her sister was likely to think there was a romance going on between them! She didn't mind sheltering an outlaw she suspected was innocent, but consorting with him was another matter entirely. Maybe she'd given him the wrong impression—that saving his life meant some sort of romantic interest on her part. She did find him attractive, but her interest in him remained strictly on a nurse-patient level.

The elaborate flip-flops her heart was making, however, seemed to belie that claim of platonic interest.

Displeased at having the conversation veer away from her favorite subject—herself—Rose Ellen drummed her fingers impatiently on the tablecloth. "What brings you to Midday, Mr. Archibald?"

He smiled. "I thought I might settle here a while. It's nice country."

"But you must have some profession...some purpose for staying."

His dark eyes widened as he looked across the table to Emma, then back to Rose Ellen. "Didn't your sister tell you?"

"Tell her what?" Emma couldn't help asking.

"About our plan."

Emma's heart froze. The man had turned lunatic! She couldn't tell what was going to come out of his mouth next.

"I've promised to help Emma turn her pasture back into farmland," he lied, nearly causing Emma to tumble out of her chair in surprise. "We're hoping to have it done in time to plant this spring."

Rose Ellen gaped at Emma, stunned. "Farming? What do you know about farming?"

Johann chuckled. "That's what *she* said. 'What do I know about farming?' she asked me. But I said, 'Miss Emma, having the right soil is half the battle.' Anyone with half an eye for farming can tell that this house is sitting on what has to be the richest planting soil in this area."

"But this is preposterous!" Rose Ellen said. "There hasn't been a farmer in our family since...since..."

"Grandfather." Emma barely remembered her father's father, but she knew the land had made him rich. Rich enough to send his son through medical college in Baltimore. "It hasn't been so long at all."

"Land likes to take a rest every now and then," Johann said.

As soon as Emma was over her shock, her mind started racing. Maybe Johann was just talking off the top of his head and trying to get Rose Ellen's goat, but his words struck a chord in her. She *was* sitting on top of some of the richest farmland in the area. And soon, especially if she was going to go ahead with her idea for a hospital, she would need the means to keep money coming in. Farming was time-consuming, but if she could find help, and manage her money carefully…

Rose Ellen sputtered in displeasure. "B-but the idea of *Emma*…well, it's simply absurd! She can't handle a farm! She knows nothing about it!"

"That's why she asked me to help her," Johann said.

"But she's a woman," Rose Ellen argued. "A *lady*. Emma wasn't raised to do that kind of work."

Emma sat up in her chair, feeling a self-confidence fueled by enthusiasm. "But that doesn't mean I can't start, does it?" Her skin fairly tingled with excitement. She could do it, she knew she could—if she found the right person to help her.

Maybe Johann was that man. Though he said he was a gambler, she knew that was a lie. Could he actually be a farmer?

Rose Ellen tossed her hands in the air and expelled a sound of pure disgust. "It appears you've all lost your reason."

Emma smiled. "We all have to support ourselves some way, Rose Ellen."

Her sister crossed her arms over her chest. "But I've told you again and again that you should come to Galveston. You wouldn't have to work there at all! We could be so happy, and you wouldn't have to be lonely anymore!"

Johann gestured around the full table. "It doesn't appear to me that Emma's exactly lonely now."

Rose Ellen squinted her displeasure at the man. "Perhaps not at the moment, no!"

Stretching, Johann pushed back his chair and interrupted Rose Ellen. "Well! After that fine pie I'm ready for a little stroll. It's a lovely night. Would anyone care to join me?"

He looked at Rose Ellen, who always did like to be singled out. But before she could give her assent, Johann blurted out, "Oh, I forgot, Rose Ellen, that you'll want to clean up the dishes."

Her face went slack. *"What?"*

"Since Emma and Lorna did all the cooking." He glanced around the table for affirmation. "Isn't that the way it works?"

Lorna and Emma grinned, while Rose Ellen turned almost green with disappointment.

"Emma, how would you feel about accompanying me?"

Emma leapt out of her chair. "I'd love to!"

Never in her life had *she* been the one singled out among a group of women by a man. She felt flattered and proud, and besides that, she was eager to talk to Johann about what he'd said. Perhaps he was only talking big to anger her sister, but she had a feeling he knew at least something about the subject he'd brought up.

He stood, brushed off his jacket, and with his cane led the way to the door. Emma followed him outside. They'd barely reached the bottom porch step when Johann took her arm and leaned against her. Up to that moment she'd almost forgotten that he was not a healthy man.

"Oh, my heavens!" she exclaimed, secure in the knowledge that they were out of hearing range. "Are you all right?"

He nodded, but his lips were compressed to a thin line, and the color had drained out of his cheeks. They both sank down to the porch steps.

"You shouldn't have come downstairs tonight," she scolded him. "I told you not to."

He sent her a wry smile. "I wanted to meet your sister."

Emma tilted her head and regarded him closely. "Be careful about tangling with Rose Ellen. She might look delicate and feminine, but as a strategist she can be as ruthless as General Sherman."

He laughed. "I don't doubt it."

"Why *did* you come down to the dinner table?"

When he looked at her, the intense warmth in his eyes was almost heartbreaking. They were sitting practically in the same place where she had discovered his body three nights ago, but the difference couldn't have been greater. Then she'd been frightened, and had wondered if he could possibly live through the night. Now she still felt a hitch in her chest that was like fright...and yet was something far more complicated.

"I wanted to start repaying my debt to you," he said.

She shook her head. "There is no debt."

"Yes, there is—and there always will be," he said, his voice husky and low. "You saved my life, Emma."

Johann had come downstairs for the sole purpose of defending her to her sister. And he hadn't fallen prey to Rose Ellen, as she'd feared. Emma could hardly contain her joy.

"Did you really mean what you said back there...about turning this land into a farm?"

He chuckled. "I was just saying what I thought might annoy your sister most."

Emma nodded. She'd assumed as much. "But if I did latch on to the idea of farming, would you know how to go about it?"

He gazed at her curiously. Then he nodded. "Yes, I would. I'm not a gambler, Emma."

She laughed. "Oh, I figured that!"

His answering smile was rueful. "In my former life, I was a foreman."

Her pulse leapt. She felt like shouting *Eureka!* and throwing her arms around the man. Her savior—the outlaw—a farmer! "I'll do it!"

His brown eyes widened. "I beg your pardon?"

"I want to become a farmer, just as you suggested."

"I wouldn't be too hasty...."

"But you were absolutely right. We need to hurry if we're going to put in a spring crop."

"Oh, well now..."

"Maybe some corn." She watched him closely for his reaction. "Or what about wheat?"

He didn't look sold on the idea. "Listen, if you want to pretend to go through with this till your sister leaves..."

"Oh, no, I'm very sincere, Johann. You see, I've wanted to start a hospital, and this will allow me to go forward with that project. The hospital will need money—especially in the beginning—and the land can provide it."

His lips screwed into a frown. "But Emma, you're forgetting one thing...."

For a moment she was so feverishly intent on her proposal that she didn't seem to hear him. Then, as the silence stretched, she became aware of him staring at her, and his words sank in. "What?"

"I'm not...well, for one thing, I'm not exactly able-bodied."

She frowned. He didn't have to remind her of another reason he wasn't at liberty to help her with her project. He wasn't able-bodied, and he wasn't free. He was here only because he was in hiding.

She sighed, and looked away toward the moonlit land in question. Suddenly her fingers itched to get to work. "There has to be a way."

"There is."

She looked up at him expectantly.

"But I'm not the man to help you," he said. "You know I'll have to leave soon. You'll need to find someone else."

In all her life, she'd never felt she had an ally besides her father. Now, in Johann she had one. She didn't want to give him up, even if she had to blackmail him into staying.

"I won't allow it." She made the declaration as easily as if she were a queen.

Lang eyed her cautiously. "Won't allow what?"

"You. To leave. You're going to stay right here and work for me."

He let out a disbelieving chuckle. "You think you'll be able to force me to stay?"

"I know I will."

He squinted. "How?"

She took a deep breath. "Because I know who you are, Lang Tupper."

Chapter Six

Maybe she expected him to be surprised. He wasn't. "I know."

Emma looked shocked. "You do?"

"The posters you left upstairs were a pretty pointed hint."

She clapped her hand over her mouth and stared at him with wide green eyes. "Gracious grannies! I forgot all about those!"

"Are you crazy, Emma?" he asked. "Don't you know what it would mean if someone saw you tearing those down?"

"No one saw me. You don't have to worry."

He didn't have to worry? Lang shook his head. "I'm not talking about myself. I'm talking about *you*."

She stiffened. "I'm really not doing anything wrong, *if* you're an innocent man. Are you trying to tell me you aren't?" Her chin lifted in challenge.

Never in his life had he been in a position of having to clear his name. He didn't like the feeling—even if Emma were the most receptive audience a supplicant could ask for. "I didn't do the things they're accusing me of."

"I knew it," she said confidently.

"How did you know?"

She didn't bat an eyelash. "Because you don't look like a murderer to me."

And as she gazed at him, he could tell that for Emma Colby, the matter was just that simple. By looking into his eyes, she believed she could gauge his innocence, just as probably by a few words from Lorna she had decided that she'd been wrongly treated. Emma would be the type to go by her gut feeling, but Lang knew from experience that instinct could occasionally lead you astray. "You can't always judge a person with just one look."

She raised a brow. "Are you trying to tell me I made a mistake taking you in?"

"No."

"So tell me the facts," she said, "and I'll decide for myself."

He hesitated. "Well, for one thing, I guess I should tell you about my brother, Amos. He's my kid brother. Five years younger than me. I tried to take care of him after our parents died...."

Understanding dawned in Emma's eyes. "He's the one in the picture!"

Lang nodded miserably. Implicating his brother didn't sit well with him. Brothers were supposed to stand up for each other, to help each other. That's what he'd always tried to do for Amos. But in the end, Amos had betrayed him. His mind still had a difficult time wrapping itself around that fact.

"Amos was always a rough kind of kid, but never bad. Not really bad. You know. Drinking. Gambling. Fist-fights."

Emma nodded understandingly.

"When he was old enough, Amos left, saying he was going to be a cowboy, and I think he did drive a herd north one year. Then last year I heard that Amos was mixed up with a vicious gang along the border, and had been involved in several thefts. I couldn't believe my kid brother would be involved in something like that, so I left my job as a farm foreman to find him. Sure enough, he was thick with a fellow named Gonzales, who had a string of thefts to his credit. I thought if I stayed with him for a while, I could convince him to leave.''

"So you joined the gang."

He nodded. "After a while, I think Amos decided that I was a nuisance. Gonzales had planned a bank robbery, which I had secretly planned to sabotage. I figured maybe a close brush with the law would scare my brother out of the outlaw life. But before I could act, the robbery went wrong. Someone shot the bank clerk. And then I was shot, too. Now I know by whom.''

Emma gasped. "You can't believe your own brother..."

Bitterness coursed through him. "He was right behind me, and that's where the shot came from. And I had hinted to him that maybe after the bank robbery we could go home, and I think he didn't want that. And anyway, he never looked back to see if I made it out of that bank.''

Emma took all this in, her eyes dark with understanding. "But how did you get away? And why did you try?''

That's what he'd been asking himself for days now. "I ran out of pure instinct, following my brother—but of course he was long gone. It was amazing I wasn't caught, but it was almost dark, and on foot I ran through the brush until I came to a farmer's house. I wondered whether I should knock on the door, but I was filthy and had blood on me. And I figured word about the botched robbery would have spread already, and a farmer might shoot first and ask questions later. So I went to the barn and I took a horse.''

Emma nodded, and though what he had done was wrong, her expression was understanding. "If you hadn't, you might have died."

"The farmer heard me as I was leaving and shot me in the leg as I was riding away. After that, I don't remember much. I don't know how I got to your house."

"Sheer willpower, it seems to me."

He shook his head. "Sheer folly, maybe. That's what the whole episode was. I should never have gone after Amos, I can see that now."

"But of course you had to try. He's your brother."

"I sometimes wonder—he seems so little like the boy I knew growing up. You see, while I was with that gang I saw a side of my brother that I'd never witnessed before. I'm beginning to realize that maybe people aren't all good or all bad, but a mix of the two. In some, with a little encouragement, the bad can take over. I guess that's what happened with Amos."

She frowned in thought as she continued to gaze at him. Then she reached out, touching his arm. The touch was like a balm that reached right down into his soul. "You tried your best for him, Lang. You can't blame yourself."

How did she know? How could she tell how he'd agonized over the way Amos had turned out, almost as if he *were* personally responsible for pulling the trigger in that bank? "Sometimes I think I didn't do enough—you know, when he was younger. That if he'd had more money, or more schooling, or more churchgoing, he would have had the good side of himself encouraged instead of the bad."

She nodded. "It's hard to shake regret."

Lang couldn't imagine that Emma had done anything to regret in her sheltered life here in this comfortable Colby house, but he did believe that she sympathized with him.

Her green eyes spoke volumes on the subject of under-standing.

"That's why I want to start my hospital here in Midday. I don't want to look back one day and realize that I saw a need and did nothing. There are people here, like Davy, who need a place to go when they're sick." She looked at him entreatingly. "You're needed here, too, Lang."

"But what use can I be to you if I'm in hiding? Every minute I stay here I'm putting you in danger."

She shook her head. "Don't worry about me."

"All right, then what about my own sorry hide? If Rose Ellen starts sniffing around, she might begin to suspect something."

Emma nodded. "I've thought of that. We'll just have to make sure no one else sees you."

"That will be difficult."

"I'm not letting you leave here, Lang."

He laughed. "You mean you're holding me hostage?"

She crossed her arms resolutely. "If you try to leave before I give you permission, I will march right up to the sheriff's office and tell him everything—even that *I* knew who you were and willingly hid you from him."

"But that's crazy!" he cried. "Besides which, it's blackmail."

She grinned in triumph. "*That's* how matters stand."

His mind reeled at what she was doing for him. "I can't let you risk so much for so little."

"So little?" Her eyes brimmed, which made him shift uncomfortably. He wasn't used to women's tears. "I don't call what you just did tonight in that dining room little. No one has stood up for me in front of Rose Ellen."

The emotion in her voice was nearly his undoing. In-stinctively, he reached out and turned her chin up to him. He shouldn't have, because now the very air seemed to pulse between them. And now he realized that for days the thought of touching her had been in his mind, tempting him to follow up on the attraction he'd felt for her from the minute he'd laid eyes on her. If he'd been a free man instead of a hunted one, he would have tucked her slender body up next to his and kissed her.

It was wrong, feeling like this. But as her eyes looked up at him, and she bit her lip tentatively, desire surged in him.

He cleared his throat, then awkwardly dropped his hand. He immediately missed the contact between them, but it was easier talking without it. "Your father stood up for you. He left you this land because he knew you would find something useful to do with it."

Her lips parted. "How did you know he left it to me?"

He shoved his free hand into his pocket. "I...just happened to read that letter Rose Ellen sent you."

She tilted her head, but didn't look offended. "Yes, I can't forget that Doc would have wanted me to make good use of his legacy."

"I've only known you for a few days, Emma, but from what I've seen, you've got it in you to rustle up a whole army of support, when and if you issue a call to arms."

She grinned and crossed her arms a little saucily. "All right, you can be my first recruit. Help me plan out this farm you were talking about."

He responded to her request with a light laugh and a mock salute. "Yes, ma'am. Just remember, I'm a conscript, not a volunteer. I'm being blackmailed into duty."

As blackmail went, though, Emma drove a pretty fair bargain.

Barton Sealy leaned on the door outside the jail, his stance belying the choppy sea of worries swelling inside him. Beneath his exterior his whole body was so tense that even his teeth hurt. Lack of money ate at him like a festering wound—and money wasn't something a Sealy should have to worry about.

Or at least, they wouldn't have in the old days. But in frighteningly quick time, the Sealys had gone from being the most prominent family in town to being flat broke—and he was the brokest of them all. Where had it all gone? In one generation—his—all the Sealy land, holdings, even the house, had slipped away from his control.

Now he'd even lost his last month's wages in San Antonio, gambling. But these days it wasn't as if he *wanted* to gamble, or enjoyed it. He'd just been trying to make some money to pay off debt. Wasn't that a kick in the head!

Now he was living off the hospitality of families and widow women who thought it was only neighborly to feed the sheriff. He'd been careful to keep his financial woes private, but he suspected that even the most civic-minded citizens were beginning to wonder why he was showing up so frequently at the dinner tables.

But what could he do? The Sealy farmhouse had burned years ago, and now he rented the old Sealy land, which he had to do to pay off debt. He supposed that he could make as much money off the land if he farmed it, maybe more, but that would take know-how he didn't possess. Meanwhile, he continued his slide into financial ruin. Combine his money problems with William's moping over that McCrae woman, and he was beginning to think that the Sealy name would sink to a pit of infamy from which it would never recover.

Lorna McCrae! What the hell was wrong with that brother of his? If the idiot had to go shooting off his seed, why couldn't he at least have aimed for someone a little richer? Not that there were any millionairesses wandering around Midday—far from it. The drought last summer had seen to it that everyone was about as poor as they could be without actually starving. Which didn't make men any more forgiving about gambling debts, more's the pity. And in the midst of all this hardship, William *would* have to go and spark some girl who wouldn't even come with a cow if he married her. They could have sold the cow, at least. Lorna McCrae just meant two more mouths to feed, a fact that Barton had made plenty clear to that fool brother of his. They were barely making do with their city-paid jobs as sheriff and deputy. They couldn't handle more trouble.

As he leaned against the door in tooth-grinding worry, it took him a moment to register a sprightly step heading toward him. He turned and noticed Rose Ellen Colby Douglas, looking as beautiful as ever, coming at him like a vision of what could have been. Seven years ago he might have married her—then he wouldn't have all these troubles! Doc had had plenty of money, he bet, and that house was sitting on rich farmland. Unfortunately, Rose Ellen had been snatched out from under his nose by Edward Douglas, a man who had plenty of money and didn't even need Rose Ellen. Barton's loss still ate at him.

And the really sad thing was that just days before, he'd ridden out to the Colby house with the pathetic, ultimately vain hope that Rose Ellen was having marital troubles and might be free again. Joe had mentioned her writing all those letters to her sister, and everybody figured the Colby girls would get money from selling their house and land. Barton had figured checking up on his old sweetheart would be worth a shot.

Even now his hopes made a traitorous leap at the sight of her, still pretty, with that flirtatious way about her.

Maybe turning on the old charm would convince Mrs. Douglas she didn't even need her rich boring husband....

He doffed his hat and grinned big at her. "Why, Rose Ellen! Pretty as ever!"

She held her hands out to Barton and sent him a cheek-dimpling smile. "Why, Barton Sealy! Handsome as ever!"

He came forward and took her hands in his big rough ones. "I bet you're the best view in the whole state of Texas!"

From the way her cheeks colored so prettily, he could tell that, as always, no amount of flattery would be too much for Rose Ellen. Maybe that husband of hers wasn't doing his job right. She soaked up Barton's words the way a rash soaks up balm.

"Would you like to come inside and sit a spell?" he asked, extending his arm courteously. He was eager to get a few moments alone with her, maybe rekindle some of the old magic between them. "I realize it's a jailhouse, but we're completely without inmates today."

She tilted her head and batted her lashes at him. "If they ever criminalized charm, Barton Sealy, you'd have to lock yourself up in that jail!"

He tossed his head and laughed, a deep husky laugh that gave away nothing of the desperation inside him. He'd become good at hiding that.

"What brings you here, Rose Ellen?" Barton asked her once he'd seated her on the waiting bench and offered her a glass of cool water. "You didn't come back to Midday for the sole purpose of breaking my heart again, did you?"

Rose Ellen dimpled and chuckled. "As if I could!"

Barton stared at her, transfixed. In his mind, it seemed as if Rose Ellen were a porcelain figurine filled with gold, and that if he shook her, coins would spill out from the soles of her feet.

"Frankly," Rose Ellen went on, "I felt I had to come and see about dear Emma."

Bart frowned at the thought of getting sidetracked by the subject of Emma Colby. "Everything's all right at home, then?"

"All right!" Rose Ellen exclaimed in dismay. "Emma's got that house topsy-turvy with her crazy ideas."

Barton shifted impatiently. Emma again! "I meant back in Galveston…everything's all right back there?"

Rose Ellen blinked her long dark lashes. "Oh, yes."

"Your husband…is he doing well?"

"Edward?" she asked, seeming surprised that Barton would care about him. "Of course. It's Emma I'm worried about. Oh, Barton, the gossip about that McCrae girl is terrible!"

At the very mention of the name McCrae, his face paled with anger, and Rose Ellen suddenly slapped a palm on her cheek and exclaimed, "Oh, I'm sorry…I forgot that William…"

"My brother hardly even spoke to that girl," he replied hotly. Then, catching himself, he forced a smile. "But I was surprised to hear that Emma would take that woman in at such a time. What was she thinking?"

Rose Ellen clucked her tongue. "Frankly, Bart, I'm afraid Emma has gone a little batty."

He laughed. As if *that* was news. "Word has it that she was in town yesterday telling everybody she was going to turn the house into a hospital."

"More like a lunatic asylum! Emma's out of control, I tell you. The house is all different, that terrible girl is there, and then there's some other little boy upstairs—goodness only knows where Emma rounded him up. And to top it all off, she's got some strange man renting out Daddy's old room—and a more bad-mannered fellow you've never met in your life!'' She looked at Bart pleadingly. ''Now I ask you, what can I do?''

''Do?'' Bart asked. ''About what?''

''About Emma!''

Barton sighed. For heaven's sake, was he going to have to waste their precious time gabbing about some thick-headed spinster woman? ''Forget about Emma. Let's talk about—''

''Emma's got some crazy notion that she can just live alone and make up her own mind about things!'' Rose Ellen shot to her feet in frustration. ''I know it's just because she's out here all alone, and vulnerable.''

Barton bit his lip, thinking. ''Then maybe you should stay a good long while, Miss Rose Ellen, and use your influence on her.''

Rose Ellen huffed. ''Emma's got some idea that she's going to make money all on her own and be independent.''

Now here was something, finally, to prick up his ears. ''How?'' He was always interested in money-making schemes.

''Well, the boarder, for one. Mr. Archibald.''

Barton considered boarders for a moment, regretting that the Sealy house had burned to the ground. He almost envied Emma, except that he suspected her enterprise was doomed. ''I can't imagine your sister profiting too well by her hospitality, if that's what you're worried about. Why, I went by the house just the other day and she didn't even offer breakfast. Or even a scoop of well water.''

Rose Ellen shook her head. ''Mr. Archibald has Emma convinced that she can make money farming the land. *Farming—Emma!*''

Bart frowned. ''Does Emma intend to marry this Mr. Archibald?''

''God forbid!'' Rose Ellen exclaimed. ''Though how

should I know? Emma no longer takes me into her confidence about anything.''

"But I thought—'' Barton cut off his words and worried his lower lip.

Rose Ellen tilted a curious glance up at him. "What?''

He felt uncomfortable prying, but he couldn't help himself. Right now the money matters of others were just too interesting. "But I just assumed that Miss Emma would have to give up the house.''

"Why?''

"Well...I just naturally assumed...most people did... that your husband would prefer to sell the land.''

"Finally!'' Rose Ellen exclaimed. "Someone who thinks as I do! That's just what I told Edward ought to be done! *I* thought it would be better if Emma came to Galveston and took care of things there, but the trouble is, *we* have no say in the matter.''

"Why not?''

"Because Daddy left that whole farm—the land, the house, *everything*—to Emma and Emma alone.''

Barton fell dumbstruck—it took a moment to completely comprehend what she was telling him. Plain, mousy Emma Colby had that big house and that farmland all to herself, on top of whatever other assets Doc had? Barton didn't know flip about farming, but if he had someone doing all the work for him, that would be an entirely different matter!

"I guess Daddy felt sorry for Emma,'' Rose Ellen went on, "because she's so...well, you know. Plain.''

"Emma? Plain?'' Barton repeated, almost gagging. Crikey, he couldn't believe the thoughts racing through his head...Emma Colby! He, who could have had Rose Ellen, the prettiest woman in the county, was now contemplating stooping to settling for her sister. "Of course she can't hold a candle to *you*, Rose Ellen. Who could? But she has other qualities that make up for her lack of beauty. She's very…'' He grappled long and hard for something that would compensate for a woman's not being pretty. The word *rich* came to mind, but of course he couldn't mention that. ''Hardworking.''

''Well, of course,'' Rose Ellen said. ''I don't mean to be uncharitable, and in her own way, Emma's as precious as she can be. All I'm saying is, it's going to be mighty difficult for a woman like Emma to find a husband, especially if she takes up peculiar notions like the ones she's latched on to lately! Especially if she sets herself to working like a common field hand. Can you imagine?''

Bart looked at her sharply. ''Who is this Mr. Archibald you were telling me about?''

''The boarder—if you could hear how rudely he spoke to me!''

Barton rubbed his clean-shaven jaw, suddenly not liking the idea of this boarder, even if he did mean money in the bank. ''When did Mr. Archibald get there?''

Rose Ellen shook her head. ''I don't know.''

''I didn't see any man there when I was there a couple of mornings ago,'' he observed.

Rose Ellen puffed out an exasperated breath. ''He seems as much a fixture as the porch columns. Why, he practically runs things, as far as I can tell. That's the trouble with women living alone, you know, they're apt to fall under any kind of influence…or that's what Edward always tells me.''

Barton's eyes narrowed. ''Have you seen them kissing or anything like that?''

Rose Ellen blushed. ''Heavens, no! Though they did take a walk together last night. But Emma isn't a flirt— you know that, Bart.''

She batted her eyes at him again, a gesture he barely noticed at first. He was too intent on Emma. Was Rose Ellen right—was Emma lonely...and vulnerable? He needed to get to her quickly, before somebody else horned in.

"Barton?"

He snapped back to attention. "You were right to come to me for help, Rose Ellen. I'd be glad to try to talk some sense into your sister. Why, a hospital and a farm—whoever heard of one little woman doing all that?"

If she could start a farm, there would be good income on that land. All he would have to do is step in and manage things.

"I could almost weep with relief!" Rose Ellen exclaimed. "Really, Barton, you don't know how hard it is to find someone to take my side in all of this. For months I've been telling Edward that we need Emma in Galveston, but he keeps saying that what Emma wants to do is none of his business. Sometimes he can be so unfeeling!"

Barton *tsk*ed sympathetically. "Which leaves *you* to worry yourself sick about your only sister!"

Rose Ellen's eyes practically had tears in them. Come to think of it, he was glad she had married someone else. Let poor Douglas deal with this vain, meddling nag.

"Would you be willing to come over and talk to Emma?" she asked. "Maybe you could make her see what a fool she's making of herself. Tell her how much happier she'd be in Galveston. And how much less lonely! I'm sure she'd listen to you." She grinned. "Poor Emma...you know, back in the old days, I used to think she was a little sweet on you...."

Barton's brows arched in surprise. "Really?"

Rose Ellen chuckled. "Yes, isn't that sad?"

It was hard to keep from rubbing his hands together with

glee—although he couldn't say he'd noticed any affection from Emma that morning he visited her. "I don't know...maybe I'll have more luck with her that way...."

Emma Colby...practically an heiress! He could still hardly believe this windfall. And lo and behold, his job was half accomplished—she liked him!

Of course, he couldn't say much for Emma herself, and he certainly wasn't doing handsprings at the prospect of bedding her. But he didn't really need to worry about that. There were plenty of pretty women elsewhere, women willing to give a man a tumble for the price of a few coins, and once he married Emma, he could sample as many of them as he pleased.

Of course, Emma did seem to have eccentric crusading ideas, which was troubling. But as her husband, he could just nip all her idiotic notions in the bud. Once he married her, what was hers would be his, and she would be sworn to obey him. And if she didn't want to obey, he wasn't one bit squeamish about knocking some sense into her.

Rose Ellen reached out to touch his arm, to thank him. "I certainly hope she'll listen to you."

He grinned, twinkling at her just as he used to. "I'm sure glad you came by, Rose Ellen. I'll see what I can do. In the meantime, I wouldn't mention all this around town. There's enough gossip about Emma already."

"I won't. I hate to think of people gossiping about the family! Don't be long coming out to see us."

"I won't," he replied. "You can bet the farm on that."

"If I had a farm," she said, winking. "Remember?"

The sheriff grinned back. "How could I forget?"

Chapter Seven

"**W**hat are you doing, Aunt Emma?"

Emma jumped in surprise. She'd been so absorbed in drawing a rough sketch of the layout of the farm's acreage for Lang that she hadn't heard Annalise come into the kitchen. Now the girl was staring up at her, her elbows propped on the small kitchen table, her inscrutable gaze fastened on Emma's face.

"I'm drawing a picture." She turned the page toward her niece. "Can you guess what it is?"

"It's this house and all of what's around it," Annalise said, not missing a lick.

"Oh." Emma was astounded by her niece's quickness— she wasn't that good an artist. "Yes, that's right."

Annalise pointed out the different landmarks that had clued her in. "That's the house, that's the barn, that's the back pasture...."

Emma nodded, impressed.

"Can I draw it?" Annalise asked. "I'm good at drawing."

Emma gave her the pencil and another piece of paper, glad for something to keep her niece occupied. Rose Ellen was upstairs with a headache, napping after her tiring trip to town. Lorna wasn't feeling well today, either. And of course, Davy and Lang were under strict instruction not to leave their rooms. A houseful of sick people was not the best company for a little girl, and Emma's mind was else-where—half the time drifting out into the fields, imagining them cultivated and blowing with wheat and corn, the other half upstairs with Lang.

She feared her interest in the man wasn't purely agrar-ian. Not that she was an authority on immoderate feelings. She had never had a real beau before, but she could swear if she had, this is exactly how she would feel. Exalted and terrified. Hopeful and despairing. She waited breathlessly for the next moment when she could see Lang, and she dreaded that she might be making a fool out of herself.

Being sweet on an outlaw showed fearfully poor judg-ment, even an outlaw who was protesting his innocence. She'd had so little experience with men. For so long she had been simply invisible around Midday, especially to the opposite sex. At dances she'd always been a wallflower, one of those young women who would try to entertain the chaperons to cover the fact that none of the young men were interested in her at all. She'd serve up punch and laugh dutifully at old people's jokes she'd heard a thousand times—anything to avoid standing at the side of the dance floor waiting awkwardly for an invitation that would never come.

Lang made her feel different. For the first time in her life. She wondered if he even realized it.

She hoped not.

Despite her determination not to encourage him, after a few moments of absently stirring beans she bolted out of the kitchen, up to his room. He answered her light knock and she slipped inside his room, grinning. She hated how she was acting—her interest in this man was so unseemly!—but she couldn't help herself.

He looked her up and down and smiled; his dark eyes always made her feel the way she had that night she'd drunk all the brandy, warm inside and light-headed. "Have you come to beat me at cards again? It's not fair, now that I've confessed to not being a gambler."

She laughed. "I'm just checking to see that you're getting your rest."

"How can I rest when you keep interrupting?"

She crossed her arms. "If you would stop getting up all the time, I wouldn't feel the need to check up on you. There's more than your own health at stake, you know. There's my livelihood and the future of my hospital!"

Lang raised his hands in surrender. "Well, when you put it like that, I'd be a cad not to sleep more. And from now on, whenever you give me directions, I'll simply say 'Yes, nurse.'"

"That'll be a switch!" she joked.

He bowed his head solemnly, as if practicing. "Yes, nurse."

She took a few steps into the room and rocked mischievously on the balls of her feet. It was ridiculous, what she was doing—attempting to flirt with her captive audience. But for some reason, she couldn't help herself. "Then you'll really rest, and not fuss like Davy?"

"Yes, nurse."

"And you'll eat everything I bring up so you can regain your strength?"

"Yes, nurse—even if you brought me a meal that wouldn't tempt the Donner Party, I'll lap it up like a puppy."

She laughed. "I'm working on one of those right now."

He nodded. "I know. I smell it burning."

Emma frowned, then stilled, sniffing. *Smoke!* Her eyes widened, and she whirled on her heel, emitting a sharp yelp of unhappiness. She streaked back down the stairs and into the kitchen, where Annalise sat calmly staring at the smoke seeping from the oven's crevices.

Emma grabbed a tea towel and yanked open the oven, releasing a plume of black smoke that permeated the kitchen immediately. Coughing, she reached in and retrieved the burned bread and tossed it to the old sawbuck table next to the stove. The loaf of pecan bread lay charred and steaming, almost as if it were laughing at her. Now she had a houseful of sick people and she'd destroyed part of their dinner.

Annalise came over and, standing on tiptoe, inspected the bread solemnly. "You could just scrape off the burnt parts."

Emma sighed, then looked down at the piece of paper in her niece's hands. It was Annalise's rendering of the farm, and though a child's drawing, it was considerably better than her own had been. While her own house had been a mere block with two chimneys, Annalise had made the house look more realistic, with the porch outlined, and flowers exactly where they were placed around the house. How could she have remembered such details from just one short day here?

"Annalise, that's very good!"

Her niece blinked at her, uncomprehending. "The cook at our house always scrapes the burnt part off if she leaves something in the oven too long."

Emma pointed to the picture. "I meant your drawing. You're a very talented girl."

Annalise smiled. "I like drawing people best. Can I draw you, Aunt Emma?"

"Of course, I'd be flattered!"

Dutifully, the little girl turned and marched over to the table again and took up her pencil. As she looked up and began to study Emma, her face fixed in concentration, Emma felt her heart twist in recognition. Annalise might look like a miniature of her pretty mother, but her serious personality reminded her more of herself at that age.

She went ahead with dinner, scraping carrots and throwing them in a pot of hot water, then decided the bread might be cooled enough to investigate it to see if anything could be salvaged. She reached to her knife block to remove the small carving knife for the delicate surgery, but found the knife missing. Her brow furrowed in thought. "That's funny," she muttered to herself. "My paring knife's gone."

Annalise looked up and practically squirmed with anticipation. "I know who took it."

"You do?" Emma was surprised.

"It was that man."

"Mr. Archibald?" Emma couldn't believe it.

"He took it last night after everyone was asleep," Annalise said, looking inordinately pleased with herself. "I saw him. I heard him and that little sick boy who Mother told me not to talk to talking through the door. It woke me up."

Those rascals! All she needed was for Davy and Lang to be in cahoots. And to think he'd just been fooling her with his "yes, nurse" routine!

Emma crossed her arms, shaking her head at her two wily invalids. Then, slowly, a different feeling began to suffuse her. Panic. Lang had stolen a *knife?* What for?

What else? was the answer that echoed through her brain.

Her hand flew to her mouth, and she felt as if all the

blood rushed out of her head at once. "Oh, my heaven!" Lang Tupper, outlaw, armed, was not a good combination.

She whirled and ran out of the kitchen at a frantic sprint. What a fool she'd been! Taking in a man she knew was suspicious...not handing him over to the sheriff when she had the opportunity...letting him make her believe that he was a wronged, innocent man! Making her wonder if he cared for her, when really he was simply biding his time, waiting to murder them all in their beds!

She hit the stairs running, tackling them two at a time, when suddenly a loud knock sounded on the door. Emma spun on her heel, her heart racing. There was another, louder knock.

No one could answer the door but herself, yet she needed to talk to Lang. Could there be some more innocent explanation for having taken the knife?

She turned, straightened her dress and patted down her hair, then bent her steps toward the door. When she pulled it open, she nearly fainted with relief to find Barton Sealy on the other side. "Sheriff! How good to see you!" She practically yanked the lawman across the threshold, and brightened to see the impressive revolver nestled in a holster at his hip.

The handsome sheriff beamed at her. "I sure hope you don't mind my coming by here, spur-of-the-moment and all."

"Of course not." In fact, his arrival seemed like a godsend, as if he'd somehow sensed her trouble and was coming to her rescue. Should she tell him right now about the outlaw? She looked up into his twinkling blue eyes, which were watching her very closely, and felt her heart do a nervous flip.

He was eyeballing her in such a strange way...was it possible that he knew something? Had Rose Ellen gone to town this morning and spilled the beans about the mysterious Mr. Archibald? Emma had feared her sister would say too much and arouse the curiosity of the sheriff...but given the unexplained knife incident, she wasn't certain that was such a bad thing.

And yet, she wasn't certain that was the reason Barton Sealy was here, either. In fact, worry about an outlaw seemed to be the furthest thing from his open, sunny smile. "My, you certainly look lovely today, Miss Emma!"

Lovely? Emma would have laughed if she hadn't been so surprised. For a moment, it seemed that shock was the only thing keeping her upright. Her tight facial muscles went slack, and she tilted her head up toward the sheriff. The kitchen where she'd been working for the past two hours was practically as hot as the oven that had been fired up all afternoon, and she felt so sweaty she knew she was barely presentable. She was wearing nothing but an old work dress, an unflattering check in a faded brown. Her hair, never her best feature, was bursting free of its combs and was corkscrewing around her face.

"Would you like something to drink, Sheriff?" she asked when she found her voice again.

"Please call me Barton, Emma."

"All right...Barton." She fought to suppress a blush. "Would you care for something to drink?"

He grinned from ear to ear. "Do you have any lemonade?"

"Well...no, I'm afraid not."

If he was disappointed by her domestic inadequacy, he tried not to show it. "Oh, well then, whatever you do have."

She scurried back to the kitchen and fetched the man a glass of water. When she came back out to give it to him, he was already settled on the settee in the parlor, inspecting the glum, formal room with intense interest. Emma was struck again by how impressive he seemed—one of those men who looked at the world about him as if it were his own personal property.

He took the water and leaned back, grinning at her again. Not knowing what else to do, Emma sank onto a chair opposite him and stared expectantly at her surprise guest. She kept expecting him to ask for Rose Ellen.

"Hope I'm not interrupting anything." His eyes almost twinkled.

"No, I was just finishing supper."

His smile widened. "Really?"

The man wanted to cadge a meal, that much was clear.

Unfortunately, supper was going to be a sad affair to-night—beans, no meat, burned bread, leftover pie. She swallowed anxiously. She couldn't turn the sheriff away from her table—that would be unneighborly. "Would you like to have supper with us?" Her voice lacked enthusiasm.

"Would I!" he repeated, laughing as if she'd just made a joke. "Why, Miss Emma, those are words to warm a poor bachelor's heart."

Her lips lifted in a sort of smile, but her mind raced at the quandary she was in. How was she going to finish the meal if she was stuck entertaining the guest? "I suppose you'd like to talk to Rose Ellen."

"Rose Ellen?" From Barton's tone, you would have thought he didn't know a woman by that name.

Emma frowned. "Didn't you see my sister in town?"

"Oh, of course," he replied. "I just didn't know whether she would be home by now."

"She's been home for hours. I believe she has a little headache, however."

He frowned dramatically. "Now, isn't that too, too bad!"

Despite his exaggerated tone, Emma got the notion that the man didn't care how Rose Ellen was feeling at all. She shifted in her seat, a little stunned by his attitude, and unsure what to do next. Maybe now would be the right time to bring up the subject of Lang Tupper…but the way the sheriff was still sitting there grinning at her made her rethink that plan.

All his attention to her was very suspicious. What was he doing here? Why had he called her lovely? After all, during his last visit he'd told her she was no spring chicken!

Maybe he was here in his official capacity, and he was just building up to asking about Lang. Emma opened her mouth to tell him about her outlaw quandary, but then the sheriff looked over at her and winked. *Winked!*

Emma was unnerved. What was the sheriff doing? Her desire to talk to him about Lang evaporated. Revealing a desperado's presence in her home wouldn't exactly show her own decision-making in the best light.

And after all, she hadn't seen Lang with the knife. She had only Annalise's word to go on, and though she loved her niece, there was no denying that Rose Ellen had prejudiced her daughter against the guests in the house. The knife story might not be true at all. Or if it was, there was no telling what Lang had been using it for. Now that she thought about it, the whole incident could be perfectly innocent.

Besides, the man sat sipping his water as if he had all the time in the world, and didn't appear particularly inclined to catch an outlaw. Maybe she shouldn't be in such a hurry to turn one in.

Before she could think of anything to say to break the awkward silence between them, Rose Ellen came rushing down the stairs in a fresh, pretty dress of blue organdy dripping with bows and all manner of furbelows. She appeared in the doorway in all her overdecorated glory, beaming with pleasure at the sheriff.

"Why, Barton! I wasn't expecting to see you so soon!"

Barton stood, looking Rose Ellen over with appreciation. It would be hard for a man not to. Emma's little sister had a perfect figure, with a tiny waist and plump little arms that had the appearance of never lifting anything more taxing than an embroidery hoop.

"I told you I would," Barton said.

So. He *had* come to see Rose Ellen.

"Emma said you had a headache. I hope you didn't get up from your nap on my account. Maybe you should go back to bed...."

Rose Ellen rolled her eyes. "That pesky old headache went away the minute I heard your horse coming up the road, Sheriff. A visit from you is better than a powder."

Emma listened to her sister's banter and felt vaguely nauseated. Marriage had done nothing to dull her sister's desire to charm men, apparently. She stood. "I'd better get back to the kitchen or we won't have any dinner to offer the sheriff."

Barton looked at her with concern. "I hope I haven't kept you, Emma. I enjoy speaking with you. Seems like we never do get a chance to talk."

Stunned, Emma almost tripped on her own feet on the way back to the kitchen...and she proceeded to forget all about that missing knife.

"My, this meal is delicious!" Barton lied enthusiastically.

Emma smiled. *My, this meal is dragging on endlessly,* she thought in despair.

It was just herself, Rose Ellen, Barton and Annalise, and

Emma missed Lang and Lorna acutely. Especially Lorna—although she couldn't blame the younger woman for being too intimidated by the sheriff's presence to come downstairs. And frankly, her culinary skill this evening wasn't lure enough to tempt a wary soul. The bread, though scraped to her niece's specifications, didn't fool anyone into thinking it wasn't burned. The carrots were stringy, and the beans were slightly overcooked. There wasn't enough pie to go around, so Emma did without. Even with her sacrifice the pieces were laughably small.

But for all that, after he'd lapped up the last bit of lip-curling tart apple on his plate, and chewed through the crust that after a day was as fit for resoling boots as for human consumption, Barton Sealy leaned back in his chair and emitted a rumbling, satisfied sound. "Mmm-mmm!"

Rose Ellen had had a fake smile splashed across her pretty lips all evening, but Annalise, her miniature double, looked at the sheriff as if the man were crazy. Emma almost laughed.

She supposed the sheriff was just being nice to her so she would go away and leave him alone with Rose Ellen, which she would have been happy to do. She still hadn't had an opportunity to talk to Lang about what he was doing with that knife. With the sheriff here, she was wary of drawing any undue attention to her boarder.

"I could use a little stretch after all this wonderful food." Barton's gaze shifted to Emma.

When those two blue eyes honed in on her, Emma felt frozen in surprise. "By all means," she said. "Feel free to take a walk, if you wish."

He chuckled. "I only wish to if you'll agree to accompany me."

"*Me?*" Emma blushed at her foolishness. The man couldn't have made himself any clearer. But why would he want to take a walk with her, when Rose Ellen, the woman for whom he'd apparently carried a torch for lo these many years, was sitting right across the table from him?

The sheriff chuckled. "Naturally, if you'd rather not..."

Emma remained glued in her seat. She knew she shouldn't turn down a moonlit stroll with Barton Sealy. The idea was preposterous. She didn't quite understand what had caused him to choose her over her sister, but this was not an opportunity that came along every day.

When she glanced over at Rose Ellen, her sister appeared to be taking the slight more placidly than expected. "Go on, Emma." She even stood and walked them to the door, as if she were chaperoning them.

Barton took her arm as they left the house, which put Emma even further on guard. Something was definitely wrong! She glanced back at the house and saw her sister watching them anxiously, straining her head forward as if to hear what they were saying.

Suddenly Emma understood. Her sister had obviously appealed to the sheriff to have a talk with Emma, like a wayward child, and the sheriff was performing the favor for his old sweetheart's sake.

"Rose Ellen tells me you have a boarder now," Barton said when they were probably just out of earshot of the front door.

Emma's whole body stiffened. At least the man didn't waste any time getting to the crux of things! "Yes."

He stopped and looked at her then. Those blue eyes that could melt the most steely feminine heart failed to perform their magic on hers. To think she'd almost turned Lang in to the sheriff this afternoon! Now the knife-wielding outlaw seemed less sinister to her than the machinations of her own sister.

As she remained silently glaring up at him, not offering any more explanation, the sheriff's expression slowly changed from wildly flirtatious to understanding. To her surprise, his smile broadened and became more genuine. "I can tell that you guessed your sister came to see me this afternoon...about you."

She nodded. "Of course."

He chuckled. "Rose Ellen told me all about some of the plans you were hatching. For the farm."

Emma felt riled, like a mother cat protecting her litter. Her farm idea was still so new, so unformed, that she couldn't bear to have someone pick it apart just yet.

But Barton didn't shoot the expected hole in her balloon of hope that she'd been floating around in all day. Instead, he looked at her with something akin to admiration. "That's smart thinking, Emma."

She gaped at him. *"What?"*

He gestured to the field to the side of her house. "I suspect that's about the most fertile land in the area. I never expected you would have the enterprise to try to make a go of it, though."

Her throat strained to swallow back her surprise. "Oh, well...I'm just starting to plan it all out."

His nod was approving. "That's the way to do it. Take your time. Plan. That's smart thinking."

For a moment it felt as if her head would swell so big she wouldn't be able to keep it upright.

"That boarder you took in was a good idea, too," he added.

"You think so?" She knew she didn't have to ask for the sheriff's approval—especially when the alleged boarder was a fiction and might be an outlaw who would kill them all—but she couldn't help marveling at how different Barton's attitude toward her was since the last time they had spoken. "After the storm you seemed to indicate that you thought I was crazy, just like everyone else in Midday thought."

"Oh, well...I'm still not comfortable about Lorna McCrae. I think you're making a mistake there, Emma." Emma bristled, but before she could retort, he calmed her by adding, "I know now, however, that you are only doing what you think is right. Out of the goodness of your heart."

"It *is* right," she insisted.

Barton tilted an amazed glance at her. "You know, Emma, I admire you."

She hesitated, not knowing where the conversation was about to turn. The sheriff was so unpredictable, it felt as if the earth under her very feet had gone squishy.

"When Rose Ellen came by today and started telling me all about what you were doing out here, I have to admit, I was with her at first. Your sister's a very convincing woman. Then I started wondering why. Why did I always follow along with Rose Ellen and her crowd, when it was really you I felt the sympathy for?"

She let out a breathy gasp of shock. *"Me?"*

He nodded. "You know, it's funny. All those years when you worked side by side with your father, I always admired you. I thought it was because you were so knowing, and competent, and smarter than other women."

Her face was burning. "Oh, I—"

He cut her off. "But I don't think it was just your smarts that caught my eye. It was you." He grinned. "I hope you'll forgive me for speaking so plainly, but you're so quiet, I think it gives a man the feeling that you don't want him to notice you. At least, that's the feeling I always got...."

As his words trailed off, Emma desperately feared that

they wouldn't start back up again, and that this startling confession of Barton's would go forever unexplained. And that just couldn't happen! Every syllable felt like a vindication—evidence that living in her sister's shadow and following the beat of her own drummer hadn't been wrong. She felt like the tortoise crossing the finish line looking back at the hare panting in exhaustion twenty yards behind her. In fact, her own personal hare was still silhouetted in the doorway, watching them intently.

She broke out in a smile that felt as if it had been twenty-eight years in the making. "But you're wrong! I always wanted you to notice me, but I never thought you did."

He shook his head in wonder and squeezed her arm just firmly enough, intimately enough, to make her jump. "It's funny how two people can walk around for years and years and never quite cross paths at the same time, isn't it?"

Not funny, tragic. But now, shockingly, it felt as if the tragedy might come out with a happy ending after all.

How strange life was—how quickly things could change!

Lang sensed he was in trouble the moment Emma stepped across his threshold.

After storming through the door without so much as her usual knock, she crossed her arms and glared at him disapprovingly. "May I ask why you find it necessary to arm yourself in my house, *Mr. Archibald?*"

Though there was a tacit agreement between them that she should call him by his fictitious name in front of the others, her emphasis on it now in private didn't bode well. Plus he didn't know what she was talking about.

He bowed deeply. "Yes, nurse."

She tapped her foot impatiently. "I'm not joking."

"And I'm not armed." In fact, he wished he were. Surely now that they were on better terms she wouldn't begrudge him a way to defend himself if he really got in a pinch—say, if that sheriff came up the stairs to investigate the new boarder. Having a lawman directly below him for hours on end had played havoc on his already strained nerves.

"Aren't you?"

He squinted at her, taking in the high color in her cheeks, her glorious green eyes, her simple checked gown that managed to make his stomach tighten with desire in spite of all its plainness. "Of course not."

"I've heard differently." After a short stare down in which neither of them gave an inch, she explained, "The knife?"

Comprehension dawned, and he smiled with relief. For a moment he'd feared Emma was going to pitch him out of the house for wielding a carbine only she could see. Now he could understand the source of her anxiety. Davy had probably told her about the knife he'd borrowed. "I'm sorry, I should have returned it."

The knife lay where he'd left it in the little drawer of the side table next to the bed. Inside this compartment he'd also put the things he and Davy had been working on—a carved horse and the beginnings of a head for a doll. Emma stepped forward to retrieve her kitchen utensil, but stopped in amazement when she caught sight of the toys-in-progress.

She lifted the horse out of the drawer and exclaimed in surprise, "How wonderful!"

It was still a rather crude figure, only half done, but Lang was pleased with how it was coming. And he was more pleased by the expression of delight on Emma's face. "I thought I'd make it for Davy. Poor kid is all at loose ends in that room by himself.''

''It's beautiful!''

He laughed. ''It's not done.''

''Oh, but you can tell how it will be....''

Her green eyes flashed to him, and he felt a reflexive tightening in his gut that he tried mightily to ignore. But ignoring his feelings for Emma was getting harder and harder.

''Davy shouldn't be out of bed, you know,'' she scolded. ''You shouldn't be encouraging him.''

''Do you really mind?''

She looked again at the horse and smiled, then idly studied the block that would be the doll's head. She touched it gently with one of her long, delicate fingers. ''Not really.''

''I thought the time would pass faster for him if I had him involved in our secret project.''

She nodded, then sighed. ''It seems I've discovered all sorts of secrets today.'' Then, when he looked at her questioningly, she crossed the room away from his prying stare.

Lang sat up straighter in bed, sensing trouble. More trouble—just what he needed! ''What did the sheriff want here?''

''How did you know it was the sheriff?''

''Davy told me. Davy knows everything, and he's especially impressed with lawmen.''

She grinned, then spun on her toes. For a moment he thought she might burst out with another of her surprising statements, but instead she closed her mouth and flung herself into her customary little chair and smiled. ''You came awfully close to getting turned in. I discovered the missing knife just before Barton arrived.''

''Barton?'' Lang asked.

"That's the sheriff."

Trouble started to pound in his head as insistently as the constant ache in his side. "I didn't know you were on first-name acquaintance."

Roses bloomed in her cheeks, and Lang knew that there was indeed rough water ahead. "He...spoke to me tonight. Alone."

Lang looked down at his hands, which lay worrying the woolen blanket—then wished he'd looked elsewhere. A man's hands told a lot about him, and his didn't speak particularly well. They were large, and sunburned, and callused from years of laboring. They were a poor man's hands, and for the past day or so he'd begun to forget that's all he was, ever had been, and ever would be. Once he'd loved a woman who'd laughed at him for daring to have feelings for a lady when he was just a foreman, and all he'd had left after she got through laughing at him was his good name to bolster his pride. Now he didn't even have that. He'd thrown all that away with these same hands that had wielded a gun in a robbery.

He forced himself to meet Emma's warm, almost jubilant gaze, and gritted his teeth. He wasn't in love with her, damn it. She'd saved his life, and he was grateful. He had to keep that in perspective.

"So the sheriff was just making a friendly call?"

Emma's cheeks reddened a little more and she nodded. "He...he's not what I thought he was. Not entirely."

Lang was uncomfortable delving into Emma's privacy this way, but unfortunately, she made no move to leave. She seemed to want a confidant. "I guess he's a big wheel around here." A grumbling resentment seeped through his tone, though he certainly hadn't meant it to.

"He's the handsomest man in Midday." Emma's voice

held a note of wonder. "His family is very well respected, too."

She didn't have to spell it out any more clearly. *Barton* was a catch. Good job, good looks, good name. Lang felt an unexpected stab of jealousy.

Not that he blamed the man one bit for wanting to court Emma. Heaven knows, if he were free and as well fixed as he'd one day hoped to be, he might have worked up the nerve to ask for that privilege himself. Maybe all women weren't as cold and hard as Lucy. In fact, he sensed that Emma was just the type of woman who would have restored his faith in women.

But that was just so much pipe dream speculation now. He had problems aplenty, and it appeared they had just multiplied. Because he was a wanted man at the mercy of a woman he barely knew, and from the ecstatic, bemused, hopeful look on her face, it appeared his Lady Bountiful was about to become the sheriff's sweetheart.

Chapter Eight

The very next morning Barton was back, bearing chocolates—the biggest box of candy Emma had ever seen. When he gave it to her, her arms practically sagged under the weight. The box, wrapped in blue paper with lacy detail and a big white ribbon tying it closed, mesmerized her.

"I asked Joe for the best box he had." Barton puffed up at the awe Emma exhibited over the simple offering.

No man had ever given her such a gift. All her life she'd watched her sister squirrel away sweets and hair ribbons and silly gewgaws bestowed on her by fawning admirers. For years, whenever Emma had opened her dictionary she'd expected a flower Rose Ellen was pressing, a gift from her latest swain, to flutter out of the pages. She'd gritted her teeth as men had given Rose Ellen books of poetry Emma knew her sister had no interest in whatsoever. Eventually, she had accepted these presents as Rose Ellen's due as the prettiest and liveliest sister, and had long ceased to expect such trivial riches to come her way.

But here was Barton Sealy, in his best suit, bringing her chocolates. She hardly knew what to say. The turnaround in his attitude was so quick, her head was spinning. She almost had tears in her eyes, and she didn't even particularly like candy. "Oh, thank you!"

"You're very welcome," he said, sending her one of his signature smiles. "It's such a beautiful morning, I'd be delighted if you'd come out for a walk with me. You could point out the different fields you have a mind to cultivate."

Emma's face brightened. "I wouldn't be boring you?"

"On the contrary. I'd be interested in hearing your plans. Most interested."

He sounded so sincere, she practically bounded down the path, bursting with ideas. Faster than a man could listen, she inundated him with her opinions and worries about cultivation and crop choices, fences and fertilization, all of which she'd gathered in the past day of reading her grandfather's antiquated farming books. They walked the length of three fields before she realized that she'd barely let Barton get a word in edgewise. "You probably think I sound foolish," she said. "There's so much I don't know—I would be better off listening than gabbing at this point."

His blue eyes laughed as he looked at her. "I admire your enthusiasm."

"Do you?" She felt a warmth seeping clear through her. "Rose Ellen hasn't been very encouraging. She doesn't approve."

He nodded. "But after a week or so, Rose Ellen will return to Galveston, won't she?"

"I suppose she will." She almost slipped and said she *hoped* she would. It would be so blissful to have relative peace in the house again!

"Then the most important consideration should be what *you* want to do," Barton admonished her. "After all, you're not proposing that Rose Ellen take up the plow."

At the ridiculous image of her sister under the yoke, she giggled, and she realized how correct his reasoning was.

In the end, she herself would be doing the lion's share of the work; she couldn't take too seriously the criticism of others—especially those who would only be watching her in the endeavor. "You're right."

How wise Barton was! The realization caught her unawares. She'd always considered him handsome and dashing and...well, rather dim. But that wasn't how he seemed now at all. She looked up at his striking features and tousled hair the color of spun gold and felt a sigh build in her breast. She was crazy—her feelings had whiplashed so quickly. Yesterday she had felt this way about Lang; but Lang didn't care for her. He was grateful, perhaps, but he'd given her absolutely no encouragement. Besides, he was a wanted man, unavailable. And meanwhile here was Barton...Adonis of her childhood dreams.

Adonis smiled down at her gently, as if sensing and basking in the admiration she silently heaped on him. "How will you manage on your own, Emma?"

Brought out of her reverie to tackle more practical matters, she bit her lip in thought. "I think I'll have to hire at least two men to begin with."

He nodded. "That's conservative, I would say."

Doubts crept up on her. Sometimes, what she was contemplating seemed the extremist kind of folly—a doctor's daughter trying to be a farmer! All so she could open a hospital the community didn't even seem to want.

"I worry about how a lady like yourself will manage it all. It would be easier on yourself if you had..." Barton's words trailed off, and he looked away from her. His jaw sawed back and forth, as if he regretted having spoken.

"Please speak bluntly, Barton," she urged. "A beginner in any endeavor needs all the guidance and counsel she can get."

He cleared his throat and continued to look out at the

fields, still hesitating. "I only meant you might need some-one who could help you…*really* help you."

"A partner, do you mean?"

He swiveled back to her, and the gaze he settled on her was both warm and assessing. A pinprick of nervousness darted through her.

"A partner, yes."

Emma nodded slowly. "I've thought about something like that. But I know so few people who—"

"I *didn't* mean a partner," Barton blurted out. When she glanced up at him, startled, he rushed on. "I meant a helpmeet, Emma. A husband. Have you ever considered that?"

For a moment she felt like embarrassment in lace-up shoes. She stared into those blue eyes as long as she dared, then cast her gaze down, dumbfounded. No one could ever have accused her of being a silly romantic, or believing that dreams could come true. But apparently, one was com-ing true right now. Astoundingly, she seemed to have wound up in the role of princess in a fairy tale—the Texas version—complete with Prince Charming and happy end-ing. Yet all she could do, unpracticed damsel that she was, was stare at her knight in shining armor's boots, which were old and worn. The heel was caked in mud, or muck, which seemed a stark contrast to the fine new wool of the trousers of his best suit.

She frowned at the incongruity. Why would a man come courting in his Sunday suit and forget to wear his best boots as well? It showed an incompleteness, she thought, and lack of eye for detail.

"Emma?"

Her blush deepened as she realized that the man had practically proposed marriage and all she could think about was his wardrobe! Her gaze rose and met his, and she felt truly, achingly awkward—all gangling arms and hands with nowhere to go. His eyes darkened and he stepped nearer to her, his intention clear. She suddenly had the urge to hop up and down, or better yet, spin on her heel and flee! Instead, she was frozen stiff, stupefied by what was happening. Her heart beat like the wings of a trapped bird; blood rushed through her head in a raging river of sound. God help her, Barton Sealy was about to kiss her!

He stepped his dirty boot forward and planted his hands on her shoulders, yanking her toward him. She toppled against his chest like an old dried tree trunk finally collapsing in a mild spring breeze; her own feet were still rooted while the rest of her tipped forward. Then his mouth descended on hers.

His firm lips met hers with deliberate accuracy, as if she'd been his lifelong target. She was startled by the strength of him, the pure brawn of his body as he bent her own inconsequential weight to his will. Because of his spectacular height, her neck cricked up at an awkward angle, making it more difficult to revel in this glorious moment she'd waited her entire womanhood for. Her first kiss.

Because *this* was her first kiss, she reckoned in that moment. You couldn't count the kiss Lang had given her. Lang had been unconscious…maybe he'd even thought she was someone else. No, Barton was the first man who, consciously and knowingly, had tugged her into his arms, so *he* could honestly be designated her first kiss.

Maybe if she informed him of that fact he would take better advantage of the honor, she thought with a twitch of frustration. For though she was intrigued by his lips, they remained completely stationary. After all these years of imagining, and reading—and frankly, after Lang's brief though entirely unofficial preview—she had expected more thrashing about, more desperate groping…more *movement*.

She made a stab at rubbing her lips against his needfully, but the effort was difficult. Barton held her in place against him so firmly, she might have been a medieval prisoner in the stocks.

Finally he pulled away, tipped her upright again and stepped back, eyeing her warily. "You'll have to pardon me, Emma. I've never been so forward with a woman."

As she stared up at his beautiful features, all the swooning emotion she probably should have felt thirty seconds before crashed over her in a shocking wave. Barton Sealy had kissed her! She wasn't dreaming. She'd kissed Barton Sealy—and *he* felt nervous about *her!*

"I've been thinking about you a lot lately, Emma."

And I've thought a lot about you all my life. She reached up to tuck a stray lock of hair behind her ear, but words failed her.

"I think we suit each other," he said. "We're different, yes, but you have gumption. I admire that."

She swallowed, or attempted to. At his words of praise, her shoulders straightened. Gumption! Suddenly that sounded like the most romantic, silly compliment man had ever paid woman.

"I know we've only spoken privately a few times," he stumbled on, "but I was wondering if you could tell me if you've ever thought of me…" If she wasn't mistaken, the man blushed. *Blushed!* "You know, that way."

What could she say? She'd not only thought of him, she'd curdled with envy when she'd seen her little sister enjoying his company, dancing with him and hanging on his arm in public. In fanciful daydreams he'd kissed her a million times, and done more than kiss her, and had proposed marriage on occasions too numerous to count. She'd even spent more idle moments than she cared to admit wondering about what Barton Sealy particularly liked to eat for breakfast, or what his favorite tune was. The very idea that he'd have to ask her if she'd ever thought of him *that* way was almost absurd, because the truth was she'd thought of him in every way conceivable.

Of course, since she'd always been aloof with him, she had no way to prove her devotion, except...

She glanced at him. "When I was sixteen, I carved your initials in a tree."

He looked at her with amusement mixed with, if she wasn't mistaken, relief. How funny, and how flattering, to think that Barton Sealy had been worried she'd spurn him!

They walked back to the house side by side, saying little. Emma was tongue-tied, not because she was embarrassed, but because she couldn't think of anything to say. She barely knew Barton, and yet here she was, practically pledged to him. The idea would have frightened her if she hadn't been so stunned. In fact, she felt more surprised than happy—but she knew when the shock wore off she would be flooded with pleasure. It was just that everything was happening so fast!

At the front porch he said goodbye to her, but didn't kiss her again. She was disappointed, but she was also unsure of kissing protocol. Maybe midmorning front-porch kisses weren't the thing.

After she'd watched him ride off to town until he was no more than a speck cresting the hill, she felt her spirits suddenly pick up. In fact, now that he was gone and she didn't have to talk to him, she felt ecstatic. She whirled, sending her skirts billowing around her, then flew through the door. Lord, she was hungry! She'd barely eaten breakfast, and so much had happened since then!

As she floated to the kitchen, she was stopped by the sight of Rose Ellen, looking resplendent and queenly in her purple velveteen dressing gown and matching slippers.

Her sister stood next to Emma's box of chocolates, now opened, staring at the contents in amazement. Her cheeks were pink when she looked up, and Emma could tell that one cheek was swollen with pilfered candy.

"I came down for breakfast and no one was here," Rose Ellen explained.

"I was out."

Her sister glanced at her suspiciously, then back down at the chocolates. "Wasn't that the sheriff with you?"

Emma smiled, unable to keep her chin from sailing just a notch higher. "Yes, that was *Barton*. He came by to see me."

Rose Ellen's long black lashes fluttered as she blinked. "He brought you the chocolates? Wasn't that going overboard?"

Emma grinned. "He said it was the biggest box Joe Spears had." It was oh so difficult not to gloat more, or even to shout to the heavens that she'd been kissed.

With difficulty Rose Ellen finally swallowed the lump of sweet confection in her mouth. "Did he say anything to you about Mr. Archibald?"

Emma laughed. "The subject never came up. Why would it?"

Her sister's face twisted in confusion. "But he must have said *something*."

"Yes, we talked a good deal."

"But what about?"

Emma smiled dreamily. "Oh, about my plans for the farm…and lots of things."

When her sister just stood there gaping at her speechlessly, Emma turned and continued on to the kitchen, where she poured out a cool glass of apple cider to take up to Lang. Then, absently mulling over the morning's events, she discovered she had drunk the cider herself. She poured another glass for Lang and went up to see him.

Strange, she thought, that just five days ago she'd never had a man look twice at her. Then the outlaw had showed up and she'd had not one but two kisses...even if only one of them really counted. She knew she was behaving like a silly schoolgirl with her head in the clouds, but this was all a new experience for her.

She sashayed into Lang's room, catching him unawares. She skidded to a stop, nearly spilling the cider. Lang stood in the middle of the room in only his trousers. All the times Emma had seen him unclothed before, he'd been lying down, helpless looking, but now she gaped at the wide expanse of his lightly furred chest in awe. The stark white bandage cutting across his torso only seemed to add to his appearance of strength.

For a moment she simply stood, her heart pounding so loudly in her chest that she couldn't think of anything else. Lord, that man was handsome! It struck her then how over-whelmingly glad she was to have saved his life. If Lang had died, the earth would have lost one of its finest spec-imens of man. Her skin felt feverish just watching him, and she wondered fleetingly what it would feel like to be held in *those* arms.

Her face paled. How terrible to have such thoughts especially when she had just been kissed by Barton. And yet, she suddenly remembered how giddy she'd been feel-ing around Lang, and confusion overtook her. Naturally she felt attracted to Lang—he was a dark, attractive stranger—but Barton was a solid Midday citizen, and she'd yearned for him for years.

Lang's dark eyes flashed at her. "Where have you been?"

His petulant tone jostled her out of her confusing thoughts.

He quickly donned his shirt. "You usually come up before now."

"Barton was here."

Lang sent her a distressed glance. *"Barton?"*

She let out a laugh. Why, Lang sounded almost jealous! "We went for a walk."

One dark brow rose curiously. "And?"

She crossed her arms. "What makes you think there's any more to tell?"

"Because walking doesn't usually make you hum with happiness, or your eyes shine."

Emma chuckled and then practically flung herself on the bed. Since Lang wasn't on it, it couldn't be too improper. "All right," she admitted in a rush as if Lang had browbeaten the news out of her, "he kissed me!"

Lang just stared at her. Apparently he didn't share her joy.

She sat up straight and tried to be more sober, but the effort was futile. That kiss had been more intoxicating than a whole snifter of brandy. At least in retrospect. At the time it was actually happening she'd been too stunned, not to mention uncomfortable, to be intoxicated. "I think he likes me very much," she said, unable to keep the breathless tone of disbelief out of her voice.

Lang didn't seem to believe it, either. "Are you sure that's what it is?"

"What are you talking about?" Emma asked.

"Emma, doesn't it strike you as strange that the sheriff is spending so much time with you so recently after my arrival here?"

She frowned, considering. Of course it was a coincidence. Rose Ellen had also brought up the subject of "Mr. Archibald." But what did it matter?

"He hasn't mentioned me?" Lang persisted.

She thought back. "Once." And she took great pleasure in puncturing the smug look that came over Lang's face. "He told me how smart I was to take in a boarder."

Lang was surprised. "That's all?"

"That's all."

He shook his head. "I don't like it."

"Like what?"

"The way he's hanging around here."

Emma tossed up her hands in frustration, then bounced off the bed in a huff. "Is it so difficult for you to believe that a man might be interested in me just for me?"

"When it's the sheriff? Yes!"

"Well, thank you!" Emma felt red with fury. "Now I can see what you really think of me. You sound just like Joe Spears—and my sister!"

His mouth popped open, then closed. "Emma, I didn't mean it that way."

"It certainly sounded like it," she retorted.

"I only meant that…well, how trustworthy is this man?"

He meant that it wasn't likely that a handsome sheriff would suddenly appear out of the blue and declare himself to her. That's what she'd thought, yet it had happened. "He's the sheriff, from one of the oldest families in the county. And he cares for me."

"Or so he claims…."

"I realize I'm a twenty-eight-year-old spinster," she raged, her chest heaving indignantly, "but stranger things have happened! Where is it written that the whole world should experience love, except for Emma Colby?"

"Emma, I never said that."

She didn't hear him. Tears burned her eyes, and she could feel her last hold on control slipping away from her. "Where are the requirements for being marriageworthy written in stone? I've never seen them! If they are available, I'd like to look over them to find out just under what circumstances I'm allowed to find a little happiness for myself!"

In a frenzy, and before she could burst out in tears, she flew from the room, shocked and humiliated by her outburst. The whole house had probably heard her raving like a madwoman!

What a fool Lang must think she was!

But what an irritating man! And how like a male to assume that *he* must be the reason for everything. The sheriff declares love for her, and Lang is at the heart of it. She let out a derisive, defensive hoot and threw herself across her bed, where she wept for longer than she had since her father died. This should have been the happiest day of her life. She should have been rejoicing at finally getting what she'd wanted for so long. She should have been reliving her first official kiss again and again.

Instead, she was confused and exhausted and emotionally drained. Worse still, she couldn't banish the image of Lang's skeptical look, and that question. *Doesn't it strike you as strange...?*

Rose Ellen consumed so many chocolates that by suppertime she was in a particularly foul humor. All through the meal—which, feeling frightfully full, she could only pick at—she pouted, by turns saying nothing to anyone and then lashing out unexpectedly at Emma, or Lorna, or Annalise. Emma and Annalise bore her criticism with disapproving frowns, but at dessert, when Lorna took a second helping of cake and Rose Ellen made a pointed remark about guests eating them out of house and home, Lorna dropped her fork and fled from the room.

Emma wondered how she came to be living in a house of overwrought nerves. Until recently, she had led such a quiet, solitary existence! But she'd finally had enough of Rose Ellen's bullying. After Annalise excused herself from the table, she eyed her sister reprovingly. "You can't go on sniping at Lorna, Rose Ellen. I won't allow it."

Astonishment and vexation glared back at her from Rose Ellen's beautiful eyes. "I can't believe you would speak to your own sister that way!"

Emma shifted uncomfortably. It wasn't easy giving her only family member ultimatums. For all their differences, she and Rose Ellen had never had a truly sour relationship, and they had even been close when they were children. "I don't want to be unkind, Rose Ellen, but your behavior is putting me in an untenable position."

"You're a fine one to lecture me on *my* behavior!" Rose Ellen railed. "The only reason I'm even here is because you created such a scandal that I considered it my responsibility to come home and set you straight."

Emma laughed.

Rose Ellen's eyes flashed. "Yes, set you straight!" she repeated forcefully. "You might be older, Emma, but I've been married and have experience of the world. And men."

At that last word, Emma felt a spike of dread. "And?"

"And from what I can see, your relationship to Lorna McCrae has loosened your moral standards! First you take in Lorna, then you start up some sort of liaison—the nature of which I still cannot fathom—with Mr. Archibald, and now you've allowed the sheriff to hoodwink you into believing he cares for you!"

Emma, who had been bristling indignantly through her

sister's speech, flushed with anger at that last accusation. "Barton *does* care for me."

Rose Ellen let out a sigh that was almost a sneer. "Oh, Emma, don't be naive!"

The doubts Lang had planted in her head that morning echoed again now, making Emma defensive. "I am not being naive. I have proof—or I did have, until you gobbled down all those chocolates."

Rose Ellen clucked her tongue dismissively. "Candy? If I had a penny for all the candy I've been given over the years, I'd be the richest woman in the state. Yet you can't think all those men really loved me."

"I didn't say the sheriff loves me," Emma said, although she assumed he did. "I said he cared for me, that's all."

"The chocolates were just meant to flatter you. Apparently the tactic worked better than he could have possibly dreamed. The man's probably jubilant!"

Emma practically leapt out of her chair. Why did everyone make it sound as if the sheriff could only be using calculation with her? "I'd watch what I said, Rose Ellen," Emma warned, raising her chin haughtily. "You might be making slurs against your future brother-in-law."

There! She'd gone out on a limb admitting the sheriff's hint at marriage, but it was high time Rose Ellen learned that she wasn't the only woman in the world who could turn a man's head.

But her sister didn't look at her with new sudden admiration, or envy. Instead, Rose Ellen's cheeks paled, and the room suddenly went still. "Oh, Emma. What have you done?"

Emma called on every last scrap of pride she had to square her shoulders and look her sister in the eye. "Nothing that I haven't seen you do on numerous occasions. I allowed a man who declared himself fond of me to kiss me.''

Rose Ellen stared at her hard for a moment. ''What did he say to you?''

''That's my business.''

''Doesn't it strike you as strange that a man who's barely paid you any attention in twenty-eight years would suddenly heap flattery on you, Emma?''

''He didn't heap flattery on me,'' Emma said. He'd told her that she had gumption, which she thought only the truth. ''We just talked like two adults.''

''About what?''

''About my plans for the farm.''

''Oh, Emma!'' Rose Ellen shook her head mournfully. Her nerves jangled with foreboding. If Rose Ellen were simply jealous, she would have continued being scornful and angry, but right now Emma detected pity in her tone. ''Barton was very interested in my ambitions,'' Emma explained. ''He thinks the farm is a very sound idea....''

Rose Ellen's patience—thin at best—finally snapped. ''That's because he plans to be the farm's lord and master.''

Emma blinked.

''Don't you see? I went to town and told him about your plans. Before yesterday afternoon, Barton Sealy didn't know you were Daddy's sole heir.''

The dizzying events of the past day reeled in Emma's mind like a funnel cloud, the bottom point of which was a devastating kernel of understanding. Barton found out she had money, and that very day he came to her house and began to court her. Her blood went cold. ''You told Barton that?''

''I thought everyone knew, but he told me everyone in town thought you would be moving to Galveston with me," Rose Ellen explained. "Which is only logical. I still think you should, especially now."

"Rose Ellen..." Emma said warningly.

Rose Ellen sighed. "Anyway, the sheriff promised he would come talk you out of your foolish plan. I should have smelled something fishy when he seemed so eager! His eyes practically glittered when I told him you had a crush on him all those years!"

Emma had to hold on to a chair to keep her legs beneath her. "You told him *that?*"

Rose Ellen looked alarmed. "Well, didn't you?"

A wave of nausea struck her like a blow. *He'd known all along.* When he'd asked her so humbly if she'd ever thought about him *that way,* he was certain of her answer. He didn't think he'd been chasing the wrong sister, or that she was pretty, and he probably didn't even admire her gumption. Gumption! That should have given her a clue right there. What man on earth ever had admired *that* trait in a woman? Joan of Arc had been burned for it, and Queen Elizabeth had died a virgin.

So, probably, would she. It had all been an act. A calculated plan, just as Lang and Rose Ellen had said. She nodded weakly, cursing herself for being all kinds of a fool.

Her sister looked almost sorry for her. And a bit angry, even. "I never did trust that sheriff!" she exclaimed heatedly. "I'm so glad I didn't marry him!"

But Emma almost had. As the scenes with the sheriff flipped through her mind, she thought glumly of how gullible she had been. Even Rose Ellen hadn't fallen for a man's flattery the way she had today. After thirty minutes of her babbling about fertilizer, a man had taken her into his arms, declared his devotion, and she hadn't detected the slightest bit of insincerity. She writhed in humiliation, realizing that only an old maid blinded by the first smooth talker ever to cross her path would behave with such astonishing credulity.

But even she had been suspicious of the man at first! Unfortunately, her caution had been thrown to the wind in the face of his supposed interest in her farm plans...and then in her.

Lang had tried to warn her, she remembered suddenly. Gently, he'd tried to shake her into understanding what her stiff-necked pride refused to let her comprehend. Her suitor had ulterior motives.

She patted a hand across her forehead, which was beaded in sweat. Her whole body felt clammy, dirty, soiled.

Rose Ellen gaped at her. "Are you all right?"

Emma nodded. "Of course. I'm not the first woman to be played for a fool, I suppose."

"How true!" Rose Ellen chimed, then slipped a hand up to cover her pink lips. "I mean...it's certainly good you're being so realistic."

"I've had a lifetime of practice."

Rose Ellen nodded. "A lot of women would go into hysterics after having been duped."

The trouble was, the numb weariness overcoming Emma *felt* like hysteria. She just wanted to hide forever. She never wanted to see the sheriff again, or anyone else, for that matter.

It was funny—she'd been Lorna's champion because she felt so sorry for her. For weeks she'd empathized with Lorna, had shaken her head at how William Sealy could be so cruel and heartless, how families could scorn someone they supposedly loved. She'd decided she knew just how she would feel in Lorna's shoes. But in reality, she didn't have a clue about the true humiliation and anger and resentment Lorna must be experiencing. She'd taken only a small taste of the full plate Lorna was getting, and her spirit felt trampled.

"I think I'll go to bed early tonight," she said, turning.

Rose Ellen's dismayed voice followed her to the door. "But what about the supper dishes?"

Emma felt too disheartened to care. "Do them, or leave them if you're too tired. I'll tend to them in the morning."

Her declaration of slovenliness apparently shocked her sister into speechlessness, because Emma made the rest of the trip upstairs in complete silence. She considered going to Lang's room to apologize to him for snapping at him this morning, but she couldn't face that humiliating task just yet.

She trudged to her room and listlessly tugged off her dress and slipped into one of her old thick cotton nightgowns. She'd been wearing the same design since she was twelve—pastel cotton print, usually little roses or clusters of violets, trimmed in white eyelet. The hem brushed her ankles, the cuffs encircled her wrists and the collar practically brushed her chin. As she glimpsed herself now in her bureau mirror, she cringed in recognition. It was a spinster's nightgown, she realized with horror, just as the long single braid hanging down her back was a spinster's practical braid. She'd never had beautiful, lush nightclothes like her sister; she'd never worn her hair loose and flowing.

And she wasn't about to start now, she thought, grumbling to herself as she climbed beneath her stiffly starched, pristine-white spinster sheets and practical gray-pink woolen spinster blanket. For twenty-eight years she had lived without illusions about herself; for one day she had slipped. If she went back to her old sensible self and stayed that way for another few decades, maybe she would be able to forgive her foolish lapse. Better to be a practical spinster than a foolish unhappy one.

The trouble was that ever since Lang had arrived, dreams she'd thought impossible had suddenly seemed eminently achievable. The hospital, the farm. Life had untapped possibilities, she'd discovered.

Maybe that's why she'd fallen for the sheriff's smile hook, line and sinker. She frowned. Perhaps it would be wise to get her life back on track, to forgo her ideas for the hospital and the farm at present, and concentrate on restoring some of her dignity. She had enough problems to tend to with Lorna and Davy and Lang without taking on bigger projects. And maybe if she renounced her hospital and farm plans, Rose Ellen would finally give up and retreat to Galveston without her.

Just as she was about to drift away into sleep, something brought her back. She sat up in bed and heard a light rapping at her door. This was probably Rose Ellen, come to lecture her about leaving the supper dishes for her to do.

"Come in," she said, more irritated than she'd meant to sound.

To her amazement, Lang slid through the door, shut it behind him and came right up to her bed, his hands behind his back. Emma, blushing, pulled her blanket right up to the top of her chin. No man had ever marched into her bedroom before! She wasn't even decent.

"What are you doing here?"

He looked at her hesitantly. "I thought I'd bring a peace offering."

Suddenly she remembered that the last time they'd spoken, she'd been screaming like a harpy at him for suggesting the sheriff might not be sincere in his affections. If only she'd listened!

A little of her outrage seeped out of her. "I'm the one

who should be apologizing to you," she said. "You were right. The sheriff doesn't care a fig about me. He just wants my land."

"I heard."

Of course. His room was directly above the dining room, and she and Rose Ellen hadn't exactly been speaking in dulcet, ladylike tones. "I'm so ashamed," she said, dropping her hands into her lap. Tears burned her eyes, and she fought them with the last spurts of strength in her exhausted body.

He sank down onto the bed next to her, and she felt a quickness in her stomach, a butterfly of awareness that caused her to cringe. *More foolishness*—just as her horrified reaction to his entering her bedroom had been. When would she learn that there was as much chance of her being ravished as there was of her walking on the moon?

"Why should you be ashamed when it was the sheriff who behaved dishonorably?" Lang asked.

Her shoulders rose in a vague shrug. "I should have known better. I should have known that no man would…"

She couldn't finish. Her cheeks burned, and her eyes remained focused on her hands. She couldn't look Lang in the eye for fear that he would detect the magnitude of her chagrin.

Then, into her open palms dropped a bluebird.

It wasn't a real bluebird, of course, though it might have been, so lifelike was the wooden carving. The tiny creature perched precariously on a small branch, glancing up at her with inquisitive life in its wooden eyes. Its tail feathers were bent, its delicate wings slightly spread as if just about to take off in flight; she sensed the potential of movement in its stance and the pert determination of its pointy beak. Or perhaps this young bluebird was just testing its feathers, gauging its strength.

Of course, the bird wasn't blue. It might have been a small robin, or a sparrow. But just as she sensed movement, she also sensed unseen color.

"Oh, Lang," she whispered. She looked up at him in surprise. She'd seen a little of his work last night, but she'd never expected him capable of this. "You're an artist!"

He chuckled. "I'm a workingman with too much idle time after harvest."

For the second time today Emma was overwhelmed by a gift, but this, she could see, had more genuine goodwill behind it than the largest box of chocolates in Joe Spears's mercantile. No one could fashion such a beautiful, intricate piece and give it away without feeling something for the recipient—even if it was pity.

She sighed, remembering that her mortification was the reason he'd given her the bluebird. "I can't accept it. It's too nice, and you shouldn't owe me anything when you were only telling me the truth."

"I was wrong."

She didn't understand. "But you heard me talking with Rose Ellen...."

He shook his head. "I meant I was wrong to let you leave with the impression that I thought you didn't deserve love. In fact, just the opposite is true. If I sounded harsh, it was only because I was jealous."

"Jealous?"

Lang's dark eyes alone could have communicated his remorse. "If I were in the sheriff's shoes, I would have declared myself years ago and proven that you were worthy of more affection than one man could even offer you."

The tears she'd been fighting back rallied, and when she felt one splash hotly onto her cheek, Lang reached across and gently wiped it away with his thumb. A flash of desire seized her even as her mind whirled in confusion. *Maybe he really does care...or maybe he just pities me....*

Her gaze fluttered down to the bluebird perched to spread its wings, then back up into Lang's dark, piercing gaze. She couldn't trust her instinct, which was telling her that the man looked at her with raw desire. The sheriff's admiration had sounded real enough, too. But Barton's kiss...*that's* when she should have smelled a rat. While she'd expected fireworks and shooting stars, from the sheriff's kiss she'd received only workmanship and a crick in her neck. She'd known it wasn't right. Only afterward had she tried to convince herself that she'd been swept off her feet.

After this harrowing day, Lang could talk about love till his tongue dropped off, and she'd never know whether or not to believe him. His kindness, his heart-stopping gaze and the hard broad muscles beneath his shirt made her want to trust his sincerity. If he'd just take her in his arms, she might see her way to making a more certain judgment....

She took a deep breath, drawing in oxygen like courage. She'd made such a jackass out of herself this day, surely one more bit of lunacy couldn't hurt. Maybe that way she could confine a lifetime's foibles to one neat twenty-four-hour period.

"May I ask you a favor?"

Lang's dark brows rose in curiosity. "Of course."

"Would you kiss me like there was no tomorrow?"

And who knows, she thought. There might not be. Because if Lang said no, she might die of embarrassment right there on her old spinster bed.

Chapter Nine

Lang didn't need to be asked twice. As soon as Emma spoke the astonishing words, he bent down to press his lips against her own parted ones. He didn't question her motives, or ask how a simple carved bird could elicit such an odd request, or wonder why the hell she was asking him of all people to kiss her. He'd already spent four long days in bed thinking way too much about Emma to refuse the opportunity she offered him.

The trouble was, he'd meant to stop with a mere brush of his lips against hers. A taste, nothing more. But a taste of Emma's sweet lips wasn't nearly enough. Her mouth was soft and warm, the movement of her lips tentative yet curious. Five minutes ago she'd seemed shocked that he would march into her bedroom; now she seemed unafraid to have him ravish her in her bed. The contradictions in her drove him to distraction, and his pent-up desire for her made him forget all about his plan to stop at a simple peck.

He pulled her gently to his arms and deepened the kiss, slanting his mouth for better access to the delectable wine of her lips. His movement shifted something between them; suddenly Emma became an active participant in their experiment. Forgotten covers pooled around her waist as she lifted her hands to encircle his nape. Her body cleaved to his like sky against the earth.

He hadn't expected the sharp stab of desire he felt as she undulated against him, or that a mere soft moan of pleasure from her would drive him to the edge of control. His groin was burning and stiff, and as they explored each other's mouths, he realized it had been a long, long time since he'd felt this strong a desire for any woman.

Not since Lucy.

The very name was like water dousing a campfire. Lucy had taken his kisses as her due, stoked his desire and affections, then turned away from him without a second glance when he'd offered her everything he had. She never dreamed of marrying a farmhand, she'd declared. She'd assumed Lang had understood that from the beginning.

He hadn't, but he'd learned the ground rules, all right, with Lucy as his master teacher. Rich gals didn't marry poor men, and kisses that meant a great deal to one person could count for very little to another.

Slowly he tore himself away from Emma's lips, savoring the last taste of her. Who knew if he would ever be allowed another? Emma wasn't Lucy...but now he wasn't even a farmhand. He was a desperado, and though he was innocent, asking a woman to care for him was close to criminal. Especially a woman who had already been as kind and generous to him as Emma had been.

When he pulled back he searched her green eyes for her reaction, but his gaze was drawn again to her parted lips, still moist and pink from their kiss.

"Oh my!" She glanced down at her arms and hands and torso as if taking inventory, then looked back up at him. "That didn't hurt one bit!"

He almost laughed. "I've never heard that particular reaction to a kiss."

She ducked her head and her cheeks pinkened. "I only meant, that was wonderful. I—I never knew..." Her words stammered to a halt, and she gazed at him with such open, trusting admiration that he was on the verge of kissing her again. "Thank you."

He shot off the bed; it was safer that way. Emma wasn't Lucy, he repeated to himself. She was both more mature and more innocent, stronger and more vulnerable. She was beautiful, and suddenly he wanted to be the man who showed her what it was like to make love. Or maybe he only wanted to forget all the problems that fate had rained on his head, or to be reassured that there was one woman in the world who was generous and good. Or that his life would go on.

But his life was a risky proposition at this point, and Emma would be a fool to love him. There wasn't much of a future in it.

Yet he couldn't bring himself to just leave her. He wanted her to know how she'd moved him. "To hell with the sheriff," he said, his voice surprisingly raspy and dry.

She smiled, and didn't seem the least shocked by the profanity, or for that matter, the sentiment.

"The man who wins you will be lucky, Emma. Don't ever forget that."

He went back to his room then, his awkward gait slowing his progress. He didn't want anyone to see him coming out of Emma's room, especially when his face was sure to have a string of troubled emotions marching across it, amounting in the end to a bad case of male frustration. Damn and double damn!

The man who would win Emma would be lucky, all right. Unfortunately, Lang Tupper was a man for whom luck was in short supply.

* * *

Emma gazed at her bluebird and suddenly felt as if she were that small winged creature, poised to take flight. At least her heart was soaring, even if she was still earthbound. She'd hoped that Lang's kiss would show her that he was more sincere than Barton, but the kiss had done more than prove a point; it had transported her. For the third time in one week, she had received her first kiss.

Because Lang's kiss was the kiss that the novelists wrote about, the daydream concoctions that reality didn't disappoint. Her lips felt warm and wet, and the desire that the mere touching of his mouth against hers had stirred in her remained with her still as she lay on her bed minutes after he was gone. Emma knew that she should feel ashamed of the liquid heat that had pooled at the core of her womanhood, but she did not. She was too fascinated, too overcome with the rush of blood through her veins, too amazed by the feeling of weightlessness that had seized her.

Lang Tupper. She mouthed the name quietly, as though she were just discovering it. Why had he left her so abruptly? Did he wish she hadn't thrown herself at him? Of course, if memory served, the man hadn't needed much encouragement....

Lang hadn't pounced on her, or clunked their bodies together like toppled stone statues, or pinned her down till her neck cramped. If she ever needed proof that he wasn't a criminal, she'd received it tonight. His kiss was gentle, not that of a hardened lawbreaking vermin. Lang hadn't demanded or pushed too far too fast; he'd simply given, offered himself to her unquestioningly, and had made certain she'd received pleasure. Her thoughts galloped ahead to wonder what other pleasures he might be able to impart.

A stern voice of propriety scolded her for such wanton thoughts. *For shame, Emma Colby!* her finger-wagging conscience screamed. But how could she really feel a shred of guilt about one even not-so-innocent kiss? She was twenty-eight, for heaven's sake. Her sister had gone through more beaux by the time she was seventeen than Emma would ever see in a lifetime. She was certain the sheriff had never kissed Rose Ellen as if she were a statue.

She grinned. Or maybe he had. Maybe statue was his style. Some swain he had turned out to be!

She couldn't believe she was laughing, when just minutes before she was wishing she could hide from the world. She had Lang to thank for that, too. To think, she'd actually wanted to sleep for a week—a week, when there was so much to do, and accomplish! Now she didn't want to waste a single minute of her life regretting what was done. She certainly wasn't going to waste precious time moping over Barton Sealy.

The next day when Emma went to town to order seed corn, she pointedly avoided the sheriff's office. Her wagon stood right on Main Street, so she didn't doubt that Barton would realize she was there. But she wasn't going to talk to him. Not even to give him a piece of her mind, which she would have enjoyed. In the interest of maintaining her dignity, she'd decided the silent treatment would get the message across to him just as well.

She marched out of the feed store, aiming her steps back toward the wagon. There was much to do at home. Lang, who was finally, tentatively, on his feet again, was marking off acreage to be plowed up. She was already way behind the other farmers in the area and would have to hustle if she wanted to have a decent crop.

As she turned a corner, she heard footsteps behind her. She whirled, half expecting to discover Barton following her, and gasped. It wasn't Barton Sealy.

It was his brother. William.

This was the first time she had seen the youth since learning of Lorna's predicament, and Emma was shocked both by how young he looked and how mature. He had the same basic features as his older brother—tall frame, blond hair, blue eyes—but on William the traits were configured in such a way as to give him the appearance of being as yet half-finished. Tufts of yellow hair tossed every which way on his head, limbs gangled like a colt's, and the blue eyes that gawked at her were as innocent as the sheriff's were calculating.

Being confronted by him was a shock. For weeks her mind had formed the most unfavorable picture of him— the seducer, the man who had abandoned poor Lorna in her hour of need. And indeed he might be all those things. But looking at him she could understand why Lorna still hankered after William, and wanted even now to believe the best of him. His appearance was that of a sweet, innocent youth.

"Miss Emma! I've been meaning to talk to you."

She lifted her chin, sniffing. She'd had about enough of Sealy men, thank you very much. "If it's about Lorna, you would do better to address her personally."

At the mention of the girl's name, his eyes became misty and expectant. "How is Lorna?"

"Pregnant with your baby," Emma stated flatly.

William's cheeks streaked red.

"Do you deny it?" she asked, indignation making her voice shrill. "Can you?"

He shook his head. "I've been wrong, Miss Emma. That's what I wanted to talk to you about." He cast a worried glance down the street toward the sheriff's door. "I've heard tell of your starting a farm."

"I am." Her spine stiffened and she strained not to throw a glance at the sheriff's door, too. Perhaps the whole

Sealy family was ready to pack their trunks and move into her home.

William's large feet shuffled on the sandy pine blanks of the sidewalk. "Oh, well, I..."

Emma waited, not helping him.

At her stern silence, he finally looked into her eyes and choked out, "I need a job. I'd take it most kindly if you'd consider me for the position of farmhand."

You could have blown her over with a sneeze! A Sealy wanted to work for *her?* For generations, Sealys had been the ruling class of Midday. Sealys had been at the battle of San Jacinto, had made buckets of money in land deals and had sent one of their sons, Barton and William's father, to serve in the state legislature. They were a step up in reputation even from the Colby family.

But William's question made her think. What had become of the Sealy fortune? Most of their land had been sold, their house had burned years ago and never been rebuilt. Barton and William lived in town, and the sheriff position couldn't pay much. The old Sealy brass was definitely a bit tarnished. No wonder Barton had been willing to seduce a woman for a parcel of rich farmland.

The anger that seethed inside her at the thought of the sheriff made her first instinct to give William a flat-out no. Her heart told her to write off the whole Sealy clan as a bad lot worthy of all the misfortune life had to throw at them. But she knew that a person couldn't be judged by the actions of their siblings. She wouldn't appreciate people lumping her character in with Rose Ellen's—and look at Lang. He was being held accountable for his brother's sins, and what could be more unfair than the position he was in?

But then, William had his own sins to account for. "I would need to talk to Lorna."

Again his eyes lit up. "Do you think she would see me?"

She sighed. A part of her wished she could tell him no, that Lorna's heart had healed and she had moved on to thinking about the future. Serve the scoundrel right. But she knew deep down this wasn't so. If William Sealy appeared at the doorstep to reconcile with Lorna, for the first time the world would witness a pregnant woman doing cartwheels.

"What do you know about farming?" she asked, getting away from Lorna and back to another issue pressing on her mind. Since she didn't know what she was doing, it would be good to have someone around who did.

"Nothing," he answered honestly.

So much for that hope. Emma screwed up her lips as she gave his physique another dismayed inspection. He was skinny, with the meagerest dusting of muscle over his bones. Davy probably had more elbow grease in him than William did; Davy probably knew more about farming, too. William's way of moving also boded ill. He hesitated and lurched forward, and looked generally as if the tiniest pebble in his path would trip him up. In short, he was probably next to useless, and that trait combined with the puppylike eagerness she detected in his eyes made him an accident waiting to happen.

And there was no way on earth she wasn't going to hire him.

"Ten acres," Lang said, pointing out from a broken, splintery fence toward the horizon. He imagined what the fields would look like in a few months, with a wheat crop in and thriving. The thought absorbed him. All his life he'd looked after other people's crops as if they were his own children, never feeling completely safe until they were grown and out of his hands. There was so much to worry about, to tend to. Weather. Insects. Fire. He already felt the pleasurable hum of anxiety in his veins. He'd first told Emma he was a gambler, and maybe he was at that. Farming was the riskiest business he could think of.

"Ten acres," Emma echoed.

He felt reassured by the mixture of worry and eagerness in her eyes as she looked over her acreage. Clearly she didn't know what the hell she was getting into, but she was right to be anxious.

"As far as I can tell, all you have in the barn of your grandfather's legacy are some spades, a mule harness and a rusty plow. Oh, and an old pair of gloves I found behind a keg of nails. You'll need to get the plow back into shape, sharpen the blades and test the harness for strength."

From the way her green eyes widened, he guessed she noted *she'd* have to do all these things. Her lips parted into a dismayed O of understanding, then a curtain of unreadable emotion fell over her eyes. Lang hoped she wasn't having second thoughts, but she had to know the task ahead of her was huge. "You'll also need a mule. Preferably two."

Slowly the look of dull shock left her and she began to nod her head. Silently he rooted for her. *You can do this, Emma.* "And since your household is growing, you'll need to expand your kitchen garden. You need more chickens in the henhouse and maybe another milk cow. I guess you've already thought about that, though."

"No, I hadn't," she admitted. "But of course it makes sense."

Lang smiled. "And on top of all this, I think I should tell you that Davy sneaked outside today while you were away."

"That rascal! I told him he couldn't go out for another two days."

"I didn't see him till he was already outside, or I would have tried to bring him back earlier."

"Thank you." Her brows knit together worriedly.

They discussed places Lang had seen where the fences absolutely needed repair, then turned back toward the house. Lang faced his upstairs exile with mixed emotions. He was jumpy just being out in the open like this. Anybody could just ride up. And yet, even taking the chance of discovery, he'd enjoyed his morning out of doors—feeling the cool spring breeze on his face, smelling the fresh air. He was lucky that he wasn't spending this day in a jail cell. He had Emma to thank for that, and for so much more. She'd saved his life; she didn't know it, but she was saving his life even now, just letting him be a part of her plans, and be a small part of the kind of work he loved.

He glanced at her, remembering their kiss. Neither had mentioned it, but the memory of it was there, alive and pulsing between them. Sometimes he thought he could tell when she was thinking of the kiss—when her eyes shone particularly bright, or when high color appeared in her cheeks when they were discussing, say, seed grade. There were moments when he wanted to pull her into his arms again and bury himself in the fresh softness of her. She was so beautiful, and kind, and warm.

And then his gaze would be drawn to the imposing brick house, and the acres of fields around it, and he would realize that Emma was more than the lonely woman whose house he had found by accident; she was only just beginning to realize how much she had, and the difference she could make.

She had that glow about her again now as she looked out on her fields, that look as if she were an upstart monarch about to seize the reins of power. "Everything feels different now!"

He tried without success to look away from her enjoying the simple sensation of the breeze on her face. "How so?"

"Now that we've got a hand to help us, I think things will move more quickly. True, he probably won't be the best worker in the county, but who knows how he might turn out with your help? Just wait and see, Lang, in a few months we'll have turned this idea of yours into a reality!"

"I wish I could see it." The bare rasp of regret sneaked into his voice.

She looked at him, and that stubborn curtain had draped over her eyes again. "What do you mean?"

He couldn't look at her. "I'll be gone."

"Not necessarily," she countered. "You could stay here...."

Lang shook his head. "You know I can't."

She turned on him in a swirl of skirts and dogged impatience. "When were you planning on leaving?"

"As soon as I can ride. It shouldn't be long now."

She stopped in her tracks, her face red. "But you can't leave so soon. We're just getting started. We haven't even put a plow to sod!"

"There is no 'we,' Emma."

She stared at him as if he were suddenly speaking Chinese to her. "But I thought you cared—" her cheeks flamed "—about what happened here."

"I do, but if I stayed, it would be suicide. And worse than that, it would bring you trouble. If I got caught here—"

"But you won't!"

He tried to remain reasonable, though his chest squeezed with longing. "Do you think the sheriff is going to believe that I stayed in your house for weeks on end and you didn't know who I was?''

"But why should I?" Her voice grew more fervent. "I go into town maybe once a week, and the talk about you has died down."

"There are people in Midday who saw those Wanted posters."

"I got rid of those pictures. Anyway, you look different from your brother. You…"

He squinted at her, mimicking Amos, and as she took in his dark brow and cleft chin, her words dissolved in the wind.

"Maybe someone will remember that the posters disappeared the day you were in town," he said, trying to bring home how precarious a position he'd placed her in. "And no matter what happens in Midday, there are probably posters in every little town from here to the border."

"Then that's all the more reason why you should stay put, right here!" she urged. "Once you leave, you'll be running again. You won't know who to trust, or where you can go."

He couldn't deny that scrap of logic. And God knows he didn't want to leave, but it wasn't as if he had a whole hell of a lot of choice in the matter. "I can't put you in danger."

"I'm not!" she insisted, with a quiet stubborn rage. "No one has mentioned the escaped outlaw."

"They will." That certainty was the thorny patch they'd never be able to get around.

"I understand," she said bluntly, studying him. "You *want* to leave."

He looked into her hurt, defensive green eyes and wished immediately that he could take her into his arms and kiss her until he'd driven the insane notion from her mind. *Want* to leave? He'd as soon want to cut off his right arm. The minute he stepped off Colby property, he would be leaving the comfort of the best home he'd ever lived in and the company of a woman he cared for deeply. He would be leaving Emma, and right now he felt as if he'd be leaving half of himself behind with her.

He would have given anything if he could stay. But he couldn't, though he obviously couldn't let Emma think that he was sacrificing himself for her sake, either. Most of all, he couldn't let her see the extent to which she now occupied his thoughts.

He cleared his throat and argued as forcibly as he could. "I can't live the rest of my life hiding in an upstairs bedroom. I can't spend the next forty years pretending to be Johann Archibald. Surely you can understand that. That's not who I am. And I can't live off a woman. I have some pride."

She looked horrified. "But you're earning your keep here—and then some! I should be paying you for all the good you've done me."

"There's still the matter of my living like a mole the rest of my life. I can't go on that way."

"But look at yourself," she argued. "You've spent several hours outside, and no one is any the wiser."

He chuckled. He wasn't the only one who'd been looking over his shoulder today. "Since you came back and found me here, you've been nervous as a mouse. Every time a squirrel chucked, you jumped. A minute hasn't gone by that you haven't tossed a glance toward the Midday road to check for someone coming up it."

"But—"

"Emma, even if all that didn't matter, you just went to town and hired the *sheriff's brother*. Ask yourself honestly how long we can carry on this farce."

Suddenly it seemed as if all the wind was sucked out of her, and she had no more argument left in her. "I can see I can't dissuade you," she said, not even able to lift her chin in her usual proud way when she conceded an argument. "But where will you go?"

"I don't know...maybe to California." She glanced at him, horrified, as if he'd just told her he was about to step off a mountain. "I might be able to make a new start there."

"But what about proving your innocence? You'll always be looking over your shoulder in California, too."

Not an hour went by that he didn't think of that. "There's a chance I would never be able to prove my innocence anyway, and might just get myself hanged for the effort. Who would believe me?"

"I did!"

"You're not like everyone else, Emma."

Tears sprang to her eyes. "If people just heard your story...about how much you cared for your brother and tried to help him...they'd never believe that you would use him as your alibi."

He shook his head, longing secretly to reach out and wipe the lone teardrop that had spilled down her rosy cheek. "I was betrayed by my own brother. How safe would it be to entrust my future to a group of strangers?"

"This is wrong, so wrong," she muttered angrily. "It shouldn't be this way."

No, he thought. In a perfect world, he could walk up to Barton Sealy, explain what had happened and be exonerated. And then he would declare his love to Emma, who wouldn't care that he was poor, jobless and homeless. She would take him in and they would live happily ever after— hospital, farm, everything.

Dear God, he thought. All his life he'd had his nose to

the grindstone. He'd never held out an impractical hope in his life—except for Lucy. And now, with gut-wrenching clarity, he knew why. Pie-in-the-sky dreams were agony.

Emma nudged the tear away from her cheek with her sleeve, then straightened suddenly. Lang expected to see reproach in those eyes, or heartbreak, or even a determined resolve. Instead, he saw terror.

She was staring at a point over his shoulder, and Lang wrenched around reflexively, swearing when he saw the man coming down the road at a fast walk. They'd been so absorbed in their argument about why he should leave, they'd forgotten to watch their backs.

His first instinct was to race toward the house as fast as his mending body could carry him. He turned, but Emma grabbed his arm with her hand, her grip surprisingly forceful.

"No," she whispered, guessing his intention. "It would only make him wonder."

Lang felt sick, especially when he saw Emma attempt to mask her fear. It was beginning. He was getting her in deeper and deeper and she didn't even seem to care. "Who is it?"

"William."

He looked at the tall youth making his way down the road and despaired for Emma's future. *This* was the man who would plow her ten acres? A flea had more meat on its body than William Sealy did. Equally astonishing was the notion that this was the man who had ill-used Lorna and crushed her heart. He was hardly a man at all, and he didn't have the countenance of a heartbreaker. As he came closer, William seemed like any open-faced country boy.

"I didn't expect you till tomorrow," Emma called out to him.

He approached Emma with an apologetic smile. "I sort

of…'' He flicked a nervous glance at Lang, then rushed on, ''Well, I couldn't wait to see Lorna, and I realized I forgot to tell you something real important.''

Emma tilted her head, curious. ''What?''

William licked his lips, combed a bony-fingered hand through his tousled blond hair and shot another glance at Lang. His eyes narrowed.

Lang froze, and for a second a flurry of panic volleyed between himself and Emma. The boy recognized him.

Or did he?

Emma stepped between them. ''This is my boarder, Mr. Archibald. Johann, this is William Sealy.''

Lang shot his hand out. ''Pleased to meet you, William.''

William grinned and pumped Lang's hand. ''Howdy.''

''Now, what was this important matter, William?'' Emma asked, drawing the boy's attention. ''Are you worried I won't pay you?''

Color appeared in the young man's cheeks. ''No, ma'am. It's only that I'll need…well, once I tell my brother, I might need someplace to live.''

''But don't you live with your brother?'' Emma asked.

His cheeks went scarlet. ''Barton always told me that he would disown me if I…'' He stared at the ground. ''Well, he just doesn't think much of…my doing field work.''

Emma studied his face, and so did Lang. It wasn't just the work Barton disapproved of, obviously. Suddenly Lang got a hint of what had turned fresh-faced William into a heartbreaking cad. Namely, big brother. The king of cads.

From the house they heard the jarring sound of the front door slamming shut, and when they turned, Lorna stood at the front of the porch, gaping into the distance. Her blond hair was pulled back in combs away from her face, but spilled down her shoulders. Light wind billowed her calico skirts around her. She lifted one hand to her cheek and used the other to tame her ballooning skirts. The last gesture pulled her dress taut over her round belly, giving the three of them a starkly clear silhouette of her condition.

William gasped, transfixed. Emma and Lang were forgotten. The young man moved forward, as if in a trance, his long legs eating up the distance between himself and Lorna in nothing flat. He reached her, and for a moment the two blinked at each other in a silent standoff, eyes brimming with unspeakable yearning. Within seconds, without words, a volume of meaning was spoken. Then, as one, they came together in an explosion of emotion and movement of arms embracing, legs entwining, head buried in shoulder and then tilted up for a kiss. A howl of regret and sorrow carried on the afternoon breeze, followed by a murmur of forgiveness. And love. When the two of them finally came together, there was no mistaking the redemptive promise of their kiss.

Observing the two safely cocooned in their own world, completely absorbed in each other and the moment, Lang felt a painful hitch in his chest. Next to him, Emma sniffled, and he turned to catch her wiping her eyes.

"That sheriff is bad news all around," he said.

She nodded, then slowly peeled her gaze away from the two lovers and toward him. "William was looking at you," she said, her voice flat. "Do you think he...?"

He shook his head. "But he might, someday."

Lang turned back to the young embracing couple, so lost in each other, with such a long, sure, loving future ahead of them. A surge of pure envy suddenly pierced his heart.

Chapter Ten

"I can't remember when I've been so happy!" Lorna exhaled a breathy sigh, replaced the dipper in the well bucket and took her eyes off William for half a second to look at Emma. "Thank you for hiring him, Emma."

No one could help being happy for Lorna and William. The two were so in love, it felt that spring had truly arrived. Neither hatchling chicks, baby kittens, or the first flowers of the season could have elicited more wistful glances from Emma. She felt about Lang the way Lorna felt about William, but she couldn't take his hand in front of the others, or even in private. When her gaze strayed to his face, as it seemed to do several times an hour, she had to force herself to look away. Lang had made it clear that he was going to leave, and that their kiss would not be repeated, however much Emma might ache for an encore performance.

"I should be thanking you. You were the lure that got him out here to work for me," Emma replied.

Surprisingly, Lorna put a comforting hand on her arm. "Maybe the sheriff will come around, Emma."

Emma blinked, horrified. Had people noticed her pining—and did they think it was for Barton?

Lorna bit her lip worriedly. "William said Barton was awful mad about his coming out here to work. I hope that he isn't punishing you for what we—"

"Heavens to Betsy!" Emma exclaimed. "The sheriff means nothing to me."

Her friend looked confused. "Then who...?"

Obviously, people *had* noticed her pining. Emma blushed furiously, and tried with all her might not to look toward Lang, who was hoeing in the kitchen garden. But it seemed her eyes just gravitated that way of their own accord.

Lorna gasped. "Oh, Emma! Mr. Archibald?"

Emma shushed her. "No, of course not. I mean—well, not really."

"But aren't you afraid...?" Lorna's face screwed up in question. "I mean, are you sure he's just Mr. Archibald?"

"Of course he's just Mr. Archibald." Emma hated to think that all this time Lorna had been secretly worrying about an outlaw living in her house. As if she didn't have enough to worry about with a baby on the way! Emma also didn't want William to guess there might be anything amiss with their boarder. "We've had no evidence to the contrary, have we?"

Lorna shook her head, seeming to breathe a sigh of relief.

The next days witnessed more activity on the Colby farm than there had been on the place in years. The air was full of the sounds of work. William and Emma patched the barn roof and fixed part of the fence line. Lang and Lorna took turns expanding the little herb and vegetable garden behind the house, exerting themselves more than anyone until Lang fashioned a tube that allowed them to plant seed without either of them having to bend over. Now that Davy was up and about, he managed to befriend shy

Annalise, and the two children helped by fetching and carrying what they could, and bringing out cool lemonade to refresh the tired workers.

Rose Ellen was the only unproductive one of the lot. Emma hadn't expected her to help out anyway, but for once her sister had a valid excuse for idleness. Rose Ellen had contracted chicken pox.

"I should have known that little urchin would spread his pestilence my way!" she moaned melodramatically the day after the disease was detected. Bored and pettish from a mere day in her room alone, she now lay across the settee in the parlor in her velvet dressing gown, her hand pressed to her forehead.

Emma shook her head. "Honestly, Rose Ellen. You're worse than Davy was. And get your hand away from your face."

Rose Ellen reluctantly did as she was told. "Davy is the reason I'm in this mess. Where is he, anyway? He said he would bring me some tea!"

"He's posing on one of the mules. Annalise is drawing him as General Lee."

She sighed. "I should have gone home. Now I'm stuck here for another two weeks, with nothing to do but watch you slide into ruin."

Emma laughed. "That's the first time I've ever heard farming referred to in quite that way."

Her sister made a tutting sound that caused Emma to smile to herself. Rose Ellen had squared herself with Lorna. Now that Lorna and William Sealy were about to be married, she considered the situation a little less shocking and even struck a maternal pose with the younger woman. But she still couldn't accustom herself to the idea of her sister taking up the plow.

"I was talking about you and the handsome Mr. Archibald."

At the mere mention of Lang, Emma had to warn herself not to fall to pieces. She still hadn't adjusted to the fact that he was going to leave her someday...especially now, after they'd worked side by side for so many days. The labor seemed to bond them, even beyond the bond their kiss had created in her heart, and yet each day, as Lang was able to perform increasingly more work for longer increments of time, she knew he was that much closer to saddling up and riding out of her life. Just thinking about that created a gully of pain in her chest, as though her heart had split in half.

She glanced away from Rose Ellen. "What about Mr. Archibald?"

"I've seen you watching him."

Emma hurriedly checked the water pitcher she'd brought in full just moments before. "You said yourself that he's a handsome man."

Rose Ellen's lips pursed. "Too handsome, if you want my opinion. Don't forget what happened with the sheriff, Emma! Some men can't be trusted, and we know nothing about Johann Archibald."

"I do." She knew he had a kind, steadfast nature, and patience few men possessed, and a pair of lips that made her swoon with fevered wanting each night as she tossed sleeplessly in her bed.

"Where does he come from?"

"Texas..."

Rose Ellen rolled her eyes. "*Where* in Texas? And who are his people? I've never met a person by the name of Archibald, never even heard tell of them."

"Even you can't know everyone worth knowing, Rose Ellen."

Her sister huffed. "You're just trying to make excuses because you're sweet on him. But mind you, there's no telling what's in that man's past. It might be something scandalous. He might be divorced!"

Emma couldn't help it. She broke out laughing.

"What?" her sister asked, stunned that a simple admonition could bring forth gales of laughter.

If Rose Ellen only knew! Emma covered her mouth to disguise her chuckles, and forced herself to present a sobered face to her sister. "I'm sorry, Rose Ellen. You could be right. I guess I need to watch my step." Before she could stop it, however, another giggle erupted from her.

Rose Ellen shifted unhappily on her seat, her face growing more heated with each chuckle from Emma's lips. Finally it looked as if she could take no more. "Everyone's having fun but me!" she burst out, beating her delicate fists against a velvet-covered pillow. "It's not fair."

Emma forced herself to stop giggling. "Rose Ellen, we're *working,*" she said in a soothing tone, knowing that if there was anything her sister hated, it was work.

Rose Ellen crossed her arms and pouted. "You smile all the time now, and so does Lorna! That gangly William practically floats around this place in a cloud. Even Annalise laughs constantly now. She hardly seems like my child at all!"

Emma smiled patiently. "You'll feel better soon."

Actually, Rose Ellen was correct. Emma was having fun. Every day she sprang out of bed, ready to hurry through the regular morning chores so she could tackle the unfamiliar new work...with Lang by her side. She had to admit that he was part of the reason she was enjoying herself so much. Even the most backbreaking tasks she went about gladly, knowing a certain pair of dark eyes was watching her closely. He cared for her, she knew he did.

Every night she went to bed exhausted, and thinking about Lang. But these days felt rich and precious. Knowing Lang could leave any moment made each hour have a breathless intensity to it. Each day was dear.

"I might feel better," Rose Ellen grumbled, "but I'll still be too spotty to go to the spring picnic Sunday. I probably won't be able to leave the house for a month!"

Emma tried to soothe her. "I know you're not used to isolation, Rose Ellen, but you'll soon be able to join the rest of us."

Rose Ellen looked at her and sniffed. That sniff was followed by another, and another, and then her sister emitted a strangled hiccup. Then all hell broke loose. As Emma watched, amazed, a cascade of tears spilled from Rose Ellen's beautiful blue eyes. She let out a heartrending throaty wail and buried her face in the blankets so that all Emma could see were her trembling shoulders.

"Good heavens!" Emma exclaimed, dropping down on the settee, where she was immediately engulfed in Rose Ellen's hysterical embrace. Her sister clung to her as a small animal would cling to its mother, seeking warmth, understanding and emotional sustenance. "Rose Ellen, what's wrong?"

A piercing sob rent the air. "I'm…so…*lonely!*"

"But I told you, you'll feel better soon, and you'll be able to go back to Galveston."

Rose Ellen shook her head frantically. "But I don't want to go back there!"

Emma's mouth dropped open. Not want to go back? Why would that be, when for months she'd been trying to convince Emma to go there? "Why not?"

"Because I feel so all alone there!"

Emma could hardly believe her ears. "But you always worried *I* would feel lonely."

"No, I didn't. I just wanted to have you with me." Rose
Ellen pulled away slightly, her lashes valiantly blinking
back the flood of tears as she mopped her sopping-wet
hankie across her red nose. "I don't have any friends in
Galveston. I've never—" Her shoulders began to quake
again "—had...any...*friends!*"

Emma was flabbergasted. "But of course you have!"

Rose Ellen tossed a challenging glance her way.
"Who?"

"Well..." Emma searched her brain for a response.
"What about Janine?"

Rose Ellen let out a disgusted sigh. "She only trotted
after me all the time because I was popular with men."

"But she writes to you...."

"That cat?" Rose Ellen bristled. "She's written me
twice since I moved away—once to tell me she'd married
the bank president and then two weeks ago to gloat about
what a scandal you were creating in town!"

Emma had never liked Janine herself, so none of this
surprised her. Still... "But what about all the men who
flock around you?"

"Since I got married, none of them care about me. A
few would call occasionally, but it was always awkward.
What was the point? And while I was carrying Annalise,
even those calls stopped."

Emma frowned. "You don't have women friends in Galveston?"

"None!"

"But you have Edward. He loves you."

Rose Ellen clucked her tongue miserably. "No, he
doesn't. All he does is criticize me and tell me I need to
get out of bed more."

Normally she would have agreed wholeheartedly with
Edward, but seeing her sister reduced to such a state made

her unusually sympathetic to Rose Ellen's aches and pains. "But surely you've explained about your headaches and your foot...."

Rose Ellen's cheeks turned bright red.

"You *have* told him, haven't you?" Emma asked, shocked that her sister would keep information about her health from her husband. Shocked that she could, even. Usually Rose Ellen burst into song about every twinge almost before it happened!

"Oh, Emma..." Rose Ellen stared down at the hands in her lap. For the first time in her life, Emma witnessed her sister looking humbled and ashamed. When she spoke again, her voice was barely audible. "I don't have headaches."

Emma gaped at her, disbelieving. "What do you mean?"

Rose Ellen shook her head. "I did twist my ankle once, but it healed just fine." She bit her lip and managed to meet Emma's gaze. "I haven't been sick a day in my life since Annalise was born. I just wanted you to come visit. You always liked taking care of people, so I thought if I were ill you'd arrive on my doorstep and things would be just like they used to be."

Emma stared at her, amazed. "How they used to be?"

Rose Ellen blinked. "You know, the happy times...you and me." Her lower lip quivered. "You were always the best friend I ever had, Emma!"

Emma was then engulfed in a viselike hug, and struggled to make sense of her sister's words. She'd never thought Rose Ellen really cared about her. All those years when she had felt overshadowed and overlooked...she hadn't thought her sister valued her at all. Apparently she'd been wrong.

She hugged Rose Ellen back, and gave her some comforting pats. "I still can be your friend. I just can't live in Galveston."

Rose Ellen sniffed resentfully. "Because of Mr. Archibald!"

Emma shook her head. "Because I have work to do. I want my life to have purpose."

Her sister sighed. "You're so high-minded, but that's because you know all about nursing people. It's easy for you! I've never had to do one important thing in my life."

Emma laughed, happy to hear her sister getting back to her old self a little. "You only have to look around you to find a purpose in your life, Rose Ellen."

"How? I'm not good at one single thing, except being pretty. What can I do?"

Emma's mind raced to come up with a talent specific to Rose Ellen. "Well…you write long, informative letters. You're good at that."

The younger woman's rosy lips hitched skeptically. "What good is that? I suspect you didn't even read some of them."

Emma swallowed guiltily. "It's a talent, Rose Ellen. Some people can't write at all—or aren't physically able to. You might visit a hospital and read and write letters for the sick there."

Rose Ellen looked distressed that a concrete idea had been set before her. "I'm so tired! I think I'll go to sleep now and think about it. You'll wake me with dinner, won't you?"

Emma nodded, and tucked the covers around her sister. "Of course."

When she left the parlor and returned to the sunshine, she felt strangely happy. She looked out on the fields and remembered rambling in the countryside as a child, with Rose Ellen toddling behind her, and when they were a little older, climbing trees and wading in the creek and even playing house on rainy days. Why had she forgotten those times? Had their more recent, troubled years made her forget that Rose Ellen was once her closest companion?

A throat cleared, nearly causing her to jump out of her skin. She turned and found Lang staring at her. She must have been very distracted not to hear his approach. For days it seemed she'd been unable to stop monitoring his every movement. Now she took in his muscular frame leaning against the porch railing and felt a shiver work through her. All her life she'd listened to preachers railing about the temptations of the flesh, but she'd never had a clue what they were talking about until Lang Tupper had kissed her. Now every time she looked at the man those remembered sermons were drowned out by a pure flood of temptation.

"I hope you're not tired," he said, seemingly oblivious to the knee-weakening effect he had on her. "There's plenty more to do by sundown."

"I'm just standing here being sentimental. Rose Ellen set me off." His brows shot up in surprise, which made her laugh. "And I've got energy to spare for work. Now that we've started, I feel elated, Lang. I think I might like farming better than nursing!"

He chuckled. "You'll have to do a lot of nursing in farming. There's plenty of patching and mending involved."

His dark eyes sparkled at her, making her insides go liquid and hot. Sometimes just looking at him, she felt as if she might turn limp and boneless, like a dumpling, even when he was talking about seemingly innocuous subjects like patching roofs and how often to rest the mules. Especially then. Talking over domestic subjects with Lang brought a fierce longing within her, making her yearn for what she knew now could never be—herself and Lang, working side by side, forever.

Tears stung at her eyes, but she couldn't let him see them.

"If you do start the hospital—"

She interrupted him. "I will."

"When you do, you'll be doing two demanding jobs. You realize that, don't you?"

She nodded. "I realize it."

"You'll need help."

She looked at him, feeling a hitch in her heart, but his eyes didn't reveal the meaning she hoped to see in them. She needed help; yet he was still going to leave her. Her heart railed against the unfairness of it. "Do you have any suggestions?"

"William's a better worker than I thought he'd be. He catches on fast. If I were you, I'd keep him and Lorna on here. That way I'd…" His eyes darkened and he looked down at the pine planks of the porch floor.

"You'd what?" Without meaning to, she stepped toward him, magnetized by hope and desire. He would stay? That couldn't be. He would…what?

He shook his head. "Well, you'd be less lonely. I wouldn't worry about you so much."

She might have been encouraged by the fact that he would think of her at all, but she wasn't. She might even have laughed at the idea of yet another person worrying about her being lonely, yet she couldn't. Lonely. Just that word struck a cold note in her heart. "I have a feeling I really don't know the meaning of loneliness yet." She would when Lang rode out.

He touched her chin with his knuckles, tilting it up. His eyes were full of unspoken emotion, but her gaze focused on his lips, warm and full. If she'd thought it would work, she would have kissed him, begged him to stay, offered him anything. She'd always heard about scarlet women who used their bodies to bring men to heel and bend them to their will. And for a moment she considered making Lang such a lurid proposition. Lord knows, it wouldn't entail doing anything she hadn't dreamed about every night now.

Trouble was, she doubted it would work. And maybe she didn't want it to. Her heart was breaking, but Lang's life was on the line. His argument that the longer he stayed the more danger he was in had a ring of truth to it. Given the choice between Lang's life and her own happiness, she knew which she'd pick. Or did she?

"Emma?" he asked. "Is something wrong?"

She smiled. "Yes—I'm going crazy as a bedbug. One minute I think you're right and that you should ride out of here as soon as possible, and the next I'm dreaming up ways to entice you to stay."

"Like how?"

She leaned back against the railing. "Well, that's difficult. You've already got the best room in the house, and my cooking is lucky to draw flies."

Lang chuckled.

She shrugged. "It doesn't leave much else…besides myself."

He stilled, and his smile disappeared.

She rushed on. "Sometimes at night I think about going into your room and offering my…favors…for you to stay. But I always lose my nerve." She laughed. "I'm not sure how persuasive a tactic it would be, anyway."

Lang wasn't laughing. When he spoke, his voice came out a rasp. "Very." He reached forward and took her in his arms, his intense gaze melting the humorous facade she'd been hiding behind.

Emma closed her eyes as Lang bent forward, and for an aching eternity she held her breath...until she felt the warmth of his lips sweep across hers. It was just a brush of skin against skin, the slightest whisper of a kiss, but there was nothing slight about her reaction. Her skin was on fire; her blood heated to a deep molten core that until Lang she hadn't known existed within her. And when he pulled away from her, her heart, which for a fleeting moment had been so full, deflated suddenly until it was just an aching pebble-sized lump in her breast.

He looked away, his expression hooded.

Emma closed her eyes once more and didn't move, remaining only inches from him. They were so close, she could feel the warmth of his body, and if she closed her eyes, she would be able to imagine that he was still about to reach out to her and kiss her again, longer this time. She could dream that he would never let her go.

The scrape of his boot as he stepped away made her open her eyes. "Lang—"

"You've got company, Emma," he said, cutting her off.

She whirled and glanced down the road, expecting to find a horse in the distance. Instead, she saw Barton Sealy about twenty yards away. Emma froze.

"Folks are always sneaking up on us," Lang drawled.

Before she could put her thoughts into any kind of rational order, the front door slammed and Lang had disappeared. Emma remained rooted where she was, unable to step forward to greet her unwanted guest. Lang and the intervening days had put all thought of Barton's betrayal out of her head, but seeing his handsome face and glib smile again brought it back to her. She stiffened with resentment.

The sheriff dismounted and doffed his hat. "Howdy, Emma," he said, grinning from ear to ear.

And why wouldn't he be grinning? The last time he'd seen her, he'd kissed her once and she'd nearly fallen over herself with gratefulness. The memory made her slightly nauseated. How happy it would have made her to tell him that she'd as soon kiss a wooden statue as him again.

"How are you, Sheriff?"

Her use of his title instead of his name caused him to blink. "I was expectin' to see you before now, to tell you the truth. I thought you'd come to town to see me."

"I went to town, but I didn't have time to drop by the jail. Since then, I've been busy."

"Oh." He looked nonplussed, then shrugged. "Well, but of course you'll be taking tomorrow off. For the church picnic."

She shrugged. "Yes, I suppose so. Lorna and William have offered to take me."

Barton's eyes narrowed at the mention of his brother in conjunction with Lorna, but he gritted out a smile. "Now, why would you want to go with them, when I'd be happy to pick you up and take you there myself?"

Emma grinned back. "How kind of you! But I wouldn't want to put you out."

"It would be no trouble."

"Oh, yes, it would. Far too much trouble," Emma insisted. "I wouldn't dream of going with you."

"But I want to—"

"No, absolutely not."

His smile faded. "See here, Emma. What's going on?"

Emma smiled pleasantly. "We've been very busy here. The farm is coming along nicely, and William has been such a help."

"I didn't mean with the farm," Barton said. "I mean...between us."

Emma's eyes widened. "Why? Was there something between us?" she asked, blinking. "Did I miss it?"

He slapped his hat against his thigh. "Gol-dang it,
Emma. You haven't forgotten that I kissed you."

She let out a breathy sigh of understanding. "Oh, that!"
She laughed. "No, I haven't forgotten."

"Well, then…"

She put a hand on his sleeve and assured him, "I still
think it would be best if I went with Lorna and William,
don't you? We wouldn't want people linking our names
together."

She nearly laughed at his pop-eyed confusion. It apparently had never entered his head that she might not want
his company. "But—"

"People are such gossips," she interrupted. "Always
trying to make out a romance where one couldn't possibly
exist!"

His lips turned down in a grim line. "I see." His eyes
narrowed, and he stared at the screen door for a moment.
"Was that your boarder I saw you with just now?"

Emma continued to stare evenly at him, hoping that she
kept the wariness out of her expression. "Mr. Archibald?
Yes, I believe it was."

"He seemed a handsome fellow."

"He's an invalid," Emma offered, her mind frozen.
Why was the sheriff looking at her suspiciously?

"A young invalid, I'd say. Has he seen some sort of
trouble?"

Emma thought she might faint. "An accident…several
years ago."

His frown deepened, and she detected more than a little
skepticism, too. "Maybe I ought to have a talk with this
man. You can't trust everyone nowadays, you know. And
there have been some bad characters prowling about

lately." *Like the outlaw Lang Tupper,* his gaze seemed to say.

But surely she was just being overly fearful. There was no reason for him to put Mr. Archibald and Lang Tupper together...unless he got a better look at him than he possibly could have from that distance. She just had to make certain he didn't get another look at Lang at all.

"Mr. Archibald has been unfailingly polite and very helpful. He helped plant my kitchen garden this week."

"Did he, now?" the sheriff asked, his voice far from interested. He looked off to the side pasture, where Lorna and William were talking by the fence, and frowned. "I think I'll have a word with my brother." He smashed his hat back on his head. "Good day, Emma."

"Sheriff."

Her heart was beating like a rabbit's as she watched him stomp over to William and Lorna. Naturally, Lorna fled soon after the hellos, but the two men talked long enough to exchange what appeared to be angry words, although she was too far away to hear. Then the sheriff mounted his horse, flicked an annoyed gaze at Emma and rode off.

Fear squeezed her chest. Maybe she should have just gone to the picnic with the sheriff. By not doing so, she may have picked up an unfortunate enemy.

She turned, ran through the front door and up the stairs. When she reached Lang's room, he was sitting in the chair she usually took, apparently waiting for her. Her expression must have told him all he needed to know about her frantic state of mind. "That was the sheriff!"

His lips twitched. "So I heard. You were wonderful, Emma."

"I shouldn't have antagonized him!" she exclaimed, pacing anxiously. "What are we going to do?"

"Nothing."

"Nothing!" she repeated. "He saw you. I think he suspects—" She cut off her words, unable to speak the dreaded words.

"We'll sit tight until tomorrow. Till the picnic."

She nodded, willing herself to be calm like Lang. "The picnic." She frowned. "Then what?"

He swallowed. "Then, while you and everyone else are occupied with stuffing yourselves and dancing, I'll sneak out."

"Sneak out," she repeated, feeling suddenly numb inside.

"That way, no one around here will see me."

Emma's insides suddenly felt like a lump of iron. She sank against his door, cold and shaky. Lang sounded so calm; he'd thought this all through, and now he was prepared to follow what was certainly a rational course of action. She'd known this moment was coming, but she wasn't ready, and she couldn't be calm. "Tomorrow is so soon!" she exclaimed. "Too soon!"

"But it's ideal. Half the county will be there. I'll be able to head out with little chance of being noticed for a good long while."

"But what about the planting?" she said, when she really just wanted to cry *what about me?* Or *what about us?*

But of course there was no *them*. Lang had made sure of that. If only he could have ensured that she wouldn't fall in love with him. Because that's what had happened, she realized now. After twenty-eight years of being wise and careful and responsible, and shaking her head over what fools women made of themselves, she'd gone and fallen in love with Lang Tupper, the worst possible choice she could have made. To say the man was without prospects was laughable. He was very possibly without a future at all.

But she loved him. Loved him the way she'd never expected to love a man since she was a silly sixteen-year-old—with every fiber of her being. Every moment of the day she thought of him; she went to bed at night dreaming of how it felt to be held in his arms; she could have written several volumes of sonnets about his handsome face, his deep voice, his uneven but still graceful walk. His kindness toward her would easily have filled a volume all itself. She'd been a different person entirely since she'd met him, a better person. He'd changed her life.

And now he was simply going to leave?

She tried to visualize tomorrow, and their parting. The terrible thing, she realized, was that she would have to leave first. It wouldn't simply be a matter of standing on the porch and waving at him till he disappeared. She would have to tear herself away from him to go to a silly dance that would be worse than torture for her.

"I can't do it!" she said, pushing herself away from the door.

Lang stood. "Yes, you can. William will help you."

William? She managed to focus her confused gaze on him, then understood. He thought she was still talking about the planting, when her mind had sped right past that issue. Lang was more important to her than her farm.

"Emma," he said gently, "we both knew this was going to happen."

She shook her head. "But so soon?"

"I'm well enough to travel. I should have left a couple of days ago. I'm just putting you in danger if the sheriff finds me out."

She didn't give a damn about the danger. "Let me go with you, then." The words had just popped out of her mouth, but after she had spoken them, the crazy thought took root in her frantic mind. She grabbed his arms. "I'll go with you!"

"No." The answer was emphatic.

"Why not?"

"Because everything you want is right here. Your house, your land, the hospital you were going to open. Isn't that what you wanted?"

"Not if you're not here!" She couldn't believe she was speaking the words and throwing herself at a man, an outlaw, who didn't—judging by the unhappy frown on his face—even seem to want her. "Please take me with you, Lang."

He stared at her long and hard, a kaleidoscope of emotions in his expression. Finally he shook his head. "I couldn't. You would regret it."

"I wouldn't!"

He laughed. "Do you remember what I looked like when I landed on your porch, Emma? That's what running from the law does to a person. You can't relax, you have to be careful going into towns, a night in a hotel is a luxury you can't afford."

"I have money."

His lips thinned. "It's not just money, it's the threat of being discovered. You can't risk being seen by the wrong people. And even beyond your comfort, I couldn't let you give up your birthright, Emma. You'd miss home, I can assure you. If I had a home this nice, I know I would."

She was losing him. She couldn't let that happen. "But I love you."

He looked at her, swallowing so hard she could follow the tortured trail of his Adam's apple up and down his throat. For a moment, it looked as if he might reply in kind to her statement, but he stopped, tilting his head and regarding her some more.

He didn't love her. His silence made that perfectly clear. She'd blurted out her confession and now it didn't even matter. He didn't want her along because he didn't really care about her. Not deeply.

Her shoulders sagged in defeat.

He didn't touch her—no fraternal pat on the shoulder, no reassuring squeeze. "Maybe it's just that I'm something different that's come your way. A little excitement, a man who's paid attention to you when you most needed it. But in a month or so, you might realize that there's less to me than meets the eye, and Lord knows, what meets the eye isn't that great. I'm just a worker, Emma. I have no home. Right now I don't even have a good reputation, or a name. Is that what you want to saddle yourself with?"

She couldn't look at him any longer. Her eyes focused on the fringed ends of the carpet at her feet, which she nudged with the toe of her boot. She tried to swallow back her humiliation—rejected by an outlaw. Somehow it was fitting, in a way. Just another milestone in the hard-luck romantic life of Emma Colby.

She bit her lip hard, and for a moment the metallic taste of blood was in her mouth. Better not to cry at this point, she decided. She'd have plenty of time for tears later. "Please try to tell William as much as you can about what needs to be done." Normally she would have asked him to tell her, but she didn't think she could stand talking business now. "And please remember to say goodbye to me before you go."

"Emma—"

She fled the room before she burst into tears.

Chapter Eleven

"Now, how could I have misplaced a whole basket of fried chicken?" Lorna wondered aloud, rushing around the kitchen. Though her hair was up and she was wearing her best dress and bonnet, she looked pinched with anxiety.

Instead of confessing to chicken theft, Emma merely shrugged. Lorna's savory bird was more useful in Lang's saddlebags than at the picnic.

Lorna put her hands on her hips. "It couldn't have just walked away!"

Davy, sitting at the table nearby and eating a pilfered piece of pie as compensation for having to stay home with Rose Ellen, swung his feet and howled with laughter. "It might have if you didn't cook it enough!"

Both women shot the boy long-suffering glances, which delighted him even more. When Lang appeared in the door, Davy laughed and asked, "Couldn't a chicken walk away if you didn't cook it enough?"

Lang appeared appropriately mystified by the question, and by the fact that Lorna was on the verge of a break-down. "Is something wrong?"

"I can't find my fried chicken!" Lorna exclaimed, gesturing to her basket. "Now all we'll have to eat is pie and biscuits—if Davy doesn't eat even that before we leave."

Lang glanced at Emma, who had just delivered the chicken to his room announcing that he would need it for his journey. His brows shot up quizzically, and she looked away. She couldn't bear the thought of saying goodbye to him.

"We should be leaving now," Emma reminded Lorna.

Lorna stopped, tears gathering. She stood in the middle of the room and flapped her hands in frustration. "Oh, I shouldn't even be going!" she exclaimed. "I knew it was a mistake. I look terrible! People will be talking about me something fierce!"

"Nonsense," Emma assured her. "William wants to show you off."

"You look beautiful," Lang said. "You both do."

Emma, her face burning, her heart aching, forced her gaze to meet Lang's. His compliment was a lie. She had spent a sleepless night, and now her face was pale, her eyes puffy, and her hair lackadaisically put up in her standard bun. She was wearing a gray dress that had been her Sunday best a decade ago. It was a strain to keep her voice steady. "I wish you were coming with us, Mr. Archibald."

Though they had agreed to keep up Lang's fictitious identity in front of everyone, Emma was sorely tempted to break that pledge right now, and throw herself at him yet again. But Lang didn't want her. He'd made that abundantly clear yesterday.

His dark eyes looked at her with understanding. "I'm afraid I wouldn't be much of a dancer in my present condition," he answered, gesturing with his cane. "But when you're whirling about today, Emma, think once of me."

Once? She would never stop thinking about him, from the moment she left till the time she returned home to the empty house. Because, no matter how many people were living here, that's how it would seem without Lang. Empty.

Unbidden, tears appeared in her eyes. "I will." Her voice cracked from the tension.

Lorna whirled on her, surprised, then her own nervous tears began to spill over.

The two of them were standing sniffling in the middle of the kitchen when William appeared at the door. "Wagon's ready. If you—" He stopped, taking in the sight of Lorna and Emma both reduced to tears. His Adam's apple bobbed up and down nervously. "What in the name of Christopher Columbus happened?"

Emma shook her head. "We misplaced the chicken."

William shifted in confusion, not certain how seriously to take the chicken crisis. "Well…we need to get a move on."

Emma couldn't believe that her last moments with Lang were going to be spent in front of all these people, but now she couldn't see a way to avoid it. She watched him sit down at the table; Davy ran over and jumped into his lap, making Emma, if not Lang, wince at the pain it must have caused him.

"Women cry all the time, don't they, Mr. Archibald?" Davy chattered. "My sisters always do."

Lang had taken to both Davy and Annalise so easily, so naturally, and in the few short days he'd been up and about, he'd become their favorite adult confidant. Both children would be devastated when they discovered him gone.

Or, more likely, *she* would be devastated. Even watching Lang and Davy together she felt as if a rope were being squeezed around her chest. It was so unfair! Lang was so good with children, he should be able to settle down and have a whole houseful of his own.

He should be able to settle down with her.

"Emma?"

She started, realizing she'd been gaping at Lang and Davy.

"You coming?" Will asked.

She nodded, and was surprised when her feet actually moved. "Goodbye," she told Lang, as informally as she could. The word was so simple, but choking it out was one of the hardest things she'd ever done. It didn't come close to expressing all that she wanted to say to him, but her tears, at least, spoke from her heart. *Be careful,* they said. *I love you.* Nothing would ever change that.

His dark eyes followed her as she scurried out of the room.

Lorna was right to be worried. It seemed every man, woman and child was gathered at Midday's church, which rested on a hill above Wally Creek, a thin strip of water that created problems in the springtime. By August, the creek was usually little more than a trickle. At the bottom of the hill, older children played a raucous game of prisoner's base, while at the top of the hill, cloths were laid out in a patchwork quilt of picnic areas, where practically every person in Midday was seated. All eyes watched with interest as Emma's wagon approached, and when William, then Emma, then Lorna disembarked, a low rustle of murmurs fluttered through the crowd.

"Oh, Emma!" Lorna whispered. "They're already talking about me something fierce."

Emma looped her arm through Lorna's and sent her a reassuring smile. "But by the end of the day they won't be. That's what this is all about."

But Lorna's blue eyes told her clearly that the younger woman wanted nothing more than to turn tail and run. And

who could blame her? All the glances they received as they
turned to begin the task of setting out their blanket and
food were disapproving, if not downright hostile, and the
look that Mrs. Dunston threw them could have turned them
to stone. Emma had thought that William's bringing Lorna
into town would begin to put an end to Lorna's ostracism,
but now she began to wonder if perhaps she'd been too
hopeful. She ached for the writhing humiliation Lorna must
be going through. And now she wondered what on earth
had made her convince her friend to come. Lorna's best
dress still tugged tightly against her middle, and her bonnet, which Lorna so prized and had decorated for this occasion, looked worn-out and limp. She'd always thought
Lorna pretty and sweet, but now, with her head hung low,
her belly bulging and tears of terror brimming in her eyes,
doom struck in Emma's heart. The fire-and-brimstone
preacher Reverend Cathcart had brought in for the occasion
would have a field day with Lorna. She looked like shame
personified.

Emma tried to busy Lorna with setting up their picnic
blanket, and was relieved when a few more wagons came
up, distracting everyone's attention temporarily. She attempted to avoid the eyes of the disapproving crowd,
though she did make brief eye contact with Barton Sealy,
who was leaning against a nearby tree, apparently enjoying
her discomfort.

"Emma Colby!" someone yelled from behind her. "Just
who I needed!"

Emma turned in time to see Constance O'Hurlihy bearing down on her. She suppressed a shudder.

Constance was outfitted in a sailor motif—blue serge
with big brass buttons, white piping and a matching hat
that looked like a French beret, the headband of which was
pulled down squarely to the middle of her forehead. She

stopped inches from Emma's face and began speaking in a rush. "We are just *besieged* with people needing help! Mr. Howard can't hear *and* he's got an uncomfortable boil on his neck that's bothering him, but if you'll take him I'll deal with old Mrs. Pettibone. I know you can't stand the way she fusses over every little thing, but then again, I'm a little more patient, I guess."

Emma listened to Constance, feeling sick as the words began to sink in. She was being requisitioned into spinster duty. She'd never minded it before, but something about Constance's bare assumption that she would drop everything to tend to Mr. Howard and his boil made her feel sick with dread. *This is how life is going to be from now till doomsday.* Looking at Constance's thin, horsey face, her nervous eyes, the sadly overdone outfits she worked on to make herself stand out, she was looking into her own future.

Except *she* didn't even have the outfits.

She glanced pointedly at the cloth she and Lorna were setting up. "I'm rather busy...."

Constance stared at her stonily. "Well! If you don't *want* to help out, I suppose I can just take care of everyone myself. But I've never known you to be so selfish, Emma."

Emma was about to suggest that perhaps Constance should stay with her, and have fun at a public gathering for once, when their conversation was interrupted.

"I have an announcement to make."

At the sound of the familiar but uncharacteristically booming voice, everyone pivoted toward William, who had surreptitiously positioned himself at the stairs leading up to the church. His slight frame looked as if it could blow over with a breeze, yet he stood erect, and waited for everyone to focus their attention on him. Which didn't take long.

"I know some of you disapprove of Miss Lorna Mc-Crae's coming here, this being a church function and all...."

His voice was quavery but determined, though Emma's knees knocked with anxiety for him. She could only imagine how poor Lorna was feeling! What did William think he was going to accomplish by bringing even more attention to them?

"And I agree, what's happened with Lorna hasn't been right." William paused, looking into each and every face. "But what I'm here to say is it hasn't been Lorna's fault. It's been mine. But now, if she'll agree to it, I intend to make it right. If she'll have me, I intend to marry Lorna McCrae on Monday, at Reverend Cathcart's."

His pronouncement was met by one sob of happiness. He walked toward Lorna through the stunned silence, although just as he arrived to give his bride-to-be a joyous hug, murmurs began again. But this time Lorna didn't hear them; she was too wrapped up in her own felicity to worry about what other people thought.

She didn't hear the approaching footsteps of Mrs. Dunston, either. "Congratulations, Lorna," said the woman who had probably not so much as nodded in passing to Lorna McCrae before. "When is your baby due?"

Lorna blushed. "In three weeks."

Mrs. Dunston nodded curtly. "That's fast, but you never can tell about those first babies. They'll come at any time. After that, it takes nine months."

Lorna stood blinking at the woman for a moment, then, when the joke finally sank in, laughed.

After Mrs. Dunston's tacit approval, a steady trickle of townsfolk began making their way over to Emma's blanket, congratulating the couple. For Lorna's sake, Emma hid her own personal sorrow over Lang as best she could. Still finding herself at another town function, talking to old folk and keeping an eye on Annalise as she quietly drew sketches, brought home how empty her life felt now that Lang was gone. Yes, she would have her farm, and maybe her little hospital, if things worked out as she hoped. Maybe she would even try to go east for a while, and study at a real nursing school in Philadelphia. But even so, would she ever be as happy as Lorna looked right now?

Charlie Atwater was just warming up his fiddle for the dancing, playing a snappy tune that eager young folks were already starting to move to, and Emma could only sip her warm lemonade and stare at them wistfully. This would be yet another function where she stood on the sidelines, wishing.

"Look, Aunt Emma—I drew Mr. Archibald!"

Emma looked at the picture, rendered so realistically by such a young hand, and felt a stabbing pain in her heart. She marveled at how well her niece had captured Lang. His eyes were the same eyes that had looked at her, his lips the same lips that had kissed her. His hair appeared to be the same unruly collection of soft dark tufts going every which way, refusing to be tamed. Emma smiled in spite of herself.

Lorna, who was leaning against William's chest and munching on a piece of pie, studied the picture with a frown. "Aren't you forgetting something, Annalise?"

Annalise inspected her masterwork with a critical eye, then let out a breath. "Mr. Archibald's got a dimple!" She reached down and with a single masterful stroke added the cleft in the chin.

"That's him exactly!" Lorna exclaimed admiringly.

The sheriff pushed away from his tree and came to inspect the picture. Emma paled, and, without knowing what else to do, dropped her glass of lemonade right onto the drawing. Everyone on the blanket sprang to their feet.

"Oh, how silly of me!" Emma said, hopping up and snatching the picture away. She shook it out, then folded it and tried to tuck it away, but when she glanced up, Barton was staring straight at her, his eyes wide with disbelief.

It was all over.

Shaking, Emma grabbed her glass and decided to refill it from the large bowl put out by the church ladies. Lorna and William were trying to pat dry the blankets with napkins, and she stepped by them as quickly as she could— but she wasn't fast enough to evade the sheriff.

"Allow me to escort you," Barton said, taking her arm.

Though he didn't exert undue pressure, Emma winced. Why hadn't she been paying more attention to what Annalise was doing, and where the sheriff was? She'd known Barton had been hanging around, apparently waiting for her to change her mind and invite him to share their lunch. Now she'd given Lang away. *Oh, Lang!* For the first time she hoped he'd left already—that he was miles away.

When they reached the table set up with water and lemonade, Barton took the glass out of her hand and looked at her, his eyes flat and serious. "I feel like a dance," he said, setting the glass down.

It wasn't a request, it was a command. In a daze, Emma allowed the sheriff to lead her to the clearing and stepped stonily into his stiff embrace.

"I wondered what happened to those Wanted posters," the sheriff said with a bitter laugh.

She couldn't look at him, and continued to stare at the buttons on his vest. *Lang,* she thought mournfully, *I'm so sorry!* But aloud she mumbled, "I'm not sure I know what you're talking about, Barton."

His hands squeezed tight on her hand and waist, causing Emma to stiffen in pain. "Don't kid me," the sheriff warned in a low voice. At his gruff tone, she looked up into his blue eyes and marveled that she could ever have found him handsome. "I know who your Mr. Archibald is. I just can't imagine what you think you've been up to."

She tilted her chin up defiantly but said nothing, admitted nothing.

His eyes narrowed. "You could be in big trouble, lady."

She tried to stay calm, though her heart was beating wildly.

The sheriff smirked. "I see! The outlaw taking advantage of the old spinster woman."

She scowled at him. "He didn't take advantage!" She spat the words out in a low voice, forgetting that she intended to admit nothing. "Besides which, he's innocent."

Barton laughed. "Is that what he told you?"

"It's what I know to be true."

"Good Lord, you're even more gullible than I thought you were!" he exclaimed, shaking his head.

Emma felt her cheeks redden with anger. "I was only gullible the day I let you kiss me. I've wised up since then. And if you're thinking you're going to catch him, it's too late."

"Is it?" The sheriff grinned. "Care to take me over to your house and prove how late I am? Care to round up a posse of these fine citizens and scour the countryside with us?"

She glared at him, hating him. She didn't know what to say or do next. Nowhere in her thoughts had she reckoned on being in this situation. She felt sick with fear.

The sheriff chuckled. "Don't worry, Miss Colby, your

precious desperado can go free if you play your cards right. I'm not interested in him.''

At first she thought she hadn't heard him correctly. She tilted a skeptical glance at him. ''Then what are you interested in?''

Blue eyes like icy chips glinted down at her. ''You.''

Emma froze, but the sheriff tugged her stumbling, leaden feet into a waltz. ''What?''

''You're surprised?'' he asked. ''You, who own all that fine red soil? Why, if the rest of the men of Midday knew you were sole owner of the Colby homestead, they'd have been flocking to your door for months.'' He grinned. ''But now it looks like I'm the lucky winner.''

She swallowed, not quite understanding. ''But I told you already I have no interest in you.''

He squinted at her. ''That was before I picked up a pair of aces in the form of a certain outlaw's identity.''

Emma's mouth dropped open as his meaning began to sink in. ''You're blackmailing me....''

''I'm just trying to *persuade* you, using other means where kisses failed.'' His smooth grin made her stomach turn.

''You expect me to just sign my land over to you? In exchange for...Mr. Archibald going free?''

''Don't be an idiot. I expect you to marry me. I don't want folks around here saying there was anything shady going on in my dealings with you.''

Shady? The man could have invented the word! Not only was he a lawman apparently perfectly complacent with the idea of criminals gallivanting around his countryside, he was willing to stoop to blackmailing a woman into marrying him! For a moment she thought she might be ill.

And then it struck her. If she didn't take the sheriff up on his corrupt bargain, Barton might round up a posse, just as he'd threatened. Lang would be caught. It would be the same as her stringing a noose around his neck herself. She might as well have let him die on her front porch that rainy night not so long ago. All her love and good intentions mixed together wouldn't amount to a hill of flop if Lang fell into the wrong hands.

To her horror, she heard herself speaking in a trembly voice. "You'd have to promise not to go after him."

"I told you I didn't give a damn about your Mr. Archibald."

She nodded, then looked up at him to try to discern whether he was lying. A man who would twist her arm this way and marry her for her money wasn't exactly trustworthy. "And you promise not to alert any sheriff in another county?"

He shook his head. "Don't be a little fool, Emma. They'd only ask why I didn't go after him when he was here."

That was true. In marrying him, she would also have a tenuous hold over him, she realized. She would be the only one who knew he'd let a notorious outlaw go free.

As much as it sickened her and galled her, she couldn't conceive of any alternative to the man's wretched proposal. "When?" She didn't even bother to state her agreement. He knew she was cornered.

"Today."

She sucked in her breath. "No!"

He chuckled. "Shy, dear?"

"You have to give me time."

A blond brow crooked suspiciously. "Time to run away with your desperado?"

She shook her head frantically, suddenly seeing it all slip away from her. Her house, her farm, her hospital. All the control she'd so recently gained over her life. Now it would all belong to Barton Sealy. Maybe he wouldn't even allow her to open her hospital. He would take over the management of the land, which she had only so recently discovered she enjoyed. Nothing in the world would belong to her and her alone.

Except her memories, she realized. Those, and the knowledge that by giving up her own freedom, Lang might have his. Maybe he would make it to California and start anew. Maybe he would even find a wife and have children.

"He didn't want me," she told Barton. "I offered to go with him, and he said I'd only hold him back, and that I'd regret it. So you can rest assured, I won't disappear."

Barton flicked an annoyed gaze toward his brother. "Tomorrow, then. We'll make it a double wedding."

Emma also looked at the happy couple and felt her heart shatter. Could she legally seal such a cold-blooded arrangement at the same time those lovebirds tied the knot? The idea seemed almost sacrilegious. Yet tomorrow was better than today, she had to admit. At least it would give her one night to prepare for the inevitable.

She glanced at Barton Sealy and paled at the idea of sharing her life with this man…and sharing her bed. Once, she'd had silly daydreams of being his wife; now the prospect was as welcome as torture.

A second later Barton motioned for Charlie to stop playing. The fiddle broke off in midnote, striking an off-pitch scratch, and Barton began to speak.

"Folks, I, too, have an announcement to make," he said, keeping an iron grip on Emma's hand. "To my happy astonishment, Miss Emma Colby has agreed to become my bride."

At these last words, a series of gasps went through the crowd, then wholehearted applause. Even a few whoops.

Emma hadn't expected this sort of reaction; then again, she was marrying the sheriff.

He grinned, and looking at Barton just then anyone might have thought it was the happiest moment in his life. And who knows that it wasn't? All those rich Colby acres... "With my brother's permission, Miss Emma and I will tie the knot in a double ceremony, and we want y'all to come out. The Sealy men will be throwing a party!"

Hats were tossed in the air, and several bachelors did a little jig in the center of the dance area. People clapped in rhythm and laughed at their antics, and Charlie started up his fiddling again with a jaunty version of "Little Brown Jug." Emma watched the joyous display in mute amazement as the townspeople celebrated her upcoming nuptials. The whole town was whooping it up, while the bride-to-be was dying inside.

"You're doing what?"

"I'm marrying the sheriff," Emma dutifully reported to her sister. "Tomorrow."

With the exception of the red pox marks, which were almost faded, Rose Ellen's face went completely pale. "But you can't!"

"Why not?"

"Emma, you don't love him. You know you don't!"

A flush of helplessness seeped over her. "I've always liked Barton."

Her sister answered with a look that indicated that Emma had gone mad. "He's a fortune hunter!"

Emma lifted her chin. "Don't other women use money to marry advantageously?"

"What advantage does he have?" Rose Ellen scoffed.

"He's handsome."

Rose Ellen rolled her eyes. "*He* would say so, at least."

"And he's from a very good family."

The younger woman jumped on that tidbit like a frog devouring a bug. "I've been thinking about that—goodness knows I've had little enough else to do—and I've concluded that there's something very suspicious about the way these Sealy men are all suddenly so eager to become penny ante farmers."

After all the backbreaking labor she'd endured, that was one insult Emma couldn't let go. "This is not a penny ante farm, Rose Ellen. If tended well, this land could yield thirty-five bushels per acre...." Her words suddenly trailed off as a wave of nausea overtook her when she realized just what she was giving up to that scoundrel. Everything she held dear. Her home, her freedom, her very self. She sank onto the blanket-draped settee and grabbed one of Rose Ellen's goose-feather pillows for comfort.

Rose Ellen dropped to her side. "Emma, are you all right?"

She swallowed with effort. "Just bridal nerves."

Rose Ellen, who had looked shocked before, now looked positively stupefied. "Oh, Emma! You haven't done anything you shouldn't, have you?"

God forbid! Their one wooden kiss had been uncomfortable enough. Contemplating the marriage bed with that man made her blood run cold.

"I don't see what the rush is, then," Rose Ellen said. "If you'd just wait, I'd be feeling a little better, and we could throw you a really nice party, with a cake and a new dress and lots of people."

"I think a lot of people will come to Reverend Cathcart's tomorrow, even without a cake. Barton invited the whole town." In doing so, she suspected he was attempting to make it as difficult as possible for her to back out. Just as, when she'd claimed a headache at the dance and wanted to leave, he'd insisted on escorting her home himself. Or maybe he'd just wanted to get a look at all the land that would soon be his. Thank heavens he hadn't argued the point when she hadn't invited him in. Having him gaze upon her house with a proprietary eye would have sent her over the edge.

Seeing that her sister wasn't going to relent and at least have a big party to compensate for her disagreeable marriage, Rose Ellen lifted her thin shoulders and sighed. "I shudder to think what Mr. Archibald will say about all this. I think he's really very taken with you, Emma."

To hear Lang's name—even his fake one—made Emma go limp with grief. "At least I won't have to tell him."

"Do you think he won't find out? Why, just five minutes ago the poor man was down here asking me where your favorite places to hide things were."

Emma sprang to her feet. "Five minutes ago! Mr. Archibald?"

"Yes, Emma." Her sister looked at her quizzically, then smiled. "I think he wanted to secret away a little present for you."

Emma felt light-headed. Lang couldn't be here, he couldn't be. It was too terrible…too wonderful. There should have been miles and miles between them by this time! She twirled dizzily and ran hell-for-leather toward the stairs, which she almost traversed in a single leap. *Here! Lang is here!* The thought pounded in her head like insistent drumbeats, swelling her heart with both fear and relief. He needed to be gone—but oh, how glad she would be to see him once more!

His door was wide open and she sped inside before skidding to a stop, practically panting. He was sitting in a chair, his long legs stretched out lazily before him and crossed at the ankles. In his lap lay the well-thumbed copy of one of her father's favorite books, *Two Years Before the Mast,* which Lang appeared absorbed in. He barely looked up when she appeared in front of him.

"Is something wrong?" he asked, almost idly, as if he had all the time in the world.

Emma nearly shrieked. "What are you doing here?"

He grinned, a warm smile she couldn't help contrasting with the sheriff's viciously cold expression. "You know, I was thinking, instead of California, perhaps I should take to the sea for a while."

He was joking. Unbelievable! "You were supposed to be gone!" Emma reminded him. "You should be halfway to San Antonio by now!"

He shook his head. "It will be safer if I wait till I'll be closer to having the cover of darkness."

Emma ran to the window, as if she needed confirmation that it was still daylight. Of course she could see his point. The church meeting would go on past dark, but she wasn't sure she could withstand the nail-biting hours until he left. Each minute he stayed would make it that much more difficult to let him go.

He stood, still a little stiff in his movement, and smiled at her fondly. "You aren't making my job much easier, bringing the sheriff around."

She looked down at her feet. "I had to leave early…and he insisted on escorting me."

"What happened?"

She glanced up and attempted a negligent shrug. "Nothing."

His brows drew together in worry. "There *is* something wrong. I should have known it the way you came running in full steam." He stepped closer. "What's happened?"

She shook her head. "Nothing."

''Emma…something's wrong.'' His piercing dark eyes looked into hers. ''Did the sheriff say something to you?''

Her cheeks burned. She longed to throw herself into his strong, supportive arms and beg him again to let her go with him, but he'd made it clear to her yesterday that he didn't want her. And she couldn't tell him the sheriff was blackmailing her, or that she was sacrificing herself for him, because if he knew, Lang might do something foolhardy like turn himself in for her sake. Or he might confront the sheriff, and the last thing he needed was for Barton Sealy to feel any more belligerent toward him.

''Did he recognize me yesterday?''

She shook her head. ''It's not what you think.''

He let out an exasperated breath. ''Then what's wrong? You're strung tight as fence wire.''

She clenched and unclenched her fists, trying to summon a little bravery to make her confession. ''I've agreed to marry Barton Sealy,'' she said in as calm a voice as she could muster.

Lang stared at her, thunderstruck. ''You've what?''

She didn't need to repeat herself; she could tell by his sickly pallor that he'd understood. ''We're going to have the ceremony tomorrow, in town.''

''Tomorrow!'' Lang shouted, even more horrified than Rose Ellen had been.

But no one was more horrified than she herself was. And the worst part of all was having to put on a brave face for Lang. She couldn't let him know that she was going to be wed against her will.

''Why?''

She lifted her chin. ''I don't want to be alone.'' It was the most plausible-sounding lie she could come up with.

He blinked in surprise. ''But you know what a deceptive man he is.''

She nodded. "I never said I was in love with him, but can you blame me for wanting to marry one of the town's foremost citizens? He'll be able to. help me with the work here once you're gone. And I've become so close to Lorna and Will, now I'll get to be part of their family, and see their baby grow up…maybe have some of my own…." At the thought of having Barton Sealy's babies, she crossed her arms to hold back a shudder of revulsion.

Lang pinned her with his dark stare until she couldn't look at him a moment longer. "This is really what you want? Marriage to a man you don't love?"

She closed her eyes and nodded slowly, wincing when Lang muttered a string of the angriest curses she'd ever heard from anyone's lips.

"I thought better of you, Emma. I didn't expect this kind of betrayal."

Her eyes swept open in shock. "Betrayal!"

"I thought you had spine. I thought you were an independent-minded woman. But you're weak."

She thrust her chin forward. "How do you reckon that?"

"Because you'd marry a man for his good looks and his social standing in the community."

"I'm just being practical."

He sneered at her flimsy excuse. "I was proud of you yesterday, Emma, when you said you wanted to come away with me."

She felt like screaming. "But you don't want me!"

"Is that what you think?"

"It's what you said," she retorted.

"I only said that you'd be tired of a life on the run. But I didn't intend for you to run off and marry the first man who asked you."

"What did you expect, that I would live and die a spinster with only a few remembered kisses to last till I died?"

"Better that than marry someone you don't love," he replied in a heated voice. Then he stopped, looked out the window absently and combed a hand through his black unruly hair. "I'd hoped..." He let out a harsh breath that was almost a laugh. "Well, never mind that now!"

Emma felt a strange foreboding. "What had you hoped?"

He shook his head. When his head swung around and his dark gaze met hers, it was heartbreaking. "Just that you were different, that's all. Less like somebody I knew once."

Cold bands encircled her heart. "A woman?"

He nodded curtly. "Her name was Lucy. She was young, and pretty...and rich. I was in love with her— wanted to marry her, in fact." He let out a bitter laugh. "I suppose you can guess what happened to that little romance."

Emma shut her eyes. "She said no."

"The most absolute no you could imagine."

Emma shivered. She wanted to shake this Lucy person until her teeth fell out. "Because you had no money?"

The look of bitterness in his face provided the answer to her question. And now Lang thought she was like Lucy. But how? How could he possibly imagine that she would treat a man she cared for so callously? "Are you still in love with her?"

"No," he replied tersely. "In fact, I got over her surprisingly quickly once I discovered how callous she was. But I've worked hard since then to make sure no woman could ever sneer at an offer I made again."

She wanted to stomp her foot at the unfairness of it. If only he *would* make her an offer! She'd run away with him, she'd go to the farthest reaches of the earth, to China, or the moon if he wanted! She...

Couldn't.

The realization shocked her. No matter what Lang said to her now, her hands were tied. She couldn't run away with Lang, because she'd promised Barton that she would marry him tomorrow. Once it was discovered that she was missing, and Mr. Archibald, too, he would know that she'd run away with the outlaw. She had no doubt that in his wrath he would have a posse stampeding after them in nothing flat. So it didn't matter if Lang took her into his arms and made her the sweetest promises her ears could hope to hear. She was stuck.

"You have to believe that I'm doing what I think best," she said, her voice full of anguish. "I didn't know it would hurt you."

His lips twisted. "Lucy said something like that, too."

"I'm not Lucy!" Emma exclaimed. "You didn't make me an offer, Lang."

"I wasn't free to," he replied. "But I hoped that if you cared for me, you would wait. I thought maybe once I got away and got settled, I could send for you."

She sucked in a breath. "Why didn't you say so?"

He shrugged. "It's just a half-baked plan, Emma. It might never come off. I might get caught in the next county. Next week I could be swinging by a rope."

"Don't say that—don't even think it!"

His eyes lit with a fire of hope, and he stepped forward so that their bodies were mere inches apart. "Do you mean that if everything worked out, you *would* join me?"

She could feel his body's warmth, and the effect on her was like a swift river's current pulling her forward, into his arms. He kissed her swiftly, harshly. She melted against him, losing herself in the feel of his lips against hers. A swirl of heat pooled deep within her. This was where she belonged, she thought dizzily, grabbing his shoulders and pressing herself against him greedily. Lang's arms around her, Lang's lips against hers, Lang's swelling need pressing into her abdomen... She should have been aghast that a man could be so familiar with her body, but his voracious, desperate kiss was matched measure for measure with her own need. She loved this man, she dreaded letting him go, and yet...

She had pledged to marry the sheriff. Lang's freedom for hers. That was the bargain.

She dropped her head, sagging against him. "Oh, Lang!"

"Will you, Emma?" he asked, as if their conversation had never been interrupted. Except that his voice was sandpaper rough, more breathless. "Will you wait for me?"

She squeezed her eyes shut, wishing hopelessly that this was all a bad dream. She would have given anything not to have to say the words that she had to speak now. But when she relented and looked into his expectant gaze, she knew there was no escaping hurting him, deceiving him. There was no way to explain what she had to do truthfully without putting his getaway in jeopardy.

"I...can't."

As the last word issued from her lips, his arms stiffened in response, and he held her away from him, a look of confusion and almost revulsion on his face. "You're still going to marry Barton Sealy?"

She nodded weakly.

He gazed on her as if she were covered in filth, and for a moment she felt as if she were. She was tainted by the bargain she'd made with the sheriff, and she'd pay dearly for it. But it was unfair of Lang to look at her as if she were betraying him when she was only proceeding with her marriage to keep him from getting caught.

He let his arms drop and shook his head. "Is the Sealy name worth that much to you?"

She gritted her teeth. "No, but my word is. I'm promised to the sheriff."

"And you don't love him."

"No."

He nodded, obviously still mystified. She couldn't blame him. He would probably spend the rest of his life thinking that she was just another woman who was no better than his old sweetheart Lucy, but there was nothing she could do about that. Her fate, inextricably linked with the sheriff's, was sealed.

"I guess I'll be leaving now," Lang said curtly. He turned, shut the book he'd been reading and placed it on the bureau. Then he turned back to Emma with an expression that was a horrible mix of anger and disappointment. "I suppose it's lucky you came back early, for at least two reasons. If we hadn't had this conversation, I might have spent a long time pining after a married woman."

The insinuation that he wouldn't pine for her now cut her to the quick. Every day of her life she would pine for him, wish that she were married to him. "What's the other reason?"

"I forgot to ask you about my gun. I assume I was armed when you found me?"

She nodded. "It's in the barn," she replied, shocked that she could even think clearly. It seemed such a long time since that blustery night he'd arrived, she'd forgotten all about hiding his gun. It was hard to believe there was a time when she'd been afraid of the man standing in front of her.

"I hid it in a stack of hay next to your horse's stall." Then she remembered. "My father's rifle is in an old cabinet out there. Take that, too."

His lips twitched up in a crooked half smile. "I only need what I rode in with." He stared at her long and hard, as if expecting her to take back her words from before, but of course she couldn't. The lopsided smile turned into a frown, and what spark was left in those dark eyes disappeared, maybe forever. He reached over to the bedpost, grabbed his hat and slammed it on his head. "Goodbye, Miss Emma."

He turned on his heel and strolled out. Emma watched him go, still slightly limping, and felt almost disconnected from what was happening. The sounds of his boots retreating down the hall and falling on the steps didn't really register in her mind as she stood frozen in place, inspecting the room that had never seemed so full of character until Lang had arrived. Just as it had never seemed quite so empty until now, when he was gone. Somewhere in the back of her mind, she heard voices speaking downstairs, and the front door shut afterward. But it wasn't until five minutes later, when the hoofbeats sounded outside and then slowly disappeared, that the fog cleared and Lang's leaving truly sank in. When she looked out the window to the darkening horizon and could no longer see him at all, that's when her heart hit bottom.

That's when she knew that her only future was as Mrs. Barton Sealy.

Chapter Twelve

"Now I know how a prisoner feels when he faces the firing squad," Emma muttered, inspecting herself in the full-length mirror in Rose Ellen's room.

"Emma!" her sister exclaimed, causing Emma to spin in surprise. She hadn't heard Rose Ellen come up the stairs. Regal even in her nightgown and wrapper, she looked at Emma in silent disapproval. "What a peculiar way to talk on your wedding day!" Her gaze swept her dress unhappily. "And what a terrible rag to wear!"

On *any* day, her sister's tone seemed to indicate.

Emma glanced down sheepishly at the gray dress she had picked to celebrate the occasion of her marriage to Barton. It was appropriately somber for her mood. Apparently the garment didn't meet Rose Ellen's standards for wedding-day apparel, but she herself couldn't work up the necessary enthusiasm to worry about what she wore. There was too much else on her mind.

Lang, oh, my love, where are you?

She shrugged to suppress the unhappiness that thoughts of Lang now brought her. Try as she might, she couldn't force herself to be unselfishly happy that he'd been able to escape. "This dress will just have to do," she told Rose Ellen.

Rose Ellen's eyes widened. "Oh, no! We can do much better."

Emma prepared herself to endure her sister pawing through her closet full of browns and blacks, but Rose Ellen didn't head for the door at all. Instead, she turned to the carved walnut wardrobe behind them and threw wide the double doors, revealing a colorful array of her own dresses. "There *must* be something here you can wear!"

Emma was shocked. Her sister had *never* offered to share clothes before; in Rose Ellen's mind, having Emma traipsing around in her frocks would have been akin to casting her pearls before swine.

Wearing them now, under the pretense of her sham wedding, didn't seem fitting for such a remarkable gesture. "Oh, no...I couldn't, Rose Ellen."

"Why not? It's your wedding day, Emma. A woman wants to look her best...and believe me, gray is not your best."

"But all your dresses are so bright, and it's so soon after Daddy passed away." Not to mention, her wedding was also a reason for mourning.

Her sister's black brows rose. "Daddy would not want you looking like a dowd, Emma."

She made one last attempt to head her sister off at the pass. "None of your dresses would fit me."

"I'm bigger since Annalise." Her sister's gaze sized her up mercilessly. "And I'll wager you've got a perfectly cute figure beneath all those frumpy things you always wear. And once we get a corset on you..."

Emma groaned and watched in helpless dread as her sister tossed out a cream silk dress with a tiny daisy print. The pressed material shone like satin. The sleeves puffed frivolously, and the neckline dipped low enough that the whole of Midday, indeed the whole world, would have its first peek at her bosoms. Emma shook her head adamantly. "That's much too…"

"Appealing?" Rose Ellen laughed. "Don't worry so much. You're allowed to be pretty one day out of your life!"

Without further ado, her sister whirled her around and at a furious speed began unbuttoning the gown Emma had on.

"Ouch! There's no hurry." Emma's words were muffled as her sister yanked the dress up over her head in one quick motion.

Rose Ellen tossed the offending gray garment to the floor. "No hurry? Heavens, Emma, you've been dawdling up here so long, you'll be late for your own wedding! Lorna's been ready since sunrise. Even Annalise is more anxious to get going than you are."

"Where's William?"

"He went to town early to make sure everything was ready. You and Lorna are to go straight to Reverend Cathcart's. The ceremony was supposed to start at noon, but I doubt you'll make it now."

Hearing the day's itinerary made her queasy. People were waiting for her. The wedding would come off, with at least a dozen witnesses to her vows. There was truly no way out. Except for feeling sick to her stomach, she was completely numb with dread.

Rose Ellen slipped a corset on and laced the breath out of her. Then she threw the daisy dress over Emma's head and set about doing up the scores of tiny pearl buttons in back. As a final gesture Rose Ellen slammed her best white straw hat decorated with clusters of pale blue grapes atop Emma's head, and locked it mercilessly in place with one of her sword-length hat pins. Then she stepped back and smiled like a master painter finishing a canvas. She clapped her hands with delight at the results.

"Emma, you're beautiful!"

When Emma didn't move, her sister spun her around to face the mirror. The image gaping back amazed her. The odd woman did almost look like a bride. The hat, of course, was perfectly silly—the oddest concoction that had ever sat on her head. But the dress wasn't as terrible as she'd anticipated. The drop neck wasn't quite as immodest as she had feared, nor were the puff sleeves as ridiculous as they had first appeared. The most worrisome aspect of the dress was the tightly cinched waist, which remained fitted around her hips, from which the full skirt flared out. She'd never seen her figure outlined so tightly, so revealingly. The fact that it would be Barton, not Lang, seeing her in this dress shot another wave of dread straight to her heart.

"You're as pale as an egg!" Rose Ellen noted, *tsk*ing unhappily. She scanned the top of her bureau for something to remedy the problem of Emma's complexion, but Emma put a stop to that.

"You've done enough, Rose Ellen. I'm just nervous." She walked over to give her sister a peck on the cheek and before she knew it, found herself embraced in a weepy, heartfelt hug. Given how tightly Rose Ellen had laced her stays, the added pressure nearly squeezed the life out of her.

"Oh, Emma!" Rose Ellen cried tearfully. "I could never do enough. I've been so selfish. If I could ever do anything to make it up to you, I'd be so grateful!"

"Nonsense, Rose Ellen," Emma said, attempting to pry herself away. Though she *did* wish there was something someone could do to save her from this marriage, she doubted Rose Ellen would be the one to save her. "What have you done that's so selfish?"

"I've wanted you to stay single so you'd go back to Galveston with me." Rose Ellen turned her tear-streaked face up to her. "Of course, you'll always be welcome at my house...though I know you'll be too busy now with all that corn and those sick people to give much thought to me."

Emma shook her head. Amazing. She would have thought the ability to find brightness anywhere would have left her when she heard Lang ride away, but Rose Ellen's exquisite pouting still had the power to provoke her—this time to smiles. "I promise I'll visit." There would probably be many times when she would want to get away from her soon-to-be husband.

For a brief moment she considered telling Rose Ellen everything—that she wasn't in love with Barton Sealy at all, that she was in love with Mr. Archibald who was really Lang Tupper, outlaw. She was tempted to explain about the blackmailing sheriff. But what could Rose Ellen do?

You've made your bed, now you'll just have to lie in it.

Emma flinched at the thought. Right this minute, she didn't want to contemplate beds...or who would be sharing hers from here on out.

She kissed her sister again and then, before she burst into tears herself, quickly rushed downstairs. Lorna was waiting for her at the front door, and practically tugged her the rest of the way to the wagon.

"Emma, you look so pretty! I'm sure Barton will be bowled over when he sees you!"

Emma frowned and clambered onto the driver seat. The sheriff couldn't care less what she looked like—he'd made that clear enough.

While Emma might have been dressed more for the part,

Lorna looked hands down more like a bride. Her best simple dress had been let out another inch around the waist
and adorned with a silk sash, to which fragrant, early-
blooming pink hyacinths from Emma's garden were
pinned. Hyacinths also adorned her bonnet. Her cheeks
were flushed with happiness and anticipation, and her smile
even brought an answering one out of Emma.

Annalise sat in the back dressed in her blue taffeta Sunday best. Her eyes flew open when she saw her aunt.
"That's Mama's dress!" she warned, as if Emma might
not have noticed.

"I have permission," Emma assured her.

"And Mama's *hat!*" The girl sized her up doubtfully,
as if she couldn't wrap her mind around the idea of Rose
Ellen parting with one of her best gowns. Emma could
hardly believe it herself. Then the girl climbed up between
jittery Lorna and Emma. "I wish Davy could be in the
wedding, too!"

Emma twitched the reins to get the horses started. At
the first jolt of the wagon, she felt sick with dread.

She tried to concentrate on her niece. It was a good sign
that Annalise was asserting herself and making a friend.
"Maybe Davy will be well in time to make it to your
wedding, Annalise."

Annalise balked at that idea. "But I won't get married
for another twenty-two years!"

Emma smiled at her, puzzled. "Why twenty-two?"

"Because then I'll be twenty-eight. Mama always says
I'm like you and that no man will want a serious girl."
She lifted her thin shoulders at the complexity of it all.
"But you're getting married now, so I guess once you're
twenty-eight it doesn't matter."

Emma shook her head, not knowing quite where to start
to straighten out Annalise's thinking. A quick glance re-

vealed that Lorna's shoulders were quaking with silent laughter. Then, without preamble, a burst of mirth burst forth from her own lips, shocking Emma. She hadn't thought she would ever laugh again. But now, when Lorna looked at her, pointed and howled, Emma laughed until she doubled over, even as the horses jogged along, speeding the wagon to her doom. She was half-hysterical from little sleep, worry and sorrow about Lang, and the idea of marrying a man she absolutely despised, but the one bright spot on the horizon was having someone to laugh with.

Two someones. Annalise started giggling, too, and looking at Emma, said, "Aunt Emma, you're crying!"

Emma shook her head, and hugged her niece to her with one arm. "Haven't you ever laughed till you cried?"

Annalise, sober again, shook her head. "I suppose you're very relieved not to be an old maid anymore. Mama said that being an old maid's worse than anything I could imagine. So I guess it must be worse even than being eaten by coyotes." She frowned. "Is it, Aunt Emma?"

Try as she might, Emma could not avoid glancing over at Lorna, and the degeneration into helpless mirth began all over again.

Thus occupied, none of them noticed as the wagon approached the dip and curve in the road that would take them around a glade of trees and set them on the final stretch to Midday. Nor did they notice the masked figure lurking in the stand of trees—until it was too late.

The large dark man jumped out in front of them, startling the horses, which reared and wheeled, nearly overturning the wagon. As the wagon lurched to a stop, the bandit raised a revolver and Lorna screamed. Emma drew in a sharp breath at the same moment that her arms practically pinned Annalise protectively behind her.

A bandit? There hadn't been a bandit in Midday in years!

Nevertheless, the three women huddled close until the man, in a gravelly voice, ordered them to lie on the wagon floor.

At the sound of the voice, disguised as it was, Emma's heart hammered wildly, and Lorna's eyes widened in shock and recognition. "Mr. Archibald!"

It was him! Lang! Emma had to bite her lip to keep from bursting into a joyous smile. He'd come back for her! At least, she assumed that's what this robbery was all about. He'd come back to prevent her from getting married. But now he might not get away.

The fool. The wonderful, handsome fool.

"Do as he says," she told her companions, and proceeded to lie on the floor. To her shock, Lang put a bandanna around her mouth, gagging her. Afterward, he quickly tied Lorna's hands loosely to the wagon, then freed one of the wagon horses from its traces.

"You come with me." He grabbed Emma's arm roughly and yanked her up to standing. Emma grunted in dismay at being manhandled this way. Didn't he know she'd go with him gladly, readily, rather than marry the sheriff?

She'd never thought that she would scowl at Lang, but scowl she did as he boosted her up on his gray mare and took the bay from the wagon for himself. At least she got a saddle! She waited for him to return to unbind her gag. There was so much she had to say to him.

But he didn't unbind her. Instead, Lang took a length of rope, tied one end around her saddle horn and the other around his wrist, then kicked his horse into a fast trot. Emma barely had time to cast a last glance back at her niece and Lorna still huddled in the bed of the wagon, blinking in shock and confusion, before she was whisked away at a gallop, the wind whipping mercilessly at her daisy wedding dress. If it hadn't been for the gag, she might have yelled like thunder at Lang for pointing guns and scaring them half to death and then hauling her off like a sack of seed corn.

Then again, she might have just whooped for joy.

"My sister has been kidnapped!"

Barton frowned as the townspeople crowded into Reverend Cathcart's house for the wedding gasped in horror at Rose Ellen's words. Or maybe some of them were simply gasping at Rose Ellen herself. He'd never seen the woman look such a sight! Her hair was unwashed and tied back in a frowsy knot, her dress was something she never would have worn to town normally, and her skin still had fading red spots on it. Not only that, she was holding the hand of her own child—whom most of the town hadn't seen—and Davy Winters, a sharecropper's boy. This was, simply, a Rose Ellen Midday had never seen—but then, she'd come to town bearing bizarre news.

"Emma was kidnapped by a man named Johann Archibald," she said heatedly, "who just until yesterday was her boarder! My daughter recognized him."

Lorna wept silently next to William. "I think he did it out of spite, because he was in love with her."

Another gasp went around, and Barton could almost read the shock in everyone's eyes. *Two men in love with Emma Colby?*

Lorna related in her quiet, halting voice the story of the kidnapping, tears gathering in her eyes when she came to the part about Emma looking back one last time as she galloped away.

"It's my fault," she confessed miserably. "When Mr. Archibald first arrived, I told Emma he could be the outlaw that everyone was talking about. But then he started being so nice and helpful. We just assumed he was who he said he was!'' She blinked. ''Emma was so kindhearted! She'd never think bad of anybody!''

Everyone assembled responded with nodding heads and murmurs of agreement.

''Emma was always so helpful,'' said Mrs. Nathan Pitts, one of the church ladies.

''Emma told me I should take whiskey for my lumbago, and darn it all if it hasn't worked!'' Joe Spears said in testimonial.

Rose Ellen scowled at their premature eulogies. ''Well! There's no sense talking about Emma as if she were dead. We simply need to go after her.'' Her blue eyes lit on Barton, who had been hanging back a little, trying to think it all through. ''Assuming this man is the outlaw Lang Tupper, aren't you going to organize a posse, Sheriff?''

Barton shifted his feet. This sure as hell put him in a spot. He shouldn't have left Emma alone, should have insisted she marry him yesterday, but he'd figured there was nothing she could do to foil his plan. That was women for you! They could always figure out a way to spoil everything. And very clever of her to arrange it so that it appeared she'd been kidnapped, instead of in cahoots with a desperado!

The little Winters boy with Rose Ellen pointed excitedly at Barton and said in a piercing voice, ''Of course you've gotta have a posse! You're the sheriff. That's what lawmen do, ain't it?''

Barton tried not to glare at the noisy little brat. God, he hated kids!

One thing was certain—he couldn't let people find out that he'd known Emma had been hiding an outlaw. That would be the end of him. Just by looking into the faces in front of him he could tell that it already struck some folks as peculiar that he'd courted Emma and hadn't recognized something untoward about that boarder of hers. But if he organized a posse and went chasing after Emma and her outlaw, and actually had the bad luck to find them, what then? Once they got back to town, those two would spill the whole story of the deal he'd made with Emma, and that would be the end of him anyway.

"Well, Bart?" Joe Spears asked. The whole room was growing impatient for his decision.

Barton felt frozen. It would be better for him if the two of them got away. Maybe the posse wouldn't find them...but how could he be sure? He could misdirect the group, but what if they figured out what he was doing? That would be bad. He could hope that another arm of the law in a far-flung county would find Lang Tupper and Emma, but those two could blurt the whole story of what Barton had done in that case, too, and sure as shootin', word of his disgrace would get back to Midday.

His fat was in the fire now. Fine thing for a man to think he's on the brink of the good life, only to have his hopes ripped out from under him! The disappointment was crushing.

Disappointment...

Just that quickly, an idea occurred to him.

He shuffled forward slowly, head bowed, then stopped next to Rose Ellen and took a long, halting breath. Then, dramatically, he collapsed his head in his hands and let out a wail. "My God, I feel responsible...why didn't I see? Why didn't I *do* something?"

For a moment, as nothing but stony silence met his outburst, Barton feared his charade wouldn't come off. Finally, however, old Constance O'Hurlihy fluttered forward, taking the bait. She patted him comfortingly on his shuddering shoulders. "There, there, Sheriff... You mustn't blame yourself."

"Who else?" he sobbed into his hands.

"Blame the outlaw, damn it, if that's who took your fiancée," Joe Spears suggested.

Mutters of agreement spread through the room.

"The man had me hornswoggled, too." He heard his brother move forward. "C'mon, Bart, let's go after the varmint. He can't have that much of a head start."

He looked up, hoping his eyes seemed suitably red. He'd rubbed them hard enough. "Will, it's your wedding day."

William looked at him, aghast. "But Bart, it's partly my fault for not seeing through Mr. Archibald. I can't get married now."

"But you have to," Barton insisted. He couldn't believe that fool Emma had put him in the position of actually advocating this marriage between his brother and some little immoral nobody from Little Sandy. Or maybe he could. He began to hate Emma more with each passing minute. "Think of your young bride, on the brink of..."

He meant to say her happiness, but as he nodded toward the McCrae woman, who was about to pop the sash on that wedding dress of hers, he didn't have to finish the sentence. The woman looked like a cow fixing to drop a calf, and given her imminent impending motherhood, no one raised a peep to suggest that William should put off his wedding another day.

Wincing at what a fool his brother was, Barton shook his head again, then lifted his chin and explained, "No, this is my tragedy. I alone must go after Emma and that outlaw who's stolen her from me."

"But you can't go alone!" Rose Ellen cried.

He sent her a stony glare, hoping to intimidate her into

complicity. "I have to," he said. "Don't worry, Rose Ellen. I promise I'll bring your sister back safe and sound."

"But wouldn't it be better—"

"This is my responsibility!"

Barton rushed out of the small house and away from the
crowd, and went directly to his horse. He needed to get
out of town quickly, away from overeager townsfolk and
especially Rose Ellen, who'd been looking at him with
something akin to suspicion.

Lord save him from troublesome Colby women!

A good long time passed before Lang thought it might
be safe to stop. And by the time he took the gag off Emma,
the woman was spitting mad and wasted no time tearing
into him.

"This is outrageous! You're mean and low-down and
every horrible filthy thing I could think of to say about
you! You're a snake and a rat! How dare you point a gun
at my little niece and Lorna on her wedding day and—"

Lang had a feeling she'd go on this way forever if he
didn't stop her, so he shoved a canteen of water in front
of her nose. "Here, wet your whistle so you can keep
howling at me some more."

Green eyes glared at him and then she grabbed the canteen and tossed down what had to be half the container,
letting streams of water dribble down the sides of her
mouth and splash down to the skin left exposed by her
low-cut dress. As she drank her fill, Lang felt his own
mouth go bone-dry.

Not that her dress was shockingly revealing or anything
near it by most standards, but for Emma it was. And much
as he hated to admit it, it galled him to think the display
had been meant for Barton Sealy. Even her silly hat, with
the damn grapes on it, which was now flopped over on one

side of her head, made him green with jealousy. He knew he shouldn't feel that way. He thought he'd had this all figured out. Only, he'd expected Emma to attend her wedding to Barton in something black and miserable—not looking daisy fresh.

He gritted his teeth as she tossed his canteen back to him and started yelling some more. "You've got nerve to beat the band, Lang Tupper! How dare you run off with me like a barbarian! Don't you know that the law will be after me? After *both* of us? I was about to marry the sheriff, for heaven's sake! You think he's going to let some outlaw just ride in and steal me away?"

Letting out an exasperated breath, Lang reached up, grabbed Emma around her tiny waist and yanked her off her horse. It felt as though he'd grabbed hold of a bird cage. "What do you have underneath that dress, iron plating?"

She grimaced. "Never mind my underwear!" Her cheeks were flushed bright red, and she slapped at her head to take off her ridiculous hat. She looked at the thing with disgust and then threw it to the ground in frustration. "Christopher Columbus, Lang! You could have gotten away—you should be halfway to California by now!"

He shook his head. "Did you honestly think I could leave you like that, Emma?"

She slammed her hands on her hips. "And do you think Barton Sealy is just going to let Lang Tupper make a fool of him?"

"How would the sheriff know I'm Lang Tupper, Emma?"

She opened her mouth to answer, then snapped it shut again, realizing she'd been caught. Finally she blurted out, "He just does. I know he does."

"Who told him?"

She shook her head. "Nobody." Her rigid straight posture collapsed in that moment. "Annalise drew your picture at the picnic."

Lang barked out a laugh. "I knew that girl had talent."

"Oh, Lang." Emma looked up at him with the most heartbreaking expression he'd ever seen. "I wanted you to get away!"

He stepped forward, wishing he could throw his arms around her and kiss her senseless. Unfortunately, there were some things they needed to get out in the open first. "Is that why you made a bargain with the sheriff?"

Her lips parted as if she might try to deny it, but then she shook her head again. "Yes. Oh, why couldn't you let well enough alone!"

"You call marrying the sheriff 'well enough'?"

Her chin jutted stubbornly. "You would have been safe."

"Did you think once I figured out your plan I'd let you sacrifice yourself for me? Is that what you think of me?"

She stamped her foot in the dirt. "You weren't supposed to figure it out!"

"But I did almost as soon as I left. Nothing you said to me yesterday made sense, given what had happened before with Barton Sealy. I knew there was something wrong."

She scowled up at him. "And now there's a lot more wrong! We'll both have heck to pay now."

Lang chuckled. "Such language! That's what comes of consorting with outlaws, Miss Colby."

She gaped at him, astounded. "How can you make jokes at a time like this? Don't you know it's only a matter of time before we'll be hauled back to Midday?"

"Nope." He leaned back on his heels. "In fact, I think we're well out of it now."

"Well out of what?" She looked around almost as if

expecting Barton Sealy to jump out from under a sage bush or prickly pear.

A creek was nearby, and Lang strolled toward it. "He's not coming after us, Emma. From here on out we have to worry more about other sheriffs than your thwarted fiancé."

Emma stumbled after him. "But that's crazy! Of *course* he'll be coming."

"You sound almost as if you want him to."

"I don't, but I know him, Lang."

He bent to fill the canteen from the clear stream, then took a long draw himself. Damn, but it had been an exhausting day. It might be early spring, but with the sun beating down, after three hours of hard riding it seemed like August. And Emma had to feel even worse than he did. A wave of guilt hit him—not his first of the day. It had almost killed him to take her hostage like that, but he'd been compelled to so that the others wouldn't think she was in league with an outlaw. She'd done so much for him—had almost given her life for him, actually—the least he could do for her was protect her reputation.

"He knows he's licked, Emma," he explained. "If Barton finds you and hauls you back, you could run around Midday telling everybody that the sheriff knew there was an outlaw in your house and did nothing about it. You could tell everyone that the sheriff blackmailed you into marrying him. You think the sheriff wants that?"

"He could also put me in jail for helping you."

"You'd still have a trial. You could tell the whole story then. Even better—you'd have a captive audience."

She worked her jaw back and forth in amazement. "I never thought of that."

"I think it's in the sheriff's best interest to let 'Mr. Archibald' get away."

"But what about…" Emma blinked. "Well, now that I think about it, I wonder who would come after me?"

"There might be someone—maybe William, I was thinking—but let's just keep riding and hope they don't find us. At least we can be fairly well assured that there's not an angry Barton Sealy tailing us. If anything, he'll be trying to make sure we're *not* followed."

"Hmm, the sheriff working on our side." Emma smiled. "That's comforting."

Lang grinned back and handed her the canteen again, watching in wonder as Emma took another long drink. She never failed to amaze him. His own brother had betrayed him, yet this woman he'd known for such a short time had risked so much to save him. He could never repay her, but if they ever got out of this mess, he intended to spend a lifetime trying.

"Pretty dress," he said, feeling a surge of pure desire hit him. Every curve on her body was outlined by the thing, especially after a day of sweating in the saddle. He was glad Barton wouldn't see her.

"It's Rose Ellen's." His raised eyebrow response brought a laugh from her. "My sister and I have a peace treaty, I think. Though I don't know how *she'll* react to my kidnapping."

"Dare we hope she'll go back to Galveston?"

Emma giggled, then covered her mouth. "I shouldn't laugh. Poor Rose Ellen. She's had a more unhappy life than I imagined."

It was hard for Lang to get himself worked up on Rose Ellen's behalf right at the moment. He was plenty worked up as it was just over her sister. Against the harsh, un-cleared landscape, she looked like a fish out of water, vul-nerable and worn. It didn't help that she was wearing the finest dress he'd ever seen her in, and that just a half day of riding had brought out an ugly blister on her hand—hands that weren't immune to work. But work was one thing, living as a fugitive was quite another.

Another wave of guilt crashed over him. He'd never known Emma outside the comfort of the house she'd lived in all her life. She'd never known hardship. And now he'd taken her away from all that, and what could he offer her in return? All he had to his name were the clothes on his back and two stolen horses...one of them hers.

She reached out and touched his hand, her eyes soft. "Is something wrong?"

Wrong? Everything was wrong! Last night he'd lain awake thinking that kidnapping Emma would solve all their problems, and maybe it had in the short run. But what if Emma tired of life on the run, or they never made it to California, or she simply tired of *him?* The responsibility for what he'd done warred with his desire to pull Emma into his arms and simply bury all his worries in her soft flesh and warm lips.

She stepped closer to him, so that he could smell the faint vestige of a tart perfume in the air. The scent was almost his undoing, but he managed to walk the razor's edge between control and insanity. Making love to Emma right here in the open when heaven only knew how many people were hunting them would have been crazy.

"I'm not mad anymore, if that's what you're worried about," Emma said. "I can see now you did the only sensible thing."

Her voice was an understanding caress that pricked the hair on the back of his neck. He clenched his hands into fists and felt his lips form into a taut line. "Even for tying up your niece?"

She smiled. "Annalise will be thrilled. She's lived

through an adventure that will have Davy pea-green with jealousy.''

''And Lorna?''

''William will comfort her, though I suppose this did put a kink in her wedding day.'' Her pink lips tilted up in a smile, bringing him just a little closer to the brink of something foolish.

He muttered, spun on his boot heel and crouched by the creek again. The canteen didn't need filling so much as he needed something to do to get his thoughts back in order. He cupped his hands and splashed the cool water against his face and neck.

''Get yourself ready for another long ride,'' he instructed Emma. ''We won't stop again till after dark.''

He glanced up at her only briefly, but in her face he caught every nuance of confusion he'd dreaded seeing. One minute he'd been talking with her, the next he was barking orders. But she had nothing on the jumble of conflicting emotions inside his own heart.

Chapter Thirteen

By the time they stopped and Emma was finally able to get down from her horse, her legs felt like cast-iron noodles. She'd never known a body could feel so stiff and weak at the same time, so heavy and yet so wobbly. If it weren't for her sister's corset—a contraption surely invented by someone who despised womankind—she was afraid she might have simply stepped off her horse and collapsed to the ground in a heap.

As it was, the inky night covered her inability to straighten up entirely, thank heavens. She didn't want Lang to think she was a weakling, which she was beginning to suspect she was. She'd always assumed the outlaw life would be something of a lark. Why else would so many be drawn to it?

Maybe because they're fools, she thought with a groan as she inched stiff-backed toward the campfire Lang was quickly and methodically setting up. Somehow he knew all about these things—fires, and navigating the open land by the stars, and what water was safe to drink. Life and its hardships had taught him how to survive, while she had lived twenty-eight years, and one measly day of roughing it was nearly her undoing. She sank to the ground, mindful of her sore behind, which felt as if it had been thrashing against a boulder all day, not a saddle. Even her hands ached from clutching the reins so tensely. And her head! She gritted her teeth, making sure not to hit the dirt too quickly and unduly rattle her headache. When she was safely settled both to her head and her behind's satisfaction, she carefully removed her hat.

As she watched Lang's progress on the fire, her brow furrowed. "Won't that draw attention to us?"

Lang didn't deny it. "It seemed to me that you could use a little warmth, but I'll make it small, so that it will burn out soon after you go to sleep."

Sleep! She'd never imagined that she'd so fervently look forward to sleeping. She felt all that she would have to do would be to close her eyes and she might never wake up. She dearly wanted slumber, yet...

Her gaze caught Lang's and her every nerve ending became a little more awake. There would be no privacy here in this tiny camp. Would Lang sleep next to her...or *with* her? She flushed at the thought, and yet she couldn't deny that she'd been dreaming about such a possibility all day long, and not with dread. She supposed running away with Lang—no matter how much he tried to disguise her going with him as a "kidnapping"—made her something akin to an outlaw's moll. Would Lang now expect her to behave like a moll?

So far he hadn't made many demands. She'd expected him to try to steal a kiss by the creek the first time they'd stopped. He'd been watching her with such hunger she wouldn't have been surprised if he'd taken her in his arms and kissed her straight into tomorrow. But maybe that's why he hadn't. They hadn't had time. But now... As she gazed into his eyes, a molten warmth pooled at her very core and radiated desire throughout her body. Hours of darkness stretched ahead of them, and surely Lang would want to take advantage of that fact.

She felt only half-ashamed at the way her blood boiled through her veins in anticipation. It would have been different if she didn't love Lang. But she did. She'd loved him enough to be willing to marry Barton Sealy, but now that he'd saved her from that, her love knew no boundaries, no reason. And in saving her from a marriage that would have been a fate worse than death, hadn't he proved he loved her, too? Surely loving a man made their relationship less sinful. After all, Lang probably would have married her himself if he'd been able to. Maybe that made her less an outlaw's moll than an outlaw's bride.

The question thrumming through her was, would tonight be her wedding night?

"Here," Lang said, handing her his canteen. "You look like you need a drink."

"I do?" Actually, water had been the last thing on her mind.

"Well…you were licking your lips."

Luckily it was dark, or Lang might have seen the fiery blush in her cheeks. Worse, he might have looked into her green eyes and detected exactly how much she wanted him. She might tell herself she was a bride, but the feelings coursing through her were definitely more on the moll side.

She glugged down a hefty draft of water.

Lang grinned and struck a match, illuminating his handsome face as he coaxed his carefully constructed fire to blazing life. Funny to think that a few short weeks ago she'd found his face so rough and wild. Now she saw strength, kindness and a sensuality that set her ablaze with a mere glance. She'd never expected to fall in love with a man like Lang, who was so comfortable with himself, so at one with the earth around him. Then again, she'd never expected she would be running off to parts unknown with *any* man. For so long, her life had centered around her little world—her father, the house and Midday. She was sad to leave those things behind, but at the same time, she felt wild and adventurous, as if for the first time she was really living.

She smiled. "I guess California needs nurses just as much as Texas does." She'd come to terms with her destination mere hours into their ride that morning, about the time she started getting sore. In fact, her only regret now was that California wasn't a little closer. "Don't you think so?" She stretched her arms and allowed herself a moment of fanciful dreaming. "I hear the country there is like Eden."

Lang blinked in surprise. "Where?"

"California. They say parts of it are just like paradise, lush and bountiful. Anything will grow there—grains, vegetables, fruits...." Her voice trailed off as Lang continued to stare at her as if she were speaking Greek to him. It was as if he'd never heard of a farm before. "Haven't you heard that about California?"

"Well...yes." But his voice held not a trace of enthusiasm for the subject.

Her lips tightened, then twisted in confusion. Perhaps he hadn't guessed that she would be so eager to go with him. Maybe he thought she didn't even want to go. "Don't worry about me, Lang. It will be better this way. Rose Ellen's always been bitter about Daddy leaving me the house and all that land. I might have made a go of it, but the future was uncertain at best." She chuckled. "Of course, it's still uncertain, but with you by my side, I have more confidence."

He frowned. "You'd give up your house to Rose Ellen, just like that?"

"Well, of course! What else can I do now?"

"What about your hospital?"

"I'll still pursue that goal, depending on where we end up. If, for instance, we're near San Francisco, then the people there will probably already have a hos—"

"San Francisco!" Lang's exclamation cut off her words. "Emma, what are you talking about?"

Her face felt frozen, in spite of the warmth from the fire. Could she have heard him wrong? "Two days ago you spoke of running away to California, so I just assumed that's where we were going."

His eyes shuttered.

"Isn't that what you had planned, Lang?"

"Sure...a few days ago."

A tremor of foreboding overtook her. "Well then, where *are* we headed?"

"*You're* headed to San Antonio."

She jumped to her feet with an energy she never would have guessed she had left in her. But even as her movements quickened, dread pounded in her heart. "And where are you going?"

"After my brother."

Emma felt sick. Lang was planning on going after Amos—the man who'd betrayed him and left him for dead—and all along had planned on leaving her behind in San Antonio. "But you can't do that!"

"I need to clear my name. It's what you suggested from the first."

Of course. Clearing his name sounded good in theory when she was sitting in her comfortable house in Midday, and appealed to her sense of high-mindedness; but now she could see the risk involved. "To get your brother you'll have to walk into a nest of outlaws. You could be killed!"

A muscle in his clenched jaw twitched. "That's a risk I'll have to take."

"Death?" she practically squeaked.

"If I don't risk it, I won't have a life worth speaking of."

She was momentarily dumbfounded. Here she was thinking that she was embarking on a grand adventure, and Lang was speaking as if he were at the end of his rope! "But I thought that's why you kidnapped me—so we'd be together when you ran off to California. I thought we were going to start anew...."

"I just didn't want you to marry the sheriff."

Slapping her might have produced a less chilling reaction. She almost wept. Lang didn't want her to marry the sheriff...but he mentioned nothing about wanting to marry her himself. Or being in love with her. She wasn't an outlaw bride, she realized. She wasn't even a moll. She again was just Emma Colby, spinster, secretly in love with a man who apparently didn't give a flip about her. If he did, why would he walk right into a lion's den?

"If I left the state with my brother still at large, I'd never be free, Emma. All my life I'd be looking over my shoulder, wondering if the law was ever going to catch up with me. That's no way to live."

"But in California—"

"California is a state, too. They could catch me there."

"What are the odds?"

"It doesn't matter. I'd always be worrying about it."

She practically quivered in frustration of his putting himself in such danger. She'd seen what a few angry men had done to his body once before. How many more bullets could Lang withstand? If anything happened to him now, what would she do?

At that terrible thought, she rushed forward and took his

hand. "You wouldn't have to worry. Even in Midday, when supposedly the whole town was looking for an outlaw, no one suspected you."

He laughed. "Sure, except the sheriff."

"I should have been more careful! I *will* be more careful in California. No one there will know us, and they won't be looking for you anyway."

Lang shook his head, and she felt the argument slipping away from her. "It'll be better this way, you'll see."

She stamped her foot. "You can't leave me in San Antonio while you go risk your life."

"I can't take you with me."

"Why not?"

"Because it's dangerous."

"All the more reason why I should be with you."

Lang took a breath for patience. "What could you do? Can you shoot a gun?"

"Of course!" He pinned her with a skeptical gaze until she practically writhed at the lie she'd told. "Well, I know how one works."

"These fellows I'm going after won't hold their draw long enough for you to bone up on an instruction book, Emma."

"All right," she conceded, "maybe I'm not the best with a gun, but I can help you in other ways."

"How?"

She swallowed. "I can cook for you and make camp so you can rest more. You'll need your strength."

She thought she detected a softening in his gaze. "Sweetheart, after one day of riding, you're practically dead on your feet. How will you hold up after tomorrow? And what do you know about cooking on the trail, or building fires, or hiding a camp so people can't trail us?"

He was right; she was useless. But at least he was calling

her sweetheart. "Nothing. But I do know that two are usually better than one."

"Not in this case," he said, shaking his head. "I'll leave you in San Antonio and come back for you when I have Amos."

The thought of being in some strange room without knowing Lang's fate was bad enough, but he just kept piling on disturbing news. "*Have* him? You mean to take him *alive?*"

He looked at her with something akin to horror. "You didn't think I'd kill my own brother, did you?"

"But he almost killed you—or as good as tried to!"

From the way his body stiffened, she could see that she lanced a part of his consciousness that he'd just as soon forget. "I wouldn't murder my own flesh and blood, Emma. I just want Amos to own up to what he's done, and let me clear my name."

"Oh, I'm sure he'll be happy to," she retorted, unable to bite back a sarcastic tone. If Lang thought he could just waltz up to his brother, slap his hand and haul him off to the nearest sheriff, he had another think coming. And if he thought that she was just going to sit idly by while he attempted such madness, he was even more wrong still!

"I won't stay behind." He opened his mouth to interrupt her again, but she rushed on. "I don't care what you say. I'm going with you, Lang. I love you."

There. She'd said it again.

Maybe this time he'd hear her.

Lang stared at her stonily for a long minute that seemed to stretch even longer as an embarrassed flush crept up her to her cheeks. She raised her chin, as if she didn't give two hoots whether he reciprocated her feelings or not.

Finally he took another deep breath and gave her one of

those looks that indicated he was running out of patience. "You should get some sleep, Emma."

What little hope remained inside her sank like a rock. *I tell him I love him, and he responds by telling me to go to bed?* She clenched her hands into fists at her sides in determination. "I said I love you, Lang."

Before the words were even out, he retorted, "I heard you."

She glared at him. "And?"

He stared back at her with his eyes burning with emotion she couldn't quite read. "And I still say you need your rest."

Fury coursed through her. "Just once I'd like to have a man respond to me the way he's supposed to!"

The stony stare remained, though one of his lips twitched. "How's that?"

"I don't know—like men respond in books! When Juliet told Romeo she loved him, Romeo didn't tell her goodnight!"

"Yes, he did."

She blinked, astonished. "He did?"

"'Sleep dwell upon thine eyes, peace in thy breast/ Would I were sleep and peace, so sweet to rest.'"

Lang grinned as Emma stared at him with slack-jawed amazement. She hadn't expected an answer at all, much less a letter-perfect recitation. At least, she thought it was letter-perfect. To her chagrin, she couldn't exactly remember.

"I only went to school eight years," Lang explained, "but I tried to make the most of them."

Apparently so! Suddenly she felt all the fight had been sucked out of her, and she gazed at him dreamily. She still knew so little about Lang. Would she always be discovering different shadings of his personality?

He squeezed her hand, and lightning snapped between them. His voice fell. "I didn't arrange the kidnapping to take advantage of you, Emma."

"Oh, but—"

Before she could state that she *wanted* him to take advantage, he cut in. "You didn't come here of your own free will."

"But—"

"I realize all that you've sacrificed for me. I won't push you for more till you're ready."

I'm ready! a voice inside her shrieked. She was surprised he couldn't hear it, but evidently he couldn't. He turned and took the blanket they'd pulled off her horse and laid it across the ground. Then he arranged the canvas saddle-bag as a pillow at the head of the blanket. The action caused desire to quicken inside her...then she realized he just meant her to lie down. Alone. She stepped forward and was rewarded with a chaste kiss on her forehead.

"Good night, Em."

Em. The new nickname warmed her. Now they were getting someplace! They were just getting there very, very slowly—too slowly. "Please, Lang, rethink finding your brother. It won't do us any good. If we just went to California..."

"And what good would that do us? You think I want to spend the rest of my life wondering if you missed your home and your farm? And what about all your plans for the hospital? I can't ask you to give those up."

"I already have! Believe me, I'm a thousand times happier with you than I ever would have been running that hospital."

"I don't want to make you give anything up," Lang said. "You deserve better than a life on the run. And besides—"

His mouth clamped shut.

Emma sensed an opening. "What, besides?"

"Nothing." His eyes had that hooded look again.

Curiosity burned in her, especially when she detected two patches of red in his cheeks. "Tell me, Lang. We might as well be honest." Honesty was perhaps their only possession at the moment.

His shoulders rose in a gesture of surrender and he said, almost as if through gritted teeth, "Well, I was only going to say that the only way that we could be legally married is if I cleared my name." She gaped at him, temporarily too stunned to speak, so he rushed on. "What I mean to say is, if we went somewhere and used false names, that wouldn't make us truly and legally married, would it? And if we had children, I'd want them to have the right name."

Marriage? *Children?* These were the thoughts that had been going on behind that taciturn expression of his? Her heart soared, and she practically twirled in happiness.

She melted against his chest, encircling him in her arms. "Lang! As if I should care—as long as we're together I couldn't give a hoot about legalities."

He looked down at her, looping his hands about her waist. She couldn't tell whether he was trying to anchor her close or keep her at a safe distance. "I shouldn't want you so much," he practically growled. "I've stayed up nights, trying not to."

"I've been fighting my own battles," she said, grinning saucily. "And losing."

He groaned. "Em, you didn't come here of your own free will."

She sidled closer, seeking his warmth. "Yes, I did. You just couldn't tell it because you were too busy kidnapping me."

A muscle in his clenched jaw twitched. In fact, his whole

body seemed tense, like an overwound watch or a cat ready to spring. Incredibly, being in the circle of so much barely leashed masculine power thrilled her more than it frightened her. Too long she'd languished miserably in the fear that her desire was one-sided, and that all her affections were doomed to go unrequited. Now, as she leaned against him, bringing him to the very edge of his last nerve, she delighted in the fact that she, too, had power over him, power she'd never guessed she possessed.

His expression was anguished. "If I make love with you now…"

Just hearing the words caused her heart to race. Yes! Here was the real adventure. She felt as if she were standing on a precipice, ready to fling herself over the edge into the unknown. "I won't regret it," she assured him with a calm that surprised her. Every particle in her body thrummed with excitement, with blind desire, with simply wanting.

And then, as if to punctuate her words, she tilted her head, perched on her toes and brazenly pressed her mouth to his. The moment their lips touched, Lang pulled her close and drank deeply of her lips, until she was almost dizzy from the kiss. Even while her heart pumped wildly, she had to remind herself to breathe. Yet Lang's lips transported her to a place where mortal concerns like breathing seemed secondary to sensation and desire. A million different impulses warred within her—to keep her lips to his, to move against him, to explore every sinew of his body. All the while, his hands raced through her hair, down her back, around her waist, cupping her bottom and pulling her shockingly close to him. Every place he touched her seemed to leave a trail of fire, to make her legs feel weaker and to cause her desire to increase.

She clung to him desperately, feeling as if she were attempting to hold on to a tornado. The torrent of shocking new sensations flooding her amazed her, as did her sudden understanding of what she needed. Lang. His body against hers. Clothing, so long her armor of modesty, suddenly seemed a hindrance, a nuisance. As if he could sense her thoughts, she felt Lang's fingers working at the tiny buttons that Rose had so expertly done up for her that morning. At the same time, she began fumbling at the much simpler task of divesting Lang of his shirt.

His chest, with its heavy dusting of dark hair, was familiar to her. The bandages were gone, and in their place remained a thick red scar, healed, but an angry reminder of his brush with death. The sight caused her throat to constrict to a lump, and she ran her finger along the jagged line.

At her touch, Lang sucked in a short breath between his clenched teeth, then pushed her dress off her shoulders. Though she wore a shift and a corset, it was still the first time she had stood in her underclothes before any man, and suddenly her skin burned so with embarrassment that she feared her whole being would go up in flames, especially since Lang's gaze was steadily focused on her breasts, which were pushed high and half exposed by Rose Ellen's infernal corset.

Embarrassed as she was, however, she wanted to be free of it. She wanted Lang against her again, so she would feel active, not like a half-dressed statue frozen in front of his dark, glittering eyes.

Then he reached out and brushed the top of her breast with his thumb, nearly causing her legs to buckle beneath her. She'd never guessed one part of her anatomy could hold such a well of feeling, but that one touch nearly was her undoing. She reached out, gripped his arm and eased him down to the blanket. The material was woefully inadequate to provide a mattress for them both, so as soon as Lang was sprawled on the ground she followed her instincts and clambered on top of him so that she straddled his lap as he unlaced her. Each progressive loosening of her bindings made her realize anew how constricted she had been, and now that she could take a real breath again, she felt as if she had air to spare for kisses. She began at his ear and worked her way down his jaw, stopping at his lips again. She couldn't get enough of his mouth, his warmth, the taste of him. Every movement of his tongue seemed designed to cause a chain reaction of desire in her body, and almost rhythmically she began to move her hips against him.

Lang groaned and tore his lips from hers. He looked almost as if he were gasping for air. "Emma, wait."

She smiled, knowing she had no intention of waiting, or being patient, or following any orders he might give her. She was being driven by pure instinct now. She pressed his shoulders down to the ground and lay full against him, reveling in the tantalizing evidence of his masculinity pressing ever more insistently against her. She reached down, but the moment she touched the evidence of his desire, a sea change occurred on that blanket.

Lang's body shuddered, and with a gravelly sound that was half moan, half roar, he turned the tables on her. In a split second she found herself on her back, Lang perched over her, his face dark and intense, yet his eyes shockingly tender and vulnerable. *Wait,* they seemed to say. *Slow down.*

But inside her was a hurricane of heat and desire and a lifetime of suppressed feminine curiosity, and there could be no holding back that storm. "I trust you," she whispered, reaching down and unbuttoning his pants. As soon as she clasped her hand around the erect fullness of him, he closed his eyes.

"Em." He ground out the word before bending to give her the most passionate kiss she'd ever received. It was the kiss of a man on the breaking point, and she surrendered to it completely, as she did to the insistent movement of their bodies, a friction that made her feel as if they might combust like the sulfur tip of a match. As an amateur student of medicine, Emma was not ignorant of the birds and the bees. She had a fairly good conception of what went on between a man and a woman, and she was ready to experience it firsthand.

But again Lang surprised her. Instead of taking her immediately, just when she thought she was at the breaking point, he caressed her in places she'd never imagined a man touching—her hips, her thighs and finally the very core of her womanhood. He stroked her until she thought she might combust all by herself, until she was senselessly pleading for more. Just when she thought she could stand the exquisite torture not one second longer, when she might explode or simply dissolve into a puddle of liquid fire, Lang parted her legs, positioned himself over her and penetrated the most intimate part of her.

Emma gasped at the unexpected shock of pain. Her body arched against his, and he stilled above her, his eyes apologetic as he murmured tender reassurances against her ear. His low, husky voice stoked the fire burning within her, until she was unable to hold herself back any longer. She braved the consequences by moving her hips, and found that she increasingly felt more pleasure than pain, and soon they were moving in tandem, in a rhythm that felt both new and as old as time. Faster and faster the sensations seemed to spiral inside her, until she was spinning out of control, afire with feelings both frenzied and poetic. Tears built in her eyes, and when she finally found the oblivion of release, moments before Lang himself tensed above her and shuddered, she knew she'd been right. She would never regret this...no matter what happened.

Barton tossed and turned on the hard, cold ground, unable to get a wink of sleep. The pitiful fire he'd managed to build didn't give off enough warmth to make a fly feel cozy, and he already wished he'd brought better food. And more of it. In his nervousness and boredom, he'd already eaten half his provisions—the best half, too. Most of the jerky was gone.

The worst of it was, he still felt like nibbling. And there was something sticking in his side.

"Damnation!" Muttering to himself, he sat up and extracted a small stone embedded in the earth beneath his blanket. "And damn Emma Colby!" he added, pitching the curse into the darkness.

It was her fault he'd reached this sorry pass. If she hadn't gone and fallen under the spell of a no-good outlaw, he'd be snoozing on a comfy feather bed in her old family house this very minute. He'd have a real blaze to warm his toes, and a goose-down pillow to rest his head on instead of a pile of dirt. Also, he'd have a woman to use for his pleasure instead of just the stars and all sorts of spooky night noises for company. Odd rustlings and hoot owls sounded around him, along with coyote howls and the east wind's disturbing lullaby. He shivered.

He'd wanted to go to San Antonio and spend a few nights in a hotel, but on second thought he'd decided against it. Midday was close enough to San Antone that someone might recognize him, and then that would put him in a pickle. How would he explain why he wasn't hunting for the man who'd run away with his fiancée? Even if he did dream up some excuse, it just wouldn't look good. People might think he was yellow.

Lord, he hated Emma Colby. He'd never liked her and had only barely tolerated the thought of her becoming his wife; but now that she'd run off with another man, his pride was stinging as if she'd been his one and only sweetheart. He thirsted for revenge, but he knew he wouldn't get it. God willing, he would never have to lay eyes on her mousy face again.

He still couldn't believe she'd done it. Run off with an outlaw—when she could have been Mrs. Barton Sealy! It didn't make a lick of sense to him. He'd offered to marry that pathetic old spinster…and she'd had the unmitigated gall to prefer a desperado, an outcast of society, a man on the run. What kind of life did she think she was going to have? Heck, the man wasn't even a very successful outlaw when it came right down to it. He'd heard the Gonzales gang had only a few bank robberies to their credit.

He just prayed that she and her inept criminal lover would have the brains to make it far away without getting caught. If either one of them was dragged back to Midday, or even somewhere near Midday, it would be curtains for him. Emma would probably blurt out the whole story just for spite. She'd been angry when he'd pressured her into agreeing to marry him, he knew. But women were like that. They didn't understand the practicalities of life.

A noise startled him. It sounded like a horse's whinny, and he bolted straight up, alert, and grabbed for his rifle. But as he squinted out into the inky black of night, he saw nothing, and he sure as hell wasn't crawling out from under his blanket. The little patch of dirt beneath him was finally feeling a little warm.

He heaved a sigh. Emma had reduced him to this— sleeping out on the ground like an animal. How long would he have to stay out here in the middle of nowhere before it would be safe to go home and tell the town that he'd given up on her? That announcement would no doubt meet with all sorts of recriminations, especially from Rose Ellen. But what did she care, really? Now *she'd* own all the Colby land and be sitting on easy street. That stuck in his craw, too.

"Bart?"

Barton nearly jumped out of his skin. In one movement he was on his feet, rifle at the ready, whirling defensively in the dark. "Who's there?"

William stepped into the dim campfire light. "It's just us."

Barton deflated in relief as he made out William and Joe. "Good Lord—you about scared the life out of me!"

Joe came forward. "We were trailing Emma and that fellow.... We expected you to be farther along now, Bart."

Barton realized the position they'd found him in and writhed in discomfort over their vaguely disapproving stares. "I, uh, stopped for the night," he said, omitting the fact that he'd stopped hours before sundown. "I thought I'd do better getting an early start tomorrow—maybe catch them unawares."

William nodded, but Joe's craggy face was still screwed up in puzzlement, as if he hadn't been convinced. What business of the old geezer's was it, anyway!

"Why did you two come after me?" he asked, ready to give them his "it's my tragedy" argument again.

"Rose Ellen didn't like the fact that you left by yourself to hunt for two people."

Rose Ellen—he might have guessed! Barton bowed his head and attempted a distraught expression. "I just thought that since this was my problem, I needed to go alone."

"It's not your fault Emma was kidnapped," William assured him.

Joe shook his head. "And Miss Rose Ellen thinks it's *not* just your problem. It's her sister that's missing, remember."

"Oh, but—"

"We're staying with you, Barton," Joe Spears declared, and his tone brooked no nonsense.

Old cuss! Barton doubted the wheezing old busybody had it in him to chase outlaws anyway—which, now that he had company, he supposed he was actually going to be forced to do. How the hell was he going to get himself out of this mess?

Emma and that outlaw of hers had better be cagey, that's all he had to say. Hopefully they'd headed straight for California and covered their trail. He and William knew next to nothing about tracking people, so they might escape yet.

"I figured they're probably headed north," Barton said. "I was going to start that way before the crack of dawn."

Joe didn't blink. "I don't know how you figured north when the tracks lead southeast, son. They're going to San Antone—might already be there, I reckon."

Barton gripped his rifle to stay calm. So much for hoping the old man was too decrepit to track anyone! Didn't he have a store to manage? Why did he have to come nosing into other people's business?

"Oh, I guess I misread them...." he muttered.

"I'll say!"

A low-pitched but very definitely feminine laugh jolted him in surprise.

"What the Sam Hill?"

Barton looked up and saw Rose Ellen swagger into the firelight. She wore the same outfit she'd worn at Reverend Cathcart's house that afternoon, only now it was a little worse for wear. Amazingly, she didn't seem to care. Despite her laughter, she wasn't smiling.

Barton shot angry looks at William and Joe. "You two didn't tell me you'd brought a damn woman along." Were they nuts?

William shrugged. "She insisted."

Rose Ellen bridled. "And I'm not just a damn woman, I'm Emma's sister. It's my job to make sure that she's found and brought back safely. Sounds like it's lucky I convinced Joe to come along, too. Even *I* could see the tracks were headed for San Antonio, Sheriff."

Barton, trapped like a rabbit in a snare, felt his lips flatten into a thin, grim line. "Then I guess we're headed to San Antone," he agreed sharply, glaring at all three of them.

His list of people to send to the devil was growing fast.

Chapter Fourteen

"We're almost there now."

Emma's stomach lurched. Skipping San Antonio had sped their trip, but considering that their destination was a criminal's roost, their imminent arrival there was a mixed blessing at best.

"Are you all right?" Lang asked, his warm, loving eyes gazing at her in concern.

Instead of thinking about the unpleasant task ahead of them, she tried to concentrate on the wonderful sensations of last night. She shifted in her saddle, still shocked at the unexpected places her body ached. But even a day in the saddle couldn't blot out the memories of being in Lang's arms and feeling completely possessed by desire. Every time he'd whispered her name, she'd felt as if she'd finally found utter contentment, even if their bed was the hard ground in the chill of a spring night with nothing but the stars as a canopy.

Lang had awakened her with steaming coffee this morning, and even though she'd spent the night on the cold hard ground, she'd felt as pampered as a queen. It was impossible to believe that after finding so much happiness this might be their last day together, even their last hour. She couldn't think about it.

"I'm fine," she said, trying to put on a brave front.

There was going to be trouble. The only question was how much. As they rode through the rougher terrain of southwest Texas, she clutched her father's rifle as though it were a lifeline. It was a lucky thing he'd thought to take it after all. At first she'd wished he'd offered her the Colt holstered in his gun belt, but she thought differently now. She liked the weight of the rifle, which made sense. It was large and heavy as lead, and she took comfort in the idea that even if she couldn't shoot the blooming thing, she might at least do some damage swinging it at any foe she happened to come up against.

Oh, Lord! The thought of actually having to inflict physical harm on someone practically made her ill. She'd never been in a fight before, or even many squabbles. Just the possibility of having to land a blow caused her arms to quiver. What possible use would she be when she actually was faced with an attacker?

Maybe Lang had been right, and she should have just stayed behind. It had been so easy to be brave thirty miles ago, when she was sitting snug in the warmth of a campfire, and when the idea of facing Amos and his criminal cohorts had been more hypothetical than real. Back then all she'd thought of was losing Lang. But now she faced losing Lang and perhaps her own life. Or what if she was caught by the outlaws and not killed?

She shuddered. *No!* She shouldn't entertain such terrible thoughts. And she couldn't let Lang see her fright or he might actually force her to stay behind; no matter how terrified she was, it would be even worse if she were separated from Lang. Especially now, when she knew exactly how happy they could be together.

And though she could rationalize her brazen descent into scarlet womanhood by telling herself that she loved Lang, and that they would be married as soon as they were certain Lang wouldn't be hanged, she couldn't be absolutely sure everything would work out so neatly. What if their lovemaking resulted in a child? The thought thrilled her to her core, but frightened her, too. She wanted to have children with Lang…but she wanted Lang to be with her to be a father to the children.

The puffy clouds of bliss she'd been floating on this morning in Lang's arms shed more and more of their silver linings the closer they came to the outlaw hideout.

"Em?" Lang looked over and pinned her with his dark gaze. She could tell by his expression that he'd been watching her for some time, and had detected her worry. "It's not too late to turn back to San Antonio."

Her spine stiffened reflexively. "It's not too late to head for California, either," she replied.

He shook his head at her stubbornness. "I should have spent longer teaching you how to shoot."

"I'll be fine." She attempted to gaze down at her weapon with a confidence she certainly didn't feel.

An hour later her confidence dropped another notch when they came to the crest of a hill. Lang reined in his horse and dismounted, then gestured for Emma to do the same. "This is it."

Emma's heart thumped slowly in her chest as she gazed down the incline toward the shack below. Could such a modest little building really be the destination she'd so dreaded reaching? The house's wooden boards were weathered and faded to a dark gray; the one window visible had half a shutter hanging lopsided; the other had fallen to the ground. The front doorway gaped open like a missing tooth. Maybe the owner had discarded the door to let some air inside. Or maybe because the shack's inhabitants didn't want to be caught unawares. In front of the house stood an old rain barrel, a few scraggly trees that could provide no shade, and three untethered horses feeding idly on crabgrass.

Lang sent her a crooked grin. "Cozy, isn't it?"

He had lived in that dump. Emma tried to absorb that fact, but it was difficult, especially when she remembered that his roommates were killers.

"What do we do now?" she asked.

He eyed her sharply. "*You're* going to do nothing."

"But—"

"I'm going to try to get a little closer."

Emma looked down the hill. The bare hill. "How?" she asked, her voice barely a squeak. "They'll see you!"

"Eventually."

Sooner than that. Emma wished her pulse would stop pounding in her ears so she could think clearly.

He touched her arm. "You didn't think I was just going to knock on the front door and ask my brother to surrender himself to the authorities, did you?"

In truth, she hadn't been thinking about anything except that she wanted to be with him for whatever happened. "Let me go with you," she pleaded. "Maybe if you had a woman with you they'd be less apt to…" The words *kill you* staunchly refused to come out of her mouth.

But his head was shaking adamantly before she could finish, anyway. "You're staying right here."

"But what if something…happens?" She choked on the last word.

"Get on your horse and ride like hell in the direction we came from."

He still thought she would be useless to him, and now he was going to make sure she was just an observer. She opened her mouth to object, but the look of anguish in his eyes stopped her. She'd never seen such bare misery in a human face before, or such raw, obvious love.

"I can't stand the thought of anything happening to you," he said. "I love you too much, Em."

The words nearly reduced her to a puddle. She sank into his arms and offered him her lips. For a brief but unforgettable moment they were consumed in each other, and she could only wish it was last night all over again. Time had seemed short, but in retrospect they had had all the leisure in the world.

They were out of time now.

He pulled away from her and without another word began his descent of the hill. As she watched him go, it felt as if her heart were being shredded with every step he took.

He loved her.

The words should have sent her into an ecstasy of happiness. How long it seemed she'd waited to hear them! Instead, she only felt helpless. He loved her, and now she was stuck here on the top of this hill, watching him walk into what could surely be a death trap. And he was doing it for her, because he wanted her to be able to go back to her old life in Midday—something she barely cared about anymore.

So anxious she was hardly aware of anything beyond her own heartbeat, she kept her eyes glued on the shack to see if anyone had spotted him yet. There was no movement inside that she could detect. By the time Lang reached the windowless side of the shack, Emma felt as if her heart were lodged in her throat.

Then a man came outside. He was a short man with black hair and dark skin. Could this be Lang's brother…or Gonzales, the outlaw Lang had told her about? The urge to shout out a warning to Lang was almost unbearable.

But from the tilt of Lang's head and the tension in his stance she could tell that he had heard the man even if he couldn't see him. Lang crouched low at one corner of the building, waiting. For Emma it seemed like an eternity until the man rounded the corner where Lang crouched, and was ambushed. Lang lunged with the assuredness of a seasoned predator, quickly covering the man's mouth, and felled him with a blow to the head from the butt of his revolver.

The speed of the attack stunned Emma. She had never imagined Lang being a fighter, which was part of the reason she'd been so worried. And yet he did away with his foe so easily she wondered if he had performed that trick before. But before she could mentally applaud or rest easy in his apparent competence, another man came out the front door. He appeared to be a cousin to the first man—only larger. Mexican in appearance. And he had a gun drawn.

She stifled a scream. What could she do? Below, Lang was tensed and ready, but again he couldn't see his opponent. What if this one was quicker?

Emma watched in mounting horror until she could stand the tension no longer and scuttled to the nearest bush down the hill. When safely lodged behind it, she looked up. No one had seen her—and Lang and the outlaw still hadn't spotted each other. She kept running. The outlaw wouldn't look for her, she knew, because he was too focused on Lang's corner. Maybe a groan from his friend as Lang attacked him had drawn him outside, or perhaps the sound of the pistol butt making contact with bone.

Her whole body was trembling, but somehow her feet managed to move, and quickly. She circled around as far as she dared to the other side of the house, hoping to sneak in from behind and provide Lang with what little reinforcement she was capable of. The rifle, which just before had seemed like nothing but a heavy stick to wield in an emergency, was now poised at the ready in her arms. She'd never thought she'd contemplate hurting anyone, but with Lang in danger, she knew she could if Lang's life were on the line. When she reached the bottom of the hill, she scooted around to the rain barrel to get into position.

And then the shooting began.

Two shots cracked through the air almost simultaneously. Emma froze in fear, especially when she saw the Mexican still crouched at the corner of the building. Then another shot rang out, and she knew it must have come from Lang, around the corner. She had to help him! But as she attempted to take aim she discovered she was too far away to trust her ability to hit anything. Taking a chance, she crept out from behind the barrel and inched as close to the man's back as she dared. And then she fired.

For a moment it felt as if the whole world had exploded. The fierce crash was almost deafening in her ears, and the kick of the rifle in her arms nearly blew her back ten feet. She stumbled against the side of the house just as a shock of red tore through the air. Blood.

The next thing she knew, she was slumped against the shack, looking at the man face down on the ground, red radiating across his shirt. Emma stared disbelieving at what she had done. Killed a man! She was half repulsed, half jubilant. She nearly cried out for Lang to ask if he was okay, but a hand across her mouth stopped her.

Her gasp was cut off by the sickeningly salty taste of hot, sweaty skin. She pivoted reflexively and looked up into the cold eyes of a man she'd never met yet could have recognized anywhere. Amos Tupper.

He had the same steely gaze as the Wanted posters had depicted, but no drawing could accurately render the danger the man exuded. He grabbed her arm so tightly tears brimmed in her eyes. She might have cried out except that he still had her mouth covered—so she reacted in the most natural way she could think of. She bit him.

Amos muttered the most vulgar oath she'd ever heard, stepped back and flapped his hand angrily. Emma seized the moment to take two steps—but that's all she managed. With catlike agility Amos grabbed her arm and sent her reeling back into his chest. In the next moment, cold metal pressed mercilessly into her temple.

"Speak and you die, little lady." He ground out the words in a voice so gravelly it caused a shiver to snake through her.

It couldn't have been ten seconds since she'd shot the man, yet it seemed an eternity. And now before she could even see Lang she was being dragged away by his brother. In awkward double step she and Amos lurched toward the closest horse. At first she didn't understand. What was he doing? Then he swung up on the painted horse, and to her horror, swung her up after him, wrenching her arm so painfully it took her breath. For a moment she thought he had broken it.

"Amos!"

The shout was Lang's. He'd seen them! Emma tried to swing around to see him, but she couldn't. Amos had her half across his lap, half hanging off the horse.

"So long, big brother!" Amos hollered. "If you want your little lady to live, you'd better stay right where you are."

The world began spinning crazily as their horse neighed and wheeled, and as Lang yelled out a reply, Amos's revolver blazed shots through the air, frightening the other horses so that they tore off into the distance. Emma felt so off balance and terrified she feared she might be sick, or fall. She would like to have fallen, in fact, but Amos had one arm clamped tightly against her middle and they tore off in a gallop before she could catch more than a last blurred glimpse of Lang.

Would it be her last?

Their tracks came to a dead end at a creek. Lang scoured the hills, but Amos and Emma were nowhere in sight.

Anguish was too meek a word for how he felt. Pain tore through his gut every time he thought of Emma out there, frightened. How could he have allowed it to happen? The gun battle was over so fast, and by the time he'd rounded the corner to see where the extra shot had come from, Amos was on the paint with Emma. Following them quickly was impossible, since he'd had to round up a horse. Now he despaired of ever finding them.

He muttered a string of curses at himself for letting Emma into this situation. He'd known she should have stayed behind. He'd feared for her safety, and worried that she would be too scared to get away if something happened to him. But now as he scanned the bare hills with sick dread, he realized there was another matter he'd never reckoned on—his own terror at the idea of losing her.

Last night had been the most wonderful of his life. His time with Emma had given him extra reason to want to live to clear his name, to live to see Emma returned to her farm, and to make her his wife. If he'd ever worried that Emma was a bit like Lucy, those worries were gone now. Emma was a different animal entirely. Her generosity alone set her apart. She'd saved his life, and given him encouragement, and when they were both finally stripped of everything except a mere blanket underneath them and the stars overhead, she'd given him herself without hesitation.

Her boldness shocked and pleased him; their lovemaking

had been both wanton and tender, both an adventure and a pledge. As they lay in each other's arms afterward, Lang had been tempted to make lavish promises he had no assurance of keeping. But Emma hadn't asked for promises, nor had she been using feminine persuasion to get what she wanted. She just wanted to be with him, through thick and through thin. To Emma, his love was his most valued possession. That realization awed him.

And now it stirred him to fear, and anger. Where could they have gone? How would he ever find them? The thought of her being all alone and terrified in his brother's clutches brought out a fury in him. It had been an hour now, and she was probably losing hope. He scanned the horizon, hoping for the slightest movement. There was nothing.

Impulsively, desperately, he called out her name—threw back his head like a wild man and shouted it into the breezy afternoon air. It was an insane thing to do, since it could very well tip off his brother that he was still being followed. But if Emma was anywhere nearby, he wanted her to know that he would hunt until he found her, no matter what.

"Sit down!"

When Amos Tupper commanded, Emma did as she was told. Now that she'd known him all of an hour, the man no longer exuded danger so much as lunacy, as if he were always on the edge of control. Plus he wore a large revolver on his hip, and didn't look as if he'd be the least bit shy about using it. He frightened her.

But she wanted to look for Lang. One hour they'd ridden, she estimated. One jostling, terrifying, bone-rattling hour swung across the front of Amos's saddle, riding hell-for-leather over dusty hills and plowing through streams.

She'd never been so glad to stop moving in her life as she'd been when Amos reined in his horse, pulled her down and shoved her into this cave. But now she realized that she was probably safer when they were out in the open. She kept trying to edge toward the mouth of the cave, so she could look for Lang. Amos would have none of it. He barked at her every time she crept so much as an inch.

"I just wanted to get a little exercise," she said.

Amos glared at her. "I'll bet!"

How could a man look so like Lang and yet be so completely different in temperament? Glancing at Amos, she thought that it was easy to be fooled into thinking he must have some of Lang's personality, yet he was as cold-blooded and mean as a rattlesnake. And he was surprisingly strong. She'd be a fool to try to cross him. But she just couldn't sit in the dark indefinitely, or she would go insane with fear.

"I need some fresh air," she insisted.

"If you ask me, you're lucky to be breathing anything."

She bristled at the implied threat. "So are you, if you want my opinion."

Amos spat, sending a thick wad of tobacco arcing through the air. It landed on the dirt inches from Emma's hand with a wet *splat*. "Why? You think that brother of mine was aimin' on killin' me?"

"No, but I was."

For a moment his hard, steely eyes bored into her, then, to her shock, he clapped his hands together once and emitted a sharp laugh. "That's a good one!"

Her face reddened. "You think I wouldn't have?"

He shook his head, still grinning like a fox. "Lady, you probably wouldn't kill a cockroach. I'll bet you're the type who steps around anthills, and can't sleep the night before you've got to kill a chicken.''

She was shocked that he was astute enough to have gauged her personality perfectly. And his reminding her of how normally peace loving she was made her marvel at her own darker side. "I killed that man today, though," she said.

Amos gaped at her. "What?"

She lifted her head high, taking what pride she could in her terrible deed. Maybe she had saved Lang's life. "Your Mr. Gonzales. I killed him."

Amos threw back his head and laughed again, a sound that practically curdled her blood. "Is that what you think?"

"I know I did. I saw the blood."

He laughed again, and his mirth was beginning to anger her. "Lady, I saw the entire gunfight. My brother shot Gonzales."

Emma hadn't dreamed pulling that trigger, and seeing the blood. "But I shot—"

"A prickly pear," Amos finished for her. Her expression sent him into new spasms of laughter. "Did you actually think you'd done any good back there?"

Her cheeks were on fire. She *had* thought she'd done good—thought she'd saved the day, in fact. When really she'd only served to get in the way. Lang might have captured his brother as planned if Amos hadn't used her as a shield to get away. How could she have been such a fool?

Amos was still enjoying the big joke at her expense. "Leave it to my brother to get involved with a woman like you!"

"What do you mean?"

"You know, the schoolmarm type. Why he'd want to saddle himself down with an old lady like you is beyond me. He should have run off to California and forgotten all about me and Texas.''

''That's what *I* told him,'' Emma said. ''I thought we should just run away.''

He raised a skeptical brow. ''Him *and* you? Pardon me, but you don't exactly look like the running type.''

''That just proves how much you know about me!''

''I've met your upstanding, goody-goody kind before, lady. Though not often, thank goodness.'' He spat again.

She lifted her chin, tempted to tell him how un-upstanding she had been last night—as if that were something to brag about! But it was, she realized. She was proud that Lang had made love to her. Not for anything would she hang her head low about the love they'd shared.

She only wished she could have done more to help Lang. *Oh, Lang!* Where was he now? What if he had been shot during the gun battle?

''Emma!''

Amos's and Emma's heads snapped up straight, and they stared at each other in astonishment.

''What the hell?''

Amos pushed to his feet and moved quickly to crouch at the mouth of the cave. He glared back at her. ''Stay there or I'll shoot you and leave you here to be some wolf's dinner.''

Emma cringed back into the darkness, yet her heart was pumping pure hope. Lang had called her name! He was nearby—he would find her!

Amos unholstered his gun, which glinted from the dying sunlight outside. Emma gasped. Did he really intend to shoot his own brother? Again? She itched to do something, but she couldn't think what. And then there were Amos's threats to leave her to the wolves. She'd heard a whole pack of them howling the night before, and they'd sounded hungry.

She looked at Amos's body, tensed like a cat's, all his concentration focused outside the cave. He knew she wasn't armed, of course, but there seemed something almost arrogant about the way he could simply growl a threat at her and then turn his back, assured that she posed no danger.

Emma glanced around her and found a weighty stone with a sharp edge and quietly lifted it. Perhaps it weighed fifteen pounds—heavy enough for her purpose. Upstanding and inflexible, indeed!

Quietly, minding her skirts, she crept toward Amos, the rock lifted and ready. Once again she heard Lang call her name, and held her breath lest Amos should turn around.

Instead, he cursed, and began muttering to himself. "Son of a bitch! What in tarnation is he doing? Doesn't he know I'm gonna hear him?"

Amos turned to spit again, and just as he noticed that Emma was not where she had been cowering before, Emma brought the rock down on the side of his head. The strike of stone to bone made a cracking sound that she would never forget, and his stunned body slumped to the cave's earthen floor at her feet. Emma stared in horror at the trickle of blood coming from the wound she'd inflicted, and instinctively she dropped to her knees to test for a pulse. Amos was still alive.

And so was Lang! Grabbing Amos's gun, she leapt to her feet again and ran out of the cave, waving her arms and hollering at the top of her lungs. "Lang! Lang!"

She nearly tripped over him. He appeared from behind a scrub oak, and yanked her toward him. "Get back!"

She flourished her gun, smiling. "We're safe!" she said, throwing herself into his arms. "I knocked him unconscious!'' She hugged him around the middle so tightly she might have cut off his circulation, but she didn't care. She was so glad to see him she never wanted to let him go. ''Oh, Lang, I was so nervous—''

''*You* were?'' Lang swore. ''I thought I'd never find you!''

''I was worried you'd been hurt.''

''I heard a gunshot back at the shack. I thought Amos had hit you.''

''No, that was me!''

She explained her blundered attempt to help, though she felt somewhat redeemed for having clubbed Amos.

''The important thing is that you're all right,'' Lang said as they stood over Amos's body. His brother grunted. ''He's beginning to come to.''

''Given the size of the lump on his head, he'll probably wish he hadn't.''

Lang nodded. ''You're one of a kind, Emma. Did you know that?''

She blushed with pleasure. If he'd told her that she was the most beautiful woman on earth, she couldn't have been more pleased. ''I love you so much, Lang. I never want us to be apart again.''

''We won't be,'' he promised her. ''Maybe you're right, and we should go to California. We can drag my brother with us if need be. All I know is, I can't stand the thought of being away from you for a single day.''

They were the most glorious words she'd ever heard. ''You won't be!''

Their lips touched, and suddenly it seemed as if they were in a world all their own, of love and enchantment, where time was an endless commodity. She reveled in the taste of him, the feel of his strong arms holding her, and the memory of their night together. The thought of the possibilities of nights to come made their embrace all the sweeter.

"I'll never leave your side, Lang."

In answer, as if a third party had entered the conversation, a bullet whizzed by their heads as a sharp crack of gunfire shattered the still evening air.

Chapter Fifteen

Lang and Emma hit the ground, whereupon Lang rolled them both away from the opening of the cave.

"Who is that?" Emma asked.

Lang shook his head, puzzled. "I don't think this is one of Gonzales's gang. I'm certain there were only three people back at the shack. Otherwise I would never have been able to follow you."

"Do you think it's the law?"

As understanding dawned, Lang looked regretfully at Emma. "I've got an idea your sheriff has caught up with us."

"Barton?" The very name filled her with dread. "But you said you thought he wouldn't come after us!"

Lang poised his gun on a rock and trained his eyes on the landscape outside the cave. "Or it could be a posse. Maybe William put some people together."

"What should we do?"

Lang's lips twitched wryly. "First, pray that whoever it is stops shooting."

At that moment, as if they didn't have enough problems, Amos turned over and groaned, clutching a hand to his head. "Good Lord!" he exclaimed groggily. "Was I shot?"

Emma looked down at him, feeling an instinctive sympathy for someone in pain. And she could afford to be sympathetic, since she had his own gun safely in her hand, trained on him. "You're not shot," she explained. "I clobbered you with a rock."

He squinted up at her, too weak apparently to care that their captor-captive positions had been reversed since the last time he was conscious. "I thought I heard a gunshot."

She nodded. "We're under fire—maybe from the law." And what shocked her most was how calm she felt with people shooting at her. How long would it be before violence seemed second nature to her? She hoped never, but she was already somewhat inured to the pressure of having guns going off around her. Or maybe she just felt safer now because Lang was beside her.

"Move back," Lang instructed his brother.

Instead of doing what he was told, Amos crouched at the mouth of the cave, much as he had when he'd been looking out for Lang. Now that they were side by side, he eyed his big brother matter-of-factly. "You should have gone away and left me be, brother."

Lang swallowed. "I intended to hand you over to the law."

Doesn't he still? Emma wondered nervously.

"The law would've caught up with me eventually."

"With me, too," Lang said. "*That's* why I couldn't leave you."

"You sure handled the boys," Amos said, expressing little grief for his compadres. He looked at Lang with grudging respect.

Their conversation was cut short as a gunshot exploded from nearby and hit the cave wall next to Lang, sending a blast of sand and chipped rock around them. Emma jumped, but leaned forward, still holding tight to Amos's gun.

"Damn!" Amos muttered. "What the Sam Hill is goin' on? Why doesn't whoever's shootin' at us just wait for dark or hunger or cold to flush us out?"

"He does seem to be in a hurry," Lang noted.

Emma paled at the thought of being *flushed out* of anywhere, as if they were rabbits.

"Why don't you shoot back?" Amos asked impatiently.

Lang's eyes narrowed. "I don't want to waste bullets."

"Well, maybe one of us should distract him. I could draw him out, I bet."

Lang shook his head. "It's too dangerous. This fellow's trigger-happy."

"Well, I can't sit around here all day with no water to clean this wound on my head," Amos grumbled. "I can't wait around forever."

Lang tossed a glance back to Emma, and she nodded. Amos's head wound was dirty from where he'd fallen. "We do need water, and some alcohol, too."

"I'll say!" Amos muttered. "I could use a drink."

That wasn't quite what Emma wanted the alcohol for, though her own nerves were wearing thin, too.

"Just give me my gun," Amos said. "I'll make him move so you can get a good shot."

Lang hesitated, then nodded at Emma.

But Emma was too horrified to follow directions. *Give Amos Tupper his gun back?* Was he crazy? The man could have killed her—and probably would when he got the chance again! Or what if he just took off running? Then they'd be back where they'd started! She returned Lang's silent command with an anguished stare.

Lang eyed her steadily. *Trust me,* his dark eyes seemed to say.

Amos shot a grin Lang's way. "Your little school-marm's got more brains than I gave her credit for. You might want to hold on to her."

"I intend to."

His brother looked at her. "If you want me to promise not to kill Lang or you, I will. It's up to you to guess whether you can trust the word of an outlaw."

"I don't," Emma said flatly. "You shot Lang before."

He squinted at her fiercely. "What're you talking about?"

Before Lang could answer, Emma jumped in. "At the bank robbery. You shot him, didn't you?"

Amos turned to Lang with a look close to raw hurt. "That what you thought?"

Lang nodded. "Was I wrong?"

"Gonzales shot you." Amos shook his head. "I thought you understood. He didn't trust you. He suspected you were going to tip off the bank clerk."

"I was," Lang said.

"I figured as much," Amos said, nodding curtly. "When we got to the bank, I didn't like the feel of the whole setup, especially that jumpy little clerk. Man made me nervous, so I shot him. I figured we could get out of there, but I didn't know that Gonzales planned on getting rid of you. Otherwise I would've tried warning you."

"But you just rode off with him—leaving Lang to die!" Emma exclaimed. As if to punctuate her words, another shot glanced off the rocks at the mouth of the cave.

"What should I have done? Got caught?"

"Yes!"

"Listen, lady, I'm sorry for getting Lang into all sorts of a mess. I'm even sorry for taking you." Amos smiled ruefully. "I wouldn't have, if I'd known how handy you were with rocks. But now we're in a spot, lady, and I'm willin' to help get us out. Once we've taken care of this hombre who's shootin' at us, figuring out who was right and wrong, and who gets away and who doesn't, will seem like a luxury."

Emma still hesitated, but another bullet chose that precise moment to skim the ground inches from her leg. With a start, she practically tossed the revolver to Amos, who hefted the weighty gun, glanced one last time at Lang, then ran in a crouch out of the cave. Suddenly it seemed almost as if fireworks were going off. Gunfire cracked through the air so quickly, Emma had no time to gauge who was firing at whom.

She crept next to Lang in time to see Amos reach a tree, then fall awkwardly. The cacophony of violence suddenly stilled, and Emma felt sick inside to see Amos slumped on the ground. There was little hope that he was alive.

"Son of a—" Lang bit off his words angrily, and she touched his arm.

His brother. Looking into his brown eyes, she could only imagine his thoughts. All his life he'd tried to take care of Amos. He'd given up his own work and liberty to rescue Amos when there was little hope of rehabilitating the scoundrel. And now this—a fittingly violent end to a life lived so recklessly. Yet there was something heroic about it, too. He'd died trying to save them.

She touched Lang's arm. He didn't look at her, but continued to watch the outside, his jaw clenched tight. "You were right, Lang. He wasn't all bad."

Lang's jaw clenched. "I'm afraid we're in a tough spot, Em."

The use of his nickname for her warmed her a little, even though her limbs quivered in fear. She looked toward the jutting boulder that Lang's eyes were trained on. "Is he there?"

Lang nodded. "We don't have many shots left. Just three."

Amos had taken his gun with its precious bullets with him. Emma swallowed. Things seemed grim, all right. "What will we do?"

As Lang was about to answer her, the sound of Barton's voice carried toward them. "You can come on out now, Emma! I killed your boyfriend, but there's no reason we can't come to some kind of agreement!"

Emma's and Lang's startled eyes met. "He thinks he killed you," she whispered, "and that I'm all alone now."

Lang brooded over this new development.

"Let me go out," Emma said quickly. "I can explain it all to him—this might all be over."

"I don't trust him," Lang said.

She didn't, either. But what choice did they have?

Barton shouted at them again. "If you come along peaceably, nobody'll need to know that you were in love with that outlaw! We can get married, just like we bargained!"

His words made her blood boil. So he thought they could just pick up where they left off—and he was going to use Lang's dead body as leverage. A wave of revulsion hit her. "And what about the fact that you were blackmailing me into matrimony?" she shouted back impetuously. "Can we tell the good folks of Midday about that?"

"Be reasonable, Emma! Running off with an outlaw puts you in no position to make threats."

Reasonable? "I was kidnapped, didn't you hear?"

"We both know that's not true."

"Don't waste your breath, Em," Lang whispered, raising his gun.

"Don't waste your bullets," she said, not wanting to see any more violence. Besides, the sheriff was her problem. "He probably doesn't think I can shoot a gun, so he'll try to come closer and reason with me."

"And then what are we going to do? Invite him to the wedding?"

"We can explain that it would be best all around to clear your name and forget all about the arrangement Barton and I had."

Lang rolled his eyes. "That won't work."

"It might."

"I don't trust him with you. I don't trust him, period."

"What can he do to me?" But as she crouched on tired, shaking legs, one possible answer to that question rang ominously in her mind, an answer reflected in the skeptical glance in Lang's eyes. But that was ridiculous. If the sheriff killed her, he wouldn't get what he wanted—her land. "We can't just sit here. If he comes up and discovers that it was Amos he shot, he'll kill you."

"I'll be ready for him."

"Lang, no." If he shot Barton, how would they ever be able to prove his innocence? No one in Midday would believe that it was self-defense.

The only thing she was certain of was that she couldn't let Lang be drawn into a gun battle, and the only way to ensure that didn't happen was to put herself between Lang and danger. Not giving herself time to think twice, she followed in Amos's footsteps and ran from the cave, ignoring Lang's string of curses that followed her. He grabbed the skirt of her dress, nearly tripping her, but Emma yanked free and ran forward. Moving quickly, she sprinted and waved her hands in what she hoped would look like surrender, careful to keep herself between Lang and the rock where Barton had been hiding.

After she'd gone twenty feet, Barton stood, his rifle raised—and aimed straight at her. As she took in the sight of a deadly weapon trained on her, Emma's legs went numb beneath her and she chugged to a stop, suddenly understanding. She could see the desperate glare in his squinty eyes. He wanted to kill her so that she would never be able to tell what he'd done, so she couldn't shame him. Whatever pride there was left in the Sealy name, he intended to preserve it through her death.

"Emma, move!" Lang urged from behind her.

But she couldn't. She couldn't even glance over at Amos, at the gun that was her only hope of self-defense. She was too stunned that she had made such a fatal error. Once again she had misjudged the sheriff completely. How could she have been such a fool? Once she was gone, what chance would Lang have? Even if he killed the sheriff, how would he ever be able to clear his name?

As the last thought passed through her mind, she was deafened by a single gunshot. Expecting to drop to the ground, Emma held her breath, waiting. It was several moments before she opened eyes she hadn't been aware of closing and saw the sheriff slumped before her, as lifeless as Amos had looked. Emma gasped in horror.

"Oh, Lang!" she cried, whirling to look at him. They would have to run, immediately. California wouldn't be far enough. They would have to go to South America.

He was at her side, but instead of taking her in his arms and giving her comfort, he yanked her back into the cave.

"Watch out!" he said as he tugged her down next to him.

Emma stared at him in confusion. "For what?"

"For whoever's shooting out there."

Suddenly she understood. "You didn't kill Barton?"

Now it was his turn to look confused. "Hell, no—I couldn't. You were in the way!"

"Then who—"

She squinted out the mouth of the cave in time to see someone coming around the rock. Emma didn't know what to expect. A stranger? One of Gonzales's gang? But the marksman was neither of those.

It was her own sister.

Emma couldn't believe her eyes. Holding a revolver limply at her side, a bedraggled-looking but straight-backed Rose Ellen stood over Barton's body, gaping in amazement at what she'd done.

"I'll be damned!" Emma exclaimed.

Both Lang and Rose Ellen stared at Emma as she stood. But Emma couldn't think twice about the curse that had issued from her lips; she was too intent on giving her sister an ecstatic, heartfelt hug. She ran up to Rose Ellen and embraced her with tears brimming in her eyes, prepared to assure her that she had saved her life and that there had been no alternative to killing Barton.

But Rose Ellen needed no comforting. "That snake was going to kill you!"

Emma nodded. "I didn't realize—"

"I knew something was fishy!" Rose Ellen exclaimed. "He told William, Joe and I to stay back at that little hovel and bury bodies while he rode ahead to find you. William and Joe are back there, but I was suspicious about Barton, so I sneaked off."

"Thank heavens you did!"

Rose Ellen pulled back, put her hands on her hips and walked away from the grim scene. "Our Barton tried to keep anyone from following you at all. Now I know why! Letting a criminal go so he could blackmail you!" Her words indicated that she'd heard the shouted conversation between Emma and the sheriff.

"But Lang wasn't the criminal," Emma explained, following her sister. "That was his brother."

Rose Ellen looked over at Amos, shaking her head. "Oh, Emma, I wish you'd told me what was happening!"

"Somehow we didn't think you'd understand," Lang explained.

Rose Ellen's jaw dropped. "But of course I—" she exhaled and twisted her lips "—wouldn't have. I'm sorry, Emma, I should have known something was wrong." Her body stiffened at what she'd done. "How will I explain to William about his brother?"

Lang's jaw tightened, and Emma knew that he was thinking about his own brother, and all the havoc Amos had wreaked. "Emma and I will explain how you saved our lives, Rose Ellen. We're grateful to you."

Saved their lives! Emma could still barely believe it. She hugged Lang tightly, daring to hope that this was the end of their problems, and the beginning of their future together. Together! What a wonderful word that was. She tilted her head up to Lang, and he bent and kissed her on the lips. For a moment she was absorbed in his warmth, and trouble fell away from her.

When Lang pulled away and cleared his throat, she looked over to see Rose Ellen gaping at them with tears in her eyes. Emma blushed. "I'm sorry, Rose Ellen...I must have been carried away...."

"Oh! I don't mind that!"

Emma bit her lip worriedly, fearing Rose Ellen would crack up. "What is it, then?"

"My dress!" She dashed a tear from her eye, and Emma realized that Rose Ellen's nerves were frayed a little. "*Look* at it!"

"I owe you a thousand dresses, Rose Ellen. You saved my life."

Rose Ellen shook her head. "*I* saved the day?" She blinked in astonishment. "I did, didn't I?"

Emma nodded. "You certainly did."

Rose Ellen's beautiful eyes were luminous with feeling. "Why, this is the first time in my life I've ever done something really useful! Now I see why you love nursing so, Emma. I feel almost tipsy with satisfaction. Just think, *I'm* practically a hero, just like you will be when you start that hospital of yours."

Emma felt equal parts happiness at the prospect of going back to the life she'd hoped for, and worry at Rose Ellen's joy over having accomplished a rather gruesome task. "But Rose Ellen, you killed a man."

"Well, I'm not in any hurry to do *that* again. But I never knew I had that kind of spunk in me, Emma. Why, I can't wait to tell Edward about how brave and heroic I've been. And all the folks back in Midday, and Galveston. Rose Ellen Colby Douglas—hero! Who would believe it?"

"I guess we'll find out," Lang said. "We should get back to the others so we can get a good night's sleep and head home tomorrow."

Home. Emma looked up at him and saw in his eyes the meaning he'd meant to convey with that simple word. Their home. The farm. Her heart brimmed with relief and happiness and love.

Epilogue

Emma sat on the rocker on the porch and opened the letter that had arrived with the bundle Constance O'Hurlihy, in her new capacity as temporary postmistress, had delivered this morning, containing the book Rose Ellen had written. The loopy handwriting made her smile in recognition. She hadn't realized until now how much she'd missed seeing it.

Dear Emma,

Here it is, my first opus—*The Vigilante Sister*. You might recognize a few characters in it, especially Ella, the sister who is abducted and rescued so heroically by Rosa Ann. (But don't worry that others will draw comparisons to you; Ella is a very minor character.) My publisher says mine is the most exciting novel he's read in years! I'm so happy, and have I already told you I'm at work on a new epic entitled *The Outlaw Upstairs?* Oh, I'm full of ideas! Really, I don't know where I get them.

I'm sorry I haven't had time to write letters, but I've been so busy. I have a literary salon each Friday. This week Annalise is going to present some drawings and recite Tennyson. What a smart child! Edward says he is very proud of us both, and he is as attentive to me now as he was when we were newly married. But I suppose you know all about doting husbands. How lucky we both are!

Your loving sister,
Rose Ellen

"Good news?"

Emma had been so absorbed in Rose Ellen's letter that she hadn't heard Lang's approach. She got up out of her rocking chair—not an easy task for someone eight months pregnant—and went to his side, thrilled to have a visit from him in the middle of the afternoon. Usually he and William were out doing repair work, especially now, after their first harvest was sold and there was plenty of preparing to do for the winter. And she was usually busy reading to their patients or helping Lorna in the kitchen. But happily, Joe Spears was her only patient. He'd fallen off a ladder at the store and broken his leg. And a steady stream of visitors this morning had managed the feat of talking the man into exhaustion.

She put her arms around Lang and sighed with contentment.

"Rose Ellen's book arrived today."

"Have you read any of it?"

Lang nuzzled the top of her head, and she squeezed him a little more tightly in return. "Parts."

"What's it about?"

She leaned back and raised an eyebrow at him. "Three guesses."

He laughed. "Rose Ellen?"

"I believe she's already hard at work on another one of the same topic."

"At least she'll never lack for inspiration."

"It's true. My sister finds herself endlessly fascinating."

Lang sent her his most heart-stopping grin. After all these months, he never ceased to surprise her. Just when Emma was sure she knew every nuance of his smile, and the tilt of his head, and the timbre of his voice, he would look at her in a new way that would melt her insides as thoroughly as a candle in a forest blaze. Sometimes she wondered if there was any limit to the myriad ways a man could tempt a woman...but she hoped not!

"If I were a writer," Lang said in a husky voice, "you would be my muse."

Was it any wonder she loved him? She'd never expected a man would look at her with the searing intensity Lang regarded her with, especially when she felt as big as a heifer. But even now Lang treated her as if she were the most desirable woman in the world, and when he looked at her with those dark eyes of his, she at least felt like the most fortunate woman in the world. Sometimes she found it difficult to believe she had started this incredible year so down in the dumps and despairing for her future, which despite a few bumps along the way had turned out brighter than she could ever have imagined.

She tossed her head a little saucily. "If you were as good with words on paper as you are with flattering me, you would be a very successful author."

He pulled her closer. "Maybe with your sister's literary blood in the family now, our child will be a writer."

Emma laughed, although talk of her child always filled her with joy, and anticipation. Sometimes it felt as if the little rascal would never come! "In that case, he or she might turn out to be a doctor, or a farmer."

Lang smiled back. "Or an outlaw?" He could sometimes refer to Amos now without so much sorrow as before.

She shook her head. "I've heard that particular trait skips a generation."

"Good."

Emma laughed, shaking her head. "Who knows? Maybe by the time our grandchildren are grown, we'll be ready for a little excitement again. You'll have to admit, being on the run brought us together quickly."

The flickering heat in his eyes revealed that Lang, like Emma, was remembering that night in early spring when they'd made love under a canopy of stars. How long ago that was! In fact, sometimes it seemed almost like a dream, yet she clung to the memory, cherishing it as she did every moment with Lang. She'd told him then that she would never have any regrets, and she never would.

"I wouldn't mind being out in the wilds again," she said, then blushed, adding, "even sleeping out in the wilds."

His dark brows arched up. "How about now?"

She looked across their cultivated fields glaring in the winter sunlight, then back at him with mild shock. "Good gracious, Lang, what are you suggesting?"

He threw his head back and laughed. "Nothing you haven't already thought of."

She blushed to the roots of her hair, yet she couldn't deny that when he moved a hand up her lower back, she felt a definite stirring of desire. "It's very cold out here...."

"Mmm..." Lang continued to caress her, and gazed at her with such burning intimacy that she feared she'd never feel cold again. "But we could make a little fire up in the bedroom."

"I'll say!" Emma blurted out, then slapped her hand over her mouth to cover her smile.

Lang grinned back at her, then reached down and picked her up in one easy movement.

"Lang!" Emma cried. "What are you doing?"

"Speeding our trip upstairs."

It was true that Emma wasn't quite so fast as she had been. "But what if Lorna sees us? Or William?"

"They'll understand."

Emma shook her head as they progressed past the parlor toward the staircase. "And what if Joe sees us?"

Lang waggled his eyebrows in a way that was half seductive, half comical. "Then by tomorrow afternoon, all the world will know that Mr. Tupper enjoys ravishing his wife after lunch."

Emma tossed back her head and laughed. "The world needs gossip, I guess."

And for once, she would dearly enjoy being smack in the center of controversy.

* * * * *

If you enjoyed what you just read,
then we've got an offer you can't resist!

Take 2 bestselling love stories FREE!

Plus get a FREE surprise gift!

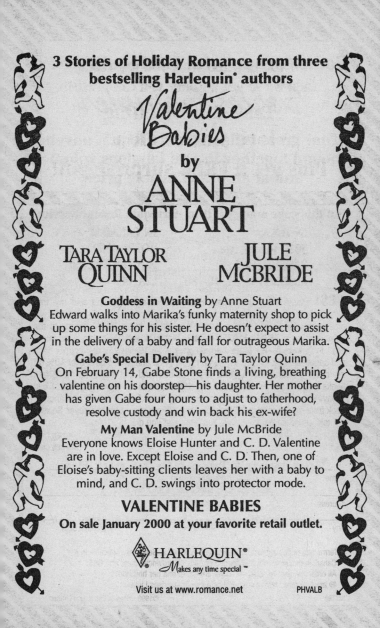

Come escape with Harlequin's new

Series Sampler

Four great full-length Harlequin novels bound together in one fabulous volume and at an unbelievable price.

Be transported back in time with a Harlequin Historical® novel, get caught up in a mystery with Intrigue®, be tempted by a hot, sizzling romance with Harlequin Temptation®, or just enjoy a down-home all-American read with American Romance®.

You won't be able to put this collection down!

On sale February 2000 at your favorite retail outlet.

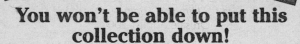

HARLEQUIN®
Makes any time special ™

Visit us at www.romance.net   PHESC

Back by popular demand are

DEBBIE MACOMBER's

Hard Luck, Alaska, is a town that needs women! And the O'Halloran brothers are just the fellows to fly them in.

Starting in March 2000 this beloved series returns in special 2-in-1 collector's editions:

MAIL-ORDER MARRIAGES, featuring
Brides for Brothers and *The Marriage Risk*
On sale March 2000

FAMILY MEN, featuring
Daddy's Little Helper and *Because of the Baby*
On sale July 2000

THE LAST TWO BACHELORS, featuring
Falling for Him and *Ending in Marriage*
On sale August 2000

Collect and enjoy each MIDNIGHT SONS story!

Available at your favorite retail outlet.

HARLEQUIN®
Makes any time special ™

Visit us at www.romance.net   PHMS